Milagro Lane

Other books by Jay Brandon:

Deadbolt (1985)

Tripwire (1987)

Predator's Waltz (1989)

Fade The Heat (1990)

Rules Of Evidence (1992)

Loose Among The Lambs (1993)

Local Rules (1995)

Defiance County (1996)

Angel of Death (1998)

After-Image (2000)

Executive Privilege (2001)

Sliver Moon (2004)

Grudge Match (2004)

Running with the Dead (2005)

Milagro Lane

A Novel

Jay Brandon

With a Foreword by
Rick Casey

San Antonio, Texas
2009

Milagro Lane © 2009 by Wings Press
Milagro Lane was first published as a weekly serial in the
San Antonio Express-News.

Cover art: "Leaving Olmos Basin" by Bryce Milligan

First Edition

ISBN: 978-0-916727-57-4

Wings Press
627 E. Guenther
San Antonio, Texas 78210
Phone/fax: (210) 271-7805

On-line catalogue and ordering:
www.wingspress.com
All Wings Press titles are distributed to the trade by
Independent Publishers Group
www.ipgbook.com

*This publication supported in part by a generous grant
from the City of San Antonio, Office of Cultural Affairs.*

Library of Congress Cataloging-in-Publication Data:

Brandon, Jay.
  Milagro Lane : a novel / Jay Brandon ; with a foreword by Rick Casey.
-- 1st ed.
     p. cm.
  ISBN 978-0-916727-57-4 (alk. paper)
 1. San Antonio (Tex.)--Fiction. I. Title.
 PS3552.R315M55 2009
 813'.54--dc22
                                    2009005130

Except for fair use in reviews and/or scholarly considerations,
no portion of this book may be reproduced in any form without
the written permission of the author or the publisher.

Milagro Lane is dedicated to my children,

Elizabeth, Sam, and Elena,

who will remember, I hope, Mission Drive-In, ElBee Magic Co., and other disappeared and yet-to-disappear sites of San Antonio; and to the people of San Antonio, who remember and have made these real and more-than-real locales into a landscape of the imagination.

Contents

Foreword, by Rick Casey	ix

Part I: The Girl in the Red Dress

The Unexpected Guest	3
"Live at 5"	9
How to Bribe a City Councilman	13
Another One Bites My Dust	20
"Alias King William"	32
Hot Mics	45
Evelyn in Sordid Splendor	56
The Employment Gap	63
Milagro Lane Explained	72
"We Have to Talk"	84

Part II: But Is It Art?

But Is It Art?	89
Island of Lost Time	101
For Love or Money – or Both	115
77 Candles	122
Stairway to Heaven	133

Part III: Elsewhen

Elsewhen	149
Where the Night Flowers Bloom	163
Questions, Answered and Un-	176
The Ties That Bind – and Choke	191
An Outfit to Make a Man Question His Gender Preference	203
A Falling Out Among Thieves?	218
Who is Estela Valenzuela?	222
The Return of *Las Dos Madres*	226
Veronica vs. the Mayor: The Finale	230
The Magic of Disappeared Places	234

About the Author	243

Foreword

San Antonio Express-News Editor Robert Rivard gets credit for the proposal: A serialized novel set in San Antonio, written in what we now call "real time," and weaving in references to events in the news. It had been done before, most famously by San Francisco novelist Armistead Maupin for his *Tales of the City*. But it had not been attempted in San Antonio. It is a testimony that Rivard did not think of me as the author. I've always been afraid of writing fiction (both unintentionally and intentionally). I have to work hard to report truth, much less create it.

But when Rivard asked if I would like to work as Jay Brandon's editor on the project, I immediately said yes. I knew Jay as a dry-witted lawyer who, remarkably, could draft proposed opinions for justices at the 4th Court of Appeals in San Antonio during his days – often a mind-numbing task – then go home and write page-turner mysteries that toured you through the city's gritty streets. I had read a number of his novels, all set in San Antonio, and both enjoyed them and learned from them.

Working with Jay was as much fun as covering San Antonio's wacky politics. I gleefully awaited each week's offering, not only eager to see where the plot was going, but also to enjoy references to such events as a police bribery scandal and Jay's insertion of real people into the story, including myself.

My greatest pleasure was putting into Jay's capable hands some material I had gathered that no competent libel lawyer would let me put into my column. The best example is the chapter titled "How to Bribe a Councilman." I had learned the details of an actual bribe, but couldn't publish them without violating my pledge not to expose my source. But here at last I was able to get the details into print. It was an example of the old saw that fiction can tell truths that journalism coughs on. In that chapter, how the deal went down, the venues at which the terms were laid out and the cash that changed hands, and even some of the dialogue, came from a real bribe paid to a real councilman. Only the names were changed, to protect the guilty. The morning the chapter was published I fantasized the politician reading it and saying to himself, "Holy shit! They know!" In reality, I have no reason to believe the miscreant ever read anything that didn't have pictures.

My other major contribution was simply to encourage Jay to tie his story to the news, and to indulge his sometimes wicked sense of humor despite his concern for the sensibilities of a family newspaper. He was confident, for example, that the paper would not print a line about a councilwoman who is also a lawyer billing one of her clients for time spent in what was decidedly illicit behavior. I assured him that I would fight for the line. The line ran: "Mr. Richard called it the sign of a good lawyer. 'Takes a drilling and keeps on billing' was the phrase he used, I believe." As far as I recall, the newspaper didn't receive a single complaint. Nor did Jay. In fact, one female reader e-mailed him to say she had eagerly shipped off the chapter to her daughter, a lawyer.

As you read the book, take some pleasure from knowing the strange manner in which it was written, in weekly chunks with relentless deadlines. It was a daunting challenge, and Jay Brandon delivered. *Milagro Lane* is as real as San Antonio itself, a city of great stories. If you enjoy reading the book half a much as I enjoyed working with its author, I'd say you're at home here even if you live elsewhere.

– Rick Casey
Houston, 2008

Rick Casey spent many years as a San Antonio journalist, including 16 years as a columnist for the *San Antonio Light* and then the *San Antonio Express-News*. He is now a columnist for the *Houston Chronicle*.

Part I

The Girl in the Red Dress

The Unexpected Guest

Everyone who was anyone came to the funeral, including at least one who didn't exist. Jerome Grohman had been a fairly young man, only 50, well-known and almost universally liked in San Antonio. After a reckless youth, he had settled down to become a civic leader with certain wayward tendencies – a sort of leaning pillar of the community – and in both aspects of his life he had made friends.

Furthermore, the Grohman family went back in San Antonio history almost as far as the city did. The Grohmans had been prominent in ranching, manufacturing and brewing, the latter of which had added to the family's fortune and to Jerry Grohman's early tendency toward carefree wildness – a quality he unfortunately had retained, as his sad death behind the wheel of his Porsche seemed to demonstrate.

Before the big public funeral came the very private viewing for the Grohman family. This served as a time of farewell and also as a dress rehearsal for the funeral, to make sure everything displayed well.

A cousin had suggested burying Jerry in the full epauletted and plumed regalia he had worn as King Antonio five years earlier. This suggestion was vetoed so resoundinglhy that the cousin almost found himself written out of several wills. Not only would such an outfit seem unnecessarily symbolic, it would be tacky. And in the Grohman family, taste ruled.

Jerry's mother, family matriarch Madeleine "Miz Maddie" Grohman, had planned the viewing quietly but thoroughly, making sure only family knew of it. That was why everyone was surprised by the appearance of the young woman in the deep maroon dress.

The woman, early 20s in age, appeared to be Hispanic, with black hair that fell in a smooth sheen to her shoulders, creamy brown skin and an aquiline nose showing off Indian heritage. She had a gift for silence and another for grace, standing at the back of the quiet downtown chapel that had opened this afternoon only for the family. The young woman did nothing to call attention to herself except stand and wear the dark red dress. She could have been taken for an apparition, a spirit of meditation.

Miz Maddie (the title persisted though she was now in her 70s) glanced that way, wondered how the girl had gotten in and whether she was lost, then returned her attention to the figure of her late son. The next time she looked back, the young woman had gone.

The large public funeral the next day at the downtown First Presbyterian Church – known as First Prez among the city's old elite as well as its rising wealthy – filled the church with the well-off and well-known. Ranking members were Sen. Kay Bailey Hutchinson, an old family friend, Congressmen Lamar Smith and Charlie González, state legislators including Jeff Wentworth, Mayor Howard Peak (a high school classmate of the deceased) and a majority of the City Council. People murmured at the brief appearance of Tommy Lee Jones, who viewed the body then quickly departed.

In this illustrious crowd, why was Madeleine Grohman's eye drawn to the young woman in the maroon dress? Somehow she stood out. Now, the young lady came forward with measured stride, stood for a long minute at the open casket, and reached briefly into it.

Miz Maddie whispered instructions to a lesser member of the family, a great-niece, who sought out the young woman. The young lady inclined her head briefly and spoke softly. Half an hour later, a time filled with praise from the minister and two or three sly references during the eulogy by an old friend of the deceased, the great-niece settled into the seat of the limousine beside Miz Maddie. The old lady seemed lost in thought so deep it might have prefaced her own passing. But after a minute she looked up, raised her eyebrow and asked a question.

The niece cleared her throat. "She said she had promised him she'd wear a red dress to his funeral."

"Indeed." The old lady's voice was surprisingly deep, and heavy with the tears she would not shed in public or even in the presence of other family. "Well done, Bridget. She sounds like an interesting young lady. Why don't you invite her for tea? At the small house."

The Grohman family had been wealthy in San Antonio for generations. In that time, they had acquired much in the way of property, and notoriously disliked letting go of any of it.

The family now owned several houses. The matriarch of the family, 74-year-old Miz Maddie, lived mainly in the Olmos Park mansion. Her late son Jerry, wild hippie that he was, had lived in King

William. But the family also owned a two-bedroom gingerbread house in the cottage area of Alamo Heights. This house stayed in the family for its address, which any Grohman child could use to attend Alamo Heights schools. It also served as a guesthouse and occasionally as a poor front. Like most old-moneyed San Antonio families, the Grohmans avoided display, didn't have their names listed on monuments, and in fact preferred to have no public life at all.

So when Miz Maddie wanted to meet the mysterious young woman who had appeared at her son's funeral, she invited her to the small house.

It was a very pleasant cottage, built in the 1920s and remodeled about every other decade since, now in an open, airy style well-suited to mild February in S.A. Miz Maddie had the tea served on the back porch, resting her dignity on a white love seat well-cushioned against its wicker frame.

The young lady arrived punctually, but took some time to reach the back. Madeleine Grohman heard her happy exclamations over small items of decoration and accessorizing. When the young lady came through the door, no longer dressed in red but in a very respectable deep blue dress that showed off her collarbones, she smiled brightly.

"You had the old wineglasses brought here," she said happily. "I'm so glad. I thought they had all broken."

Miz Maddie's eyes narrowed, but she wouldn't ask the question. "Hello, my dear, thank you for coming. May I ask your name?"

"Estela Valenzuela. I'm very glad to see you, Miz Maddie."

Estela had an accent only when she said her name. In English, like so many San Antonians, she had no accent, or so many traces that they cancelled out.

"I couldn't help noticing your remarkable dress at my son's funeral," Miz Maddie began at once. "It drew my attention."

"I'm sorry." Estela blushed slightly, a neat trick that turned her brown cheeks orange. "But I promised Jerry. He said once he'd always wanted a woman in a red dress to appear at his funeral. I bought as dark a red as I could find, and it would have been letting him down not to wear red. He wanted to make people think he'd had a wild, mysterious past, I think."

And perhaps he had, his mother thought.

"I also couldn't help noticing the way you looked at him. Clearly, you weren't a stranger. Yet I've never heard of you. Tell me, how did you and Jerry know each other?"

Estela considered the question.

"I suppose you would say he was my mentor."

"Ah." Miz Maddie, in the course of her long life, had known many men who had mentored young ladies, sometimes for years and quite attentively. Some of these had been good men, who loved their children and stood beside their wives in church on Sundays. But their mentees were precious to them, too. As long as the men remained good providers and devoted to family in public, their more private relationships only very rarely occasioned divorce or murder.

In Miz Maddie's circles, such things could be taken in stride. She found herself pleased for her son. Miz Maddie had always been an absolute paragon of propriety. More than anyone knew, she had lived vicariously through her son during his wild youth. While reprimanding him and putting restrictions on his trust funds, she had smiled inwardly.

Her life had grown much duller after Jerry had gone respectable. She was glad to learn that his reformation hadn't been complete.

She smiled at the lovely young lady.

"Tell me about yourself, dear. Where are you from?"

"West," Estela said.

"Oh? Santa Fe? Colorado?"

"Farther. Much farther."

Gabe Grohman remembered that he used to love going to his grandmother's home in Olmos Park. The old two-story stone mansion had seemed as exciting as a castle, with passages to be explored, parapets offering regal vistas, and a yard full of adventure.

Now, pacing in the front parlor two weeks after his father's funeral, Gabe wondered when the drafty old house had turned so gloomy. Miz Maddie hadn't bought heavier drapes – she had the same furnishings she'd had for decades – and the maids still meticulously cleaned everything, including the windows.

Vines had crept up the outside walls, and the trees around the house had inevitably grown taller, but that didn't account for how the sense of adventure had fled.

Maybe, Gabe thought wearily, at the age of 24 he had simply grown up. Horrible thought. "I feel older than I've ever been," he said.

"That's because you are, dear," his stepmother said helpfully.

Gabe shot what would have been a withering glance at anyone paying attention, which seldom described Evelyn Grohman. Evelyn was only a dozen years older than Gabe, the same number of years she'd been married to his father. Evelyn had not exactly been a trophy wife. Marriage to her seemed to have been designed to prove that Jerry had left his wild past behind. Not that Evelyn hadn't been pretty. She certainly inspired fantasies in Gabe in his teens.

But almost immediately after the honeymoon, she'd grown a tad plump, more than a tad distracted, and very self-indulgent.

She and Gabe cordially disliked each other, the same relationship Evelyn and his father seemed to have enjoyed over their last couple of years. In the past two weeks, though, she'd cried more public tears than any other member of the family. But then, the will hadn't been read yet.

"Has either of you met that girl in the red dress?" Maddie Grohman asked. Increasingly, Gabe's 74-year-old grandmother did that, entered a room already talking, as if she had no time to waste.

"Who?" both Gabe and Evelyn asked, startled.

"Estela Valenzuela. I've just had tea with her. Delightful girl."

Quickly, Miz Maddie filled them in on her meeting with Estela. "She and Jerry knew each other. She said they met in San Francisco, though I don't see how that could be. At any rate, he was a sort of mentor to her."

"In what?"

"Don't get that sulky look, Gabriel. It's so unattractive. She's a lovely girl, with excellent manners. I'm going to take her to the next meeting of the Friends of the McNay."

"What?" Now Evelyn sat up and took notice. She had no interest in any art that couldn't be worn, but still, her mother-in-law had never offered to introduce her to the Friends.

"Delightful girl," Maddie repeated, and left the room abruptly.

"This is intolerable," Gabe burst out.

"Just the word!" Evelyn agreed, coming to her feet. "The will not even read yet – I mean, your father not even cold, and Maddie bringing this stranger into the family! How do we even know she knew Jerry?"

"We don't," Gabe said angrily. "Who is this girl? What does she want?"

Evelyn poked him in the chest and said conspiratorially, "Gabe, you have to check her out."

"I intend to."

"I don't mean that."

"Neither do I. But I'll find out where she's from and what she wants. Trust me."

Outside the door, Maddie Grohman smiled. She would never hire a detective or ask prying questions herself. Even if certain personal information might be needed to protect the family from blackmail or scandal, she would have found it demeaning to dig into someone's background, become a common snoop.

Besides, it was much easier to trick one's family into doing it.

"Live at 5"

The man on the street has given way to the person in the mall, so that's where a reporter goes to gather opinions. Spot interviews quickly revealed that San Antonians greeted a new mayor's race with their usual level of informed enthusiasm:

"Who?"

"When?"

"You're kidding. The mayor's elected?"

"Cut!" Veronica Lewis, reporter for NewsBeat6, KSAN-TV, dropped her microphone in disgust. Veronica was 27, a veteran by TV news standards. She had logged five years in Beaumont right out of Angelo State University, where she had majored in drama.

She wore a long blue blazer over a plain white blouse. Below, half-covered by the jacket, were black leotards. On screen, only the blazer would show. Viewers also wouldn't see that her running shoes needed cleaning.

"Hey, you looked good on that take, Veronica," her cameraman Bruce said helpfully. Veronica wasn't appeased.

"Isn't there anybody in this mall who has an opinion?"

She stood in front of the Gap in Rivercenter and peered both ways, hoping to see someone who looked articulate. In her earpiece, someone from the station told her they'd be coming to her live in 90 seconds.

Back at KSAN, the director in the control booth asked, "Are we ready with that live feed?"

"Better be," said the console man, flipping a switch.

On thousands of screens all over San Antonio, Veronica Lewis suddenly appeared, staring into the camera. As soon as the red light on Bruce's camera came on, the citizen Veronica had lined up for a spot interview turned and ran.

Desperately, Veronica shot out her arm and grabbed the nearest bystander. He happened to be a young man wearing an earring at the top of his ear, "short" pants that fell almost to his ankles, and a black T-shirt with red letters saying, "Don't make me get ugly with you."

"Sir, do you have a favorite candidate in the mayor's race?"

"I don't like that sleazy one."

"Uh..." Veronica felt reluctant to name a candidate who might fit this description. "Do you mean City Councilman Heimer, or Esparza?"

"Yeah, the sleazy one with the bad hair. I'm going to vote for Mayor Peak again."

"Well, you know you can't do that?"

"Who says? You gonna tell me how to vote, lady?"

Veronica gave the camera her serious gaze. "And that's the Beat from the Street."

Back at the station, Roger, the news director, said, "Let's can this feature. It's getting on my nerves. And fire that idiot Virginia."

"Yeah, but she looks good," his male assistant said. "You know, pretty but not overboard. Like I can watch her without making my girlfriend jealous."

"Hmm," said the news director. There are intangibles in the news business. The assistant had just described exactly the kind of person who came across well on TV.

When Veronica returned, Roger called her into his office. Veronica felt the ax hovering. She had a probationary contract, which gave her the same job security as one of Blackbeard's deckhands.

"Virginia, I've tried to bring you along, give you the benefits of my experience, teach you the business..."

In her two months at the station, Veronica had seen the news director twice.

"It's Veronica, sir."

"I know it is, but we don't have any choice."

In serious discussions, Roger didn't let himself get distracted by listening to the other person. "We need production. We're coming into a sweeps month. We've been promoting our coverage of 'Undercover Policewomen: How Far Will They Go?' and our other special features for weeks. It's time for you to give us something."

She hoped he didn't mean what she thought he meant. But he did.

"Come up with something juicy in the next two weeks, Virginia, or you're out."

Veronica Lewis refused to ask God for help. She felt quite certain that coming up with something "juicy" for sweeps month was not a project in which God would be interested. Nevertheless, she went to church Sunday morning.

Since moving to San Antonio two months ago from her introductory TV job in Beaumont, Veronica had taken to sampling churches. This was in part a spiritual quest, partly a way to meet people and get to know the city, and partly just the following of a newswoman's instincts. She had tried Grace Baptist Church (the faith in which she'd been raised), First Presbyterian downtown, the giant Alamo Heights Methodist Church (known even to some of its members as the Methodome), and even a Mass at Mission San Juan.

Veronica made herself a quick breakfast in the sparkling kitchen of her garden home in the Great Northwest, not taking any care to be quiet. A wrecking ball through the window wouldn't have awakened her roommate on a Sunday morning.

Then Veronica deviated from her usual course, driving east toward downtown. She followed Culebra inward, not coming across any sanctuaries that particularly tugged at her soul until, getting close to downtown, she saw on her left the domes of the Little Flower basilica.

Perfect. This was a neighborhood where, if spiritual enlightenment didn't descend on her, she might at least see a robbery in progress and get some video. (Veronica already had the North Sider's prejudice that crime happened constantly in those parts of town she never visited.)

The 70-year-old shrine, undergoing restoration, was beautiful, with its vivid stained-glass windows, soaring ceiling, and tall shrine dominating the altar. Veronica lapsed into reverie during the Mass.

Afterward, she lingered. Veronica was one of the last to leave, and was delayed further by a large man who had trapped the priest.

"Tell me what to do, Father. Now the offer's out there, I've got to say yes or no, and either way I'm screwed, excuse my French."

The priest spoke in a much softer voice, obviously in a platitude that didn't satisfy his parishioner. The man, tall with broad sloping shoulders, leaned down, large hands running around the brim of the hat he held.

"But this man is a powerful elected official, Father. Wouldn't God want me to tell somebody? Or would that be like snitching?"

As for so many people, schoolyard ethics clashed in the man's heart with what the Church taught.

Veronica crept closer. She needn't have worried about missing a word, because the big man's voice didn't seem to have a lower volume.

"I think, John, this would be best raised in confession," the priest murmured.

"But I haven't done anything yet, Father. I want to know what to do."

Veronica came closer. "I couldn't help overhearing. I think I can help you."

The large man looked at her in surprise. Then he looked back at his priest. "Is this one of those new nuns who don't wear habits?"

Father Dominicus looked Veronica up and down, her long legs, her skirt a few inches above the knew, her slender arms and shining face, nose almost twitching at the scent of a story. The priest shook his head no.

"Come," Veronica said, taking John by the arm. "I think we may be the answer to each other's prayers."

As the two disappeared, a late arriver hurried up the steps of the basilica.

"Would you hear my confession, Father? I couldn't get by here yesterday."

The priest rolled his eyes. "Oh, no, Estela. Please, Estela, I don't have time. I have to be at a CYO meeting in two hours."

Estela Valenzuela smiled and took her confessor's arm. "Come hear me, Father. I have a lot to tell you."

How to Bribe a City Councilman

First, there must be a go-between. Don't worry, there will be. If you want something, want it publicly, the go-between will find you, and explain how the councilman can help. It's up to you. You can accept the councilman's help, or you can make your application through the normal process.

This had been John Marroquin's dilemma. Once the approach came, he knew he had to take the offer. If he didn't, the offer would be made to some other contractor, who would win the city grant – federal money, but disbursed by the city – without the formality of the city staff's intervention.

"All right," John said. "But how do I know you can deliver?"

The go-between smiled.

At the next meeting, John met the councilman. Sort of. John and the go-between, who happened to be the councilman's cousin and had obtained several small city contracts himself, were having a leisurely breakfast at Earl Abel's one Wednesday morning.

Earl's is popular for breakfast, especially with a certain crowd who likes biscuits and gravy and power. The councilman made an entrance. You couldn't miss him – a tall, gangly man, deeply browned, who seemed to know everyone intimately, including the busboys. He made his way slowly to the table with his cousin and the mark.

Cousin Henry quickly made introductions. The councilman gripped John's hand hard and looked him in the eye – for the last time. The rest of the meal, while cousin Henry talked, the councilman turned his chair away from the table, waved and called to people across the room, and occasionally walked away to have another conversation.

Later, if anything happened, he would certainly be able to deny that he'd overheard his cousin making the offer. His only reason for being there, after all, was to prove that his cousin could deliver him. Cash bribes come only with unwritten guarantees.

"The councilman works very hard for the people of his district. Eighty-hour weeks, even 90. For which he's paid $20 a week. Disgraceful. So when he can help someone, he has a suggested contribution level. Ten percent. You have applied for a block grant of

$250,00 to build low-income housing."

Henry let the contractor do the math. He could still make a profit. But could these guys deliver? "This project isn't even in the councilman's district."

"Don't worry. He's the go-to guy on projects like this. It will never even go to the staff for their approval."

"All right. We have a deal. What next?"

"Let me work. I'll be in touch."

A few days later, Henry and John met at Pico de Gallo near downtown for lunch. The councilman didn't come anywhere near this meeting, at which payment details were worked out. "Half up front," Henry said, scribbling in a notebook like a bookie. "*Bueno?* Can do?"

"*Si*," said the contractor, and he had never said the syllable with greater anxiety.

They next met downtown at the Plaza Club, atop the Frost Bank Tower. At an early lunch, John spotted cousin Henry and strolled close to him. He opened his jacket to reveal a thick brown legal-size envelope. Henry glanced at it and could see it held a stack of crisp hundred-dollar bills. His face showed alarm.

"Not here, you fool! Come to my office, 5:30 this afternoon."

"Only if he's there."

Henry shook his head slowly. "You and he will not meet again."

"Then he will not meet my friends in the brown envelope."

Cousin Henry studied Contractor John, who had a new strength in his gaze. Big boy thought he was a player now. Henry smiled inwardly. Once the contractor was in, he was dirty. He could do no damage.

"Come at 5:30," he repeated.

How to get the bribery on videotape

- Be outside the cousin's office, in long perspective. Get footage of the three men going in separately. When the councilman comes out, you get very lucky, he puts a brown envelope to his lips and kisses it quickly. Great visual.

- Put the camera in his face and ask what's in the envelope, now concealed in his pocket. The councilman smiles broadly and starts sweating.

• Sample exchange:

"What are you talking about?"

"The envelope you just kissed for the camera, councilman. How much money is in it?" you ask into your microphone, then extend it toward the councilman.

Still smiling, still sweating, he mumbles an evasion and turns away, almost running. Let the camera follow him.

• How do you get the bribery on videotape? Be the one who set up the whole sting.

"Nice work, Veronica!" the news director exclaimed when his reporter returned to the station with the footage. "Great stuff. Now get me more."

Madeleine Grohman drove Estela to the McNay Art Museum, circling the grounds to the Jones Building at the very back so that Estela felt as if she were literally being taken behind the scenes at the storied old home.

Maddie shepherded her charge past the unusual brick columns and the small white elephant statues, tusks lowered as if fending off intruders, and into the airy library where the board of the Friends of the McNay met monthly.

The Friends love new members," Maddie said graciously, but once inside she watched Estela more closely than any other observer.

Estela appeared young and impressionable, her eyes taking in every detail of the beautiful room. the girl remained gracefully silent except when addressed, a sign of a good upbringing or shyness, either of which was attractive in a young woman. Then again, her attitude might have been a matter of cunning stealth, Maddie thought. As if to provide a contrast, Lulu McDaniel, this year's chairman of the Friends, appeared. Lulu had been the queen of every room she entered since at least the age of four, and it would have taken a much stronger character than Lulu's to change the attitude created by seventy years of such treatment.

Maddie wondered if Lulu even realized that in her normal posture her nose was the most elevated part of her body.

"Well, and who have we here? Fresh blood? Thank you, dear Maddie, I'm sure we can use fresh ideas."

Said with an edge that meant quite the opposite. Lulu had enjoyed the Friends' reputation of being impossible for newcomers to penetrate.

Estela said softly, "The McNay and its Friends have had a wonderful run without my help."

"Oh, have you seen some of our exhibitions, my dear?"

"Not in quite some time. I haven't been back in town long. But for example, I did see the Rodin exhibition. Wonderful."

"Thank you. But I thought you hadn't been here?"

"I saw it in San Francisco, where it began," Estela said modestly.

"Ah." The others watched Lulu for reaction. She said studiously, "We thought it important to bring that here. No reproduction can give you the full impact of a piece like 'The Thinker'. You have to stand in the room with it. The size, for one thing…"

"Yes, and the texture," Estela said quietly, looking at Lulu as if impressed by her insight.

Lulu looked shocked. "You mean you've touched it?"

Estela ducked her head. "They had a pre-exhibition showing for some art students. I understand this came from M. Rodin's explicit instructions. He wrote, 'One must see the daubs of paint, even the artist's sweat imbedded in the pigment. And one must feel my work not only with the heart but with the hand.' Sculpture should be touched."

"I've never read that," Lulu said, musing.

"My own translation," Estela shrugged.

Lulu gave the girl a sharp glance from under lizard lids and went to the podium to organize her notes. Miz Maddie looked at Estela with an odd feeling of pride. For just a moment she thought she saw something familiar in the young woman's face.

After the meeting, the two of them wandered the McNay grounds. It was February, but the kind of spring day that San Antonio can throw any time, like an impromptu fiesta. "You made quite an —" Maddie began, then noted Estela taking a deep breath.

"What is it?"

"Can't you smell it?" Estela said wonderingly. "Rain coming. There, the first drop. See?"

"Rain has a smell? I've had sinus problems all my life, but today —"

"Don't you know?" Estela sounded shocked and sorrowful. "It's the freshest smell there is. Smell it!"

A fragrance did fill Maddie's nostrils, one she had smelled before but never identified. "Is that rain? It smells like new life."

And Maddie felt how old she was to encounter something so new. She watched Estela move around the pond, her eyes darting with the fish. The scene took the old lady back to a feeling but not a specific scene. For a moment, she felt the nearness of love.

Another drop landed on Miz Maddie's wrist, but it wasn't rain. "Jerry," she said softly.

Out of sight in the bushes bordering Austin Highway, Evelyn kept the binoculars fastened to her eyes. "What are they doing?" her stepson Gabe asked.

"They're looking in the pond."

"Maybe this girl buried something there," Gabe whispered. "Something she stole from Dad." In fact, Gabe still harbored a suspicion that his father's death hadn't been the result of his dad's own carelessness, but there was no evidence to support that hunch.

"Maybe she'd push Maddie in if there weren't so many witnesses." Evelyn voiced a thought she'd had several times, but said it as if shocked.

"This is getting us nowhere," Gabe said angrily, pulling a leaf from his hair. "We've got to track her to her lair."

"Yes," Evelyn said. "You do."

"Why, Madeleine Grohman, whatever are you doing here?" Helen Burns, whom Maddie had known for decades, looked as startled as if she'd peeped in a brothel window and spotted 74-year-old Maddie playing the piano.

Maddie looked around the Oak Park H.E.B. where the two stood, shopping carts side by side, and wondered if the store had a reputation of which she wasn't aware. Did respectable people shop some place else? "Just buying groceries, Helen."

Helen looked startled, then put her head back and laughed. She walked off down the aisle shaking her head as if to say, "Good one."

Maddie felt offended. True, she hadn't done her own grocery shopping in quite some time, but did people think of her as being above that sort of thing? She wasn't. In fact, Maddie was quite enjoying her spin through the aisles. There seemed to be more foods than there had been the last time she was here, and certainly more packaging. She had forgotten that even tin cans have a distinctive smell. And when she got to the produce section – oh, my. Maddie just stood and breathed deeply.

When she emerged carrying plastic bags, the sun was setting beyond Nacogdoches Road and the junior school. The deep blue sky was clear except at the horizon, where a few low, dark clouds caught the last of the sun's rays, smoldering with that fire.

Maddie stood in the parking lot and stared.

She realized she was the only one appreciating the display when a hurrying shopper bumped her. Maddie sighed. We're a long time in the ground, she thought. Got to see every sunset.

In the car she started crying again. She cried for herself, for life never being long enough, but mostly for her son Jerry. She'd had Jerry for 50 years, a long time. She felt sorry for young Gabe, who'd only had his father for the 24 years of Gabe's life, not nearly long enough. Not the best of years, either.

A father and son don't have a real conversation until the son is almost grown, if then. Gabe had never seen his father at his best, as a wild but essentially decent young man with a gift for amazingly kind gestures.

Maddie drifted through the large, gleaming kitchen of her Olmos Park home. Her thoughts still full of Jerry, she opened the door of her study and gasped.

Estela Valenzuela stood in the middle of the room with her hands clasped behind her back. Today the girl wore a simple yellow dress that made her skin look browner and her face as fresh as a schoolgirl's. "You asked me to come, remember?"

Over in the corner, sitting silently on the window seat, sat Jerry Grohman, his eyes deep rifts of sorrow, deeper than the living can grieve. Death was supposed to end suffering, at least. Just Jerry's luck, death had only deepened his pain. He had held this family's life and future in his hands, and had blown it. He stared helplessly at his distracted mother, wishing he could hold her.

"You know what I just did?" Maddie asked wonderingly. "I

bought groceries. I watched the sunset. What's happening to me?" She stared at Estela. "What have you done to me?"

Estela crossed the room and touched the older lady's arm. "You're drawing life close, I think. Because you miss him. I know. I miss him too."

"But you didn't even know Jerry."

"Oh, I did, Miz Maddie. Believe me, I did."

Maddie's lawyer could have told her that this is what con artists always say, and Maddie was no innocent to be taken in by a stranger. But she found the girl's touch reassuring. Of what, she couldn't say.

Over in the corner, the ghost sighed audibly and disappeared. Estela glanced at the window seat. Her eyes, too, held tears.

The tender scene that might have ensued was ended by a shattering sound from the front of the house, the plaintive wail of a heart-torn woman.

Another One Bites My Dust

Veronica Lewis enjoyed her new reputation as a sharp investigative reporter. Other reporters watched her closely, as at a City Hall news conference when Veronica began questioning District Councilwoman Suzanne Pierce.

Ms. Pierce, a corporate attorney and partner at the prestigious old firm of Burke & Dale, at the age of 36 was young and tight. Tight with the city's money, in tight with the business establishment, and generally tight-lipped. She worked out every day instead of lunching. And she had a very tight grip on the lead in the as-yet-undeclared race to be the next mayor of San Antonio.

"Ms. Pierce, would you release your billing records if asked to do so?" Veronica asked brightly.

"While I believe wholeheartedly in the concept of full disclosure, I owe discretion to my clients, and the city attorney has ruled that my billing records are not matters of public record."

Veronica made a mark in her notebook. Since everything she said and heard was recorded on videotape, the notebook was useless, but Veronica thought it added the perfect touch to her gutsy reporter image.

She contined to stare at Suzanne Pierce, who made a tiny hand gesture that the television reporter took to mean that they would continue the interview privately. Later that afternoon when Veronica dropped by Ms. Pierce's office in the Weston Centre, her interpretation proved correct.

"We'll go off the record," the city councilwoman said. She lounged back in her large desk chair and undid her jacket buttons, but continued to look tight. "If this were the good old days and we were men, I'd offer you a cigar. Come to think of it, that's what with-it women do now, isn't it? Want a cigar?"

"No thanks. I want to talk about your billing. I talked to the former managing partner of your firm, Branch Richmond. He's a wonderful old gentleman, isn't he? Charming way with a story."

"Yes, he's become quite the raconteur since he lost his mind," Suzanne Pierce said acidly.

"Some of his old friends say he had an epiphany of honesty since he retired."

"His specialist calls it an early onset of Alzheimer's."

"At any rate, he talks quite freely about any subject. Told me, for example, about coming into your office one day unexpectedly and finding you in a compromising – and quite athletic, according to him – position with an important client. Later he checked your hours and found you'd billed the client for your time during that hour."

"Are you calling me something?" Ms. Pierce asked tightly.

"Not yet. Mr. Richard called it the sign of a good lawyer. 'Takes a drilling and keeps on billing' was the phrase he used, I believe."

"That would be between me and the client, wouldn't it?"

"Yes, but your other billing records would be more interesting to voters. Such as the several times you billed a client for time during City Council meetings you attended."

Suzanne Pierce stared silently, then said slowly and deliberately, "I have dual thought processes. It's a rare attribute, but one shared by many of the nation's best attorneys. I can think about more than one thing at a time. While someone is droning on about the city budget –"

"I'll bet you can talk out of both sides of your mouth at once, too," Veronica smiled. She imagined it as a very sly, smart smile, and she wished she had a camera on her. "I can't wait to hear you explain this dual thought process thing to voters. I, for example, took it to mean either that you were cheating a client or that you were representing a client's interest while casting your vote."

"What do you want?" the attorney said.

"Do whatever you think best."

"You know, your revealing this could cost me the mayor's race. But let me tell you, Veronica, it would be the city's loss, not mine. I would make the best mayor this city's had in a quarter century."

Veronica smiled attentively. Ms. Pierce glared at her. "But that's not as important as sweeps month, is it?" she said bitterly.

Veronica thought Suzanne Pierce would have made a perfectly typical mayor. She had a politician's habit of saying the obvious aloud.

As the young TV reporter left, Ms. Pierce asked, "Who put you onto this story?"

"I have my sources," Veronica said smugly. And she wished she knew who that source might have been.

The Grohman family had earned its fortune the old-fashioned way: they dug it out of the ground. The Grohmans began quarrying limestone on land leased from the city of San Antonio in the 1850s. Following generations became great salesmen.

Grohman limestone went into San Antonio's earliest fashionable stone homes. As the city grew, the stone built mansions in King William in the 1870s to 1890s and in Monte Vista in the 1920s. Then the family branched out into other building materials. Its fortune was as solid as the earth. And, as occasional in-laws discovered, Grohmans clung to that fortune with a rock-like grip.

Evelyn Grohman, screaming again, rushed into Madeleine Grohman's antique-furnished study. "My lawyer's just read the will to me! Your son – your horrible, selfish son! Do you know what he left me?"

"Some lovely memories, I'm sure," Miz Maddie replied quietly.

The young, over-indulged Evelyn quivered like a tuning fork. "A life estate!" she screamed. "Do you know what a life estate is?"

Of course the matriarch of the Grohman family knew, but Evelyn went on.

"He left everything to his children. That's how he put it: 'my children,' as if I had nothing to do with them."

"Two of them you didn't, Evelyn."

"Everything to them, and I get a life estate. I get to use the house and the money as long as I live, then it all goes to them!"

"Isn't your life long enough, Evelyn?"

Evelyn wouldn't listen. "None of you ever treated me like a member of this family." She finally noticed Estela Valenzuela standing quietly near the desk. "Now you bring in this stranger, this tart, and leave me out in the cold. This was probably your idea, wasn't it?"

"I never talked to Jerry about his will," Estela said quietly.

Evelyn glared at her, at the young woman's use of her late husband's first name, at her presence in the old house, at – at everything about her.

Evelyn turned back to Miz Maddie. "Well, you can keep it all. The ranch, this house, the cars, the jewelry – actually, I would like the diamonds. But I won't put up with this! You know what I'll do? I'll live forever, that's what I'll do. I'll buy myself whatever I want."

Evelyn's face grew redder as she thought furiously about how to exact revenge on her late husband. "I'll get fat! Then again, I might go a different direction, if you know what I mean, and I think you do.

"You haven't seen the end of Evelyn Grohman." She rushed out of the room.

Miz Maddie, apparently unfazed by the tirade, observed, "That will be a more impressive and truthful exit line if she does get fat. Actually, it's a little too easy to see the end of her already."

Estela laughed. Maddie gazed at her gratefully. "What are we to do, Estela?"

"Whatever I can do to help, I will," Estela said earnestly.

It is with just such lines, Miz Maddie's old friends would soon tell her, that an infiltrator begins worming her way into an old woman's confidence.

Later that evening on the Channel Six news, Veronica Lewis observed for the camera: "With Councilman Esparza facing bribery charges, and Councilwoman Suzanne Pierce's lead in the mayor's race shrinking daily as more allegations about her business affairs surface, new mayoral candidates are emerging from untraditional sources.

"MacArthur High School football coach Del Rivera is said to be considering the run, and today at Fort Sam, Commanding General 'Hawk' Bintner held a press conference to announce he will seek the office upon his retirement.

"Tomorrow night, more revelations. As regular viewers know, we here at SpySix News have set a few traps for local politicos. Tomorrow: Who has fallen for them, and who has not!"

In her small living room in a carriage house in King William, Estela Valenzuela turned off the TV. She paced the old wooden floor, home to many a groom and maid. But Estela was no servant. Alone, she lost the modest look she had displayed all afternoon in the Grohman house. Her eyes, more hazel than brown, grew sharp.

"The old lady likes me," she said. "But will she tell me anything?"

In the corner, the ghost of Jerry Grohman whispered, *"Milagro Lane."* Estela's eyes took on a faraway glow.

Gabe Grohman stood with Jessica Ambrose outside one of the most popular restaurants in San Antonio.

"What do you think? Does this look okay?" he asked.

The sign advertising a hamburger, french fries and a medium drink for $1.99 made Gabe skeptical, but he was rather charmed by the advice painted on the side of the building: "Turn on Lights for Service."

Jessica peered over her sunglasses. "I think we can count on not seeing Stephanie or Patty or your grandmother. Come on."

And so, feeling adventurous, they walked boldly into the Malt House.

"Oh, my God," Jessica said at once.

Gabe and Jessica had known each other since Alamo Heights High School, from which they'd both graduated seven years earlier. At the University of Texas they'd occasionally seen each other at parties, laughed over old times and tacitly acknowledged how sophisticated they'd both become.

After college they'd gone into their respective family businesses: Gabe into Grohman Manufacturing, Jessica into marriage. She'd married Jim Ambrose, one of the old crowd and vaguely a friend of Gabe's. She'd done the social thing, Junior League, charity boards, laughed and lunched and tennised. Gabe had worked desultorily.

One night at a martini party they'd looked into each other's eyes and seen deep-seated boredom and a mutual adventurousness neither had ever suspected. Shortly thereafter they'd had the first of their lunches.

That one had been at the New Braunfels Smokehouse in Sunset Ridge, to look casual, but they'd seen ten people they knew and realized this couldn't work. After their affair became real, they turned openly secretive.

Gabe and Jessica no longer talked at parties. Where once they'd been huddled in deep conversation, now they only smiled and nodded. People who noticed such things – that is to say, women – assumed either that they'd had a falling out or the relationship had deepened in private. So now when Jessica and Gabe had lunch, it was in Boerne or some place even more remote, such as the south side.

Today they cruised the west side, and stopped at a whim at the old Malt House. Looking for a low dive where they couldn't possibly be recognized, they stumbled into an institution. Inside, the large front room was crowded, with lots of tables leaving little floor space. Icicle lights hung from the ceiling of the room divider, though Christmas was three months past. Bright white light bounced off the white walls, and the linoleum floors and hard ceiling kept the constant chatter confined, so the noise level was similar to a high school cafeteria.

"What's the matter" Gabe asked after Jessica's outburst.

Dropping her sunglasses back over her eyes, Jessica whispered, "It's Alex Briseño. We've met. You know Jim does a lot of business with the city."

"It's okay," Gabe said. "Look, it's a big group. Probably a farewell party. He won't see us. come on, let's get a table."

Jessica pulled her black leather coat tighter around her and kept her sunglasses on. She was blonde and beautiful and had style, so incognito was not her best thing. Seated in a booth, she smiled brightly at Gabe. He smiled back and took her hand. After a few minutes they looked at the eclectic menu.

"Goodness," Jessica said, gazing over the offerings: seafood, hamburgers, enchiladas and American favorites. "Do you think it would be okay to order Mexican food?"

While the heiress pondered whether good Mexican food could be had in San Antonio's biggest barrio, a staffer arrived late at the long table set up for the city manager's party. Marty Brewer was young but looked tired: a veteran of City Hall, in other words.

"Councilman Carter sends his regrets," she said to Briseno.

"Does he indeed?" the longtime city manager said with a smile, as if he could speak his mind now that he neared retirement. But ever discreet, he didn't.

Terry Brechtel, who would replace Briseno as the city manager, didn't notice her boss's tone.

At the adulterers' table, Gabe suddenly echoed Jessica's first exclamation.

"What?" his partner asked anxiously, looking around.

"It's her. The girl I told you about. Estela Valenzuela. Is she following me?"

Gazing around the room, Jessica said, "Darling, I think it's more likely you've stumbled into her lair."

"Duck," Gabe said in an urgent undertone. "She's coming this way."

They hid behind their menus. Giggling, Jessica reached out from under hers and took Gabe's hand. This was the adventure of having an affair. Estela didn't glance at them as she took a seat behind Gabe.

"This is a small town," Gabe Groman muttered. he sat in a booth at the Malt House, back to back with Estela Valenzuela, pretty sure she hadn't noticed him, but afraid to turn his head.

His lover Jessica Ambrose smiled at him her smile that had been rendered dazzling by thousands of dollars worth of braces and caps. Under the table, she slipped off her shoe and ran her stockinged foot around Gabe's ankle.

This was one advantage in being the boyfriend, rather than the husband. They felt an obligation to be frisky with each other. Gabe felt sure Jessica would never have done this with her husband in public. But then, she probably didn't consider the Malt House public, since she felt safe from being seen by anyone she knew.

Then Gabe was surprised to see a stranger approaching: a man of about 30, with light brown skin and very black, stiff hair; a thin man, but with wide cheeks, as if nature intended him to be fat but he resisted. He wore a look of amazement. Gabe quickly ducked his head.

"Estela!" the man exclaimed.

Estela's face went through a rapid series of reactions: surprise, pleasure, then some trepidation.

"Juan! This *is* a small town! But aren't you supposed to be in California? Is it Dr. Juan now"

"I'm still working on my dissertation," Juan Palomo said lightly, but in such a way that Estela knew not to inquire further. "I'm working on it here."

"In the Malt House?" Estela laughed.

"*Y tu, Estela?* What are you doing in San Antonio?"

She shrugged. Juan's eyes narrowed in speculation.

Across the busy main room of the Malt House, across an expanse of Formica-topped tables pushed closely enough together that a child could easily have skated across them from the door to the back, two uniformed San Antonio police officers finished their lunches. A Hispanic sergeant and an Anglo patrolman, they spoke to each other in low tones and resolutely didn't look around at the other patrons. When the waitress brought coffee, the sergeant asked for the check.

"It's taken care of, Manuelito."

"We're not taking any freebies, Anna," the sergeant said stiffly.

The waitress smiled. "Since when?"

"You know since when."

"Well, you'll have to take it up with the gentleman over there. He paid your check. And that table and that table and the one over there wanted to."

The two officers looked around the room for the first time. Patrons smiled, toasted with their iced tea glasses, and one lady gave them a thumbs up. After a moment the officers returned the salutes.

Estela watched this brief scene of reconciliation – only weeks after a police bribery scandal – over Juan's shoulder. Her eyes grew a little moist as he said, "Tell me what you're doing here, Estela. But I'm afraid it has to be fast. I've only got 49 minutes."

"Important appointment?"

"No, I'm a teacher. At Lanier."

Estela stared. "Teaching *high* school? What are you doing, penance? Working undercover? Is this for your thesis?"

Juan smiled rather sadly. "Maybe all those things. But I really am teaching. History and government."

"You'll be a good teacher, Juan. Who should know better than me?"

"Where are you living, Estela? Near here?"

"King William."

"King William? Isn't that a little..." Juan groped for the right disdainful word.

"What's wrong with King William? It's a fugitive hide-out."

"And are you exploring the whole city, Estela? Have you found your way to Milagro Lane?" Juan said the phrase like a password or an inside joke.

In the next booth, Gabe felt a sudden chill. The phrase echoed in his memory, so evocative he thought he should place it.

Jessica had just murmured something to him, a sibilant, husky whisper. Gabe stared blankly at her. Luckily, Jessica found dumbstruck looks on men arousing. She took them as tributes.

"Let's go, lover," she whispered, taking his hand.

Yes, Gabe wanted to leave with Jessica. But even more, he wanted to get to his street map.

"*Milagro Lane,*" he repeated silently to himself.

Of the former leading contenders in the San Antonio mayor's race, one was edging closer to indictment than to electoral victory, and the other, Councilwoman Suzanne Pierce, saw her candidacy ridiculed as more and more questions arose about her law practice and personal ties to business leaders. In support, KSAN-TV had started a daily "Pierce Responds to Charges" segment that began to verge on satire.

Councilwoman Pierce watched reporter Veronica Lewis host this jolly segment every day on the channel 6 news and smoldered. As Pierce's numbers shrank, her thoughts of mayhem grew. "How hard could it be?" she said aloud, glaring at the screen in her office. "Stupid criminals get away with it all the time."

As the traditional candidates faded away, contenders who in the past would have been considered marginal stepped forward. Maybe they were still marginal, but they got better publicity in this campaign. General A. E. "Hawk" Bintner's press conference announcing his candidacy actually drew air time.

The Commanding General of Fort Sam Houston, set to retire at just about the time of the election, appeared in full uniform. Bintner looked very impressive standing at the head of a conference table in a conference room where charts and flags gave the impression of war planning. His thick gray eyebrows emphasized blazing blue eyes atop a nose that could have accounted for his nickname.

"Since coming to San Antonio three years ago I have thrown myself into civic affairs and into local history. San Antonian has enjoyed several reputations through its long history: party town, cradle of Texas liberty, bastion of patriotism. Margaritaville, Fiesta Town, *Mañana* Land.

"But first – and still – it has been a military town. This city was established as a fort. For its first decades the commander of the presidio set civic policy. Maybe it's time to resume that custom.

"San Antonio has high energy but traditionally low performance in matters such as education. A city with high potential but lack of focus." General Bintner looked sternly into the camera and thrust a finger down at the table. "Exactly the type of young person, in other words, who blossoms in the armed forces of these United States."

"Or gets sent to reform school," muttered Marty Brewster. The young but veteran city staffer watched the press conference on the television in the office of District 6 City Councilman Ramon Carter. Marty had worked for Carter for two years and felt secure in her job since the councilman faced only token opposition for re-election. As long as he kept turning down those debate challenges, he was pretty safe, which meant so were Marty and her colleagues.

What a pain it would be, she thought, if some earnest leader with ideas like this General Bintner were elected mayor. Maybe next time around they should urge Carter to run for mayor. Thinking this insane thought, Marty laughed out loud at herself.

Then Veronica Lewis appeared on screen. "Tomorrow we begin a feature spotlighting the city council races. First up will be incumbent District 6 councilman Ramon Carter, and his very interesting community strategy for re-election."

Marty Brewster's eyes widened in horror. "No!" she screamed at the screen. "No, no no."

Her colleague Jack Jeffers came racing in. "What happened?"

"Someone said his name on TV," Marty wailed, and they both groaned.

On screen, the anchor thanked Veronica and said, "Back to the mayor's race: another unusual mayoral candidate is MacArthur High School football coach Del Rivera. A legend in the making at MacArthur, where he took the young team to the 5A state finals for the first time in decades, Rivera says he has been urged to run by many civic leaders and organizations."

Cut to a serious man of 40 or so, gray at the temples showing under his black baseball cap. Rivera seemed uncomfortable on camera, but spoke earnestly. "I see these kids carrying their backpacks and gym bags and already, at such young ages, they seem burdened by responsibility. I want to see what we as parents and teachers and as a city can do to relieve some of that burden, for all our kids."

In the studio, watching him critically, Veronica thought the coach spoke well but could have been taken more seriously if he'd been wearing something other than those tight, gray coach's shorts. Well, maybe the city was ready for a leader in shorts. God knows we'd done <u>guyaberas</u> to death.

Her thoughts returned to Councilman Carter, and her eyes narrowed. He had proven hard to get, and Veronica was getting good at getting people. She wasn't ready to give up on this one yet.

This was a special called meeting, not the regular monthly secret meeting of the Rich People Who Think They Run San Antonio.

In the 1950s and early '60s these meetings were held at Earl Abel's, at a table for four in the front room. Those were the days when they really did run San Antonio, and power wasn't ashamed of itself. The four white guys in charge didn't mind being seen together. Now the group has expanded and gotten secretive.

Roughly a dozen people attended this one. The leaders included a few women, even a couple of Hispanics, but the guys who had run the city half a century earlier would have still felt pretty much at home.

The meeting wasn't actually in San Antonio. It was at a private home in the Argyle area of Alamo Heights. It was a recently built home, a rarity for that area. One 50-ish man stood talking to the owner, who was of similar age.

"You know, this is very strange, but I can't remember what used to be on this lot. I know I must have seen it a thousand times, but for the life of me. . . ."

"That's because we bought the memory site as well," the proud owner said with a wink.

"The what?"

"The memory location. We didn't want people complaining that we'd torn down some historic home or, you know, comparing ours with what used to be here, so we bought out the whole memory site."

"Wow, that's great. I didn't know you could do that."

"Oh yes." The owner was in full imaginative form now. "The technique used to be very expensive when it first came out, but like everything else, it's gotten cheaper. Aging of the baby boomers and so forth, you know, memory isn't worth nearly what it used to be."

The visitor considered the possibilities. "Do you think they could make everybody forget my first wife?"

"Give them a call," the host urged. "I've got their card around here somewhere. If I can remember where I put it . . ."

There was no president to call the meeting to order, and in fact no order, because none of these people would take instructions from any of the others. But gradually, one topic would dominate and people would draw together. In this case, of course, it was the mayor's race.

"I still think Suzanne Pierce can be saved," one man said grumpily.

"Her soul, maybe. But if you're talking about her campaign, you're delusional."

"So that takes care of both our candidates," one woman observed, though she sounded determined rather than resigned. "I think we should back General Bintner now. He's got to be pro-business."

Everyone in the room was, of course, a business person. A banker, construction company chief, developers and a big-time real estate broker. There was a complete absence of elected officials, and surprisingly, only one lawyer – who hadn't practiced law in years, and so was tolerated by the elite.

"I don't know. I've heard peculiar things about him," the banker said of the general. "I'm throwing my votes behind the football coach. Once we give him a game plan, he'll go with it. He's used to it."

"How many votes do you control now, John?" another man asked.

John, a former banker and current deal-maker nearing 70, calculated quickly. "Used to be I could count on three, but my wife went for Kay Turner last time, so I guess it's down to me and my secretary."

Others nodded soberly. The fact was that San Antonio had been uncontrollable for some years now. Too many constituencies, too much feisty independence. The youngest man sighed and said to his friend, "I miss the good old days."

"Brent, the good old days ended when you were about eight."

"I know, and I miss them."

Estela Valenzuela knelt in the confessional at San Fernando Cathedral, which she considered her "other" parish. Because of its proximity to her King William home, she could rush here when she felt in quick need of absolution.

"Bless me, Father, for I plan to sin."

On the other side of the screen, Father Garcia sighed. "I've explained again and again, Estela, you cannot confess and be forgiven for something you haven't done yet."

"Why not? I just want a little insurance."

"But it's very difficult to demonstrate true repentance when you still plan to do it."

"Oh, believe me, Father, I'm sorry already."

But the priest remained firm. Estela finally rose, saying, "All right, I'll be back."

She went out into the odd urban serenity of Main Plaza. Behind her, Father Garcia said, "Oh, I'm sure of that." And sighed.

"Alias King William"

It was perhaps no coincidence that Estela Valenzuela had chosen to live on a street that had worked undercover for more than a century. Historical rumor claimed that the German-speaking immigrants who had built the neighborhood just south of downtown in the 1870s had originally named the street Kaiser Wilhelmstrasse. That was not true. The street had indeed been named for Kaiser Wilhelm of Prussia, but had from the beginning carried an Americanized version of the name: King William.

During the Great War, when anything that hinted of German sympathy suddenly became *verboten* in this country, the name of the street had in fact been changed to Pershing Avenue. But that name had not lasted, and King William had re-emerged. By now it was a fashionable and lovely neighborhood, but still with pockets of bohemian quirkiness.

During San Antonio's long and colorful history, many a bad man and shady lady had appeared there, changed names, and tried to lead a respectable life thereafter. King William, as far as we know, is the first entire neighborhood ever to do so.

Estela lived on King William Street itself, behind one of the most elegant houses, in a small carriage house. The house, which the owners rented to her, consisted of a small front room, bedroom and bathroom in back, and kitchenette. Basically a large stand-alone dorm room, the house suited her perfectly. It was old, its windows opened, it was centrally located.

April found Estela wearing blue jean shorts, a coral-colored, ribbed top, and no shoes as she sat at the computer in her bedroom. She liked the idea of retreating here to scour the Internet with no one looking over her shoulder. Or perhaps Estela's preference for a bedroom office was genetic. Her mother, the artist, always said she did her best work in the bedroom. If anyone fell into this trap with a look or an off-color remark, the artist would add in her loftiest accent, "I mean, of course, my subconscious mind working on a problem while I sleep. What did *you* think?"

Estela smiled at the thought of her mother. She had come to San Antonio partly to escape her mother and partly to find her again. But now she searched for something else, scouring the Internet for indexes to old deeds and wills.

She was interrupted by a voice calling through her front window, doing a Marlon Brando impression. "Hey, 'STELA! We're going to go look at some mediocre Hispanic art. Wanta come?"

Estela popped out of the bedroom and saw Jaime Jones and Ramos Ramos, the gouged-canvas and string-mud-and-matchstick artist, respectively, leaning in her window. The "boys," who were well into their forties, had eked out livings in the art world their whole lives, usually supplementing that income by waiting tables, but lately Jaime's massacred-canvas works were enjoying a vogue, even in soulless cities such as Dallas.

"No thanks," Estela said. "I've got some on my walls, I'll just look at it."

"Hey!" Jaime Jones said, pretending offense, since some of the art in question was his. Ramos Ramos, who had been born Anglo – in New Jersey, no less – smiled silently.

The boys waved 'bye and Estela decided to take a break. There was a lot of material online, but she had to go to the Bexar County Archives at the courthouse, and possibly to the UTSA and Daughters of the Republic of Texas libraries as well. She felt sure the documents she sought had never been put online. They might have been missing altogether.

As Estela left her house she felt observed, and remembered suddenly that she was following a path staked out by the late Jerry Grohman. And look where it had gotten him. She looked around and saw nothing but a beautiful spring day resting lightly on a lovely neighborhood. Nevertheless, she walked a little more briskly than usual.

A block down she passed one of the most elegant Victorian mansions in the neighborhood, the West home. Tour bus drivers liked to tell their audiences that the former owner was buried in the house's yard, sitting in her Ferrari. This was a colorful lie. Ms. West was actually buried in an east side city-owned cemetery. In her Ferrari.

Hitting her stride, Estela swung on down King William, walking by the home of nationally known criminal defense lawyer Gerald Goldstein. But sight of the attorney's residence momentarily darkened Estela's thoughts. She hoped she wouldn't need Mr. Goldstein's services. She thought again of Jerry Grohman.

Far across town, in her Olmos Park home, Miz Maddie Grohman suddenly looked startled, and turned to her grandson Gabe. "Did you feel that? Oddest feeling. As if the whole foundation shifted."

Juan Palomo had a second job. This saved him the trouble of getting a life. It now seemed rather impulsive that he'd moved back to San Antonio and started teaching at Lanier High School. He looked up a few of his old friends and found little in common with them, and as a teacher it was hard to make new friends. Teachers spend their days with students, not other adults.

He'd spent eight years in California, attending Stanford, going on to graduate school, teaching, losing his accent. He'd had a love affair that had ended badly: they'd gotten married. There'd come a point where he and Janelle both knew they had to take the relationship to the next level or lose it. But married in haste, they repented by the next weekend. Both realized that marriage had not been the correct next step in their relationship. Breaking up was.

After that Juan had rapidly gotten sick of everything Californian, and had come home. And one night his old friend James Boren, who now owned a limousine service, asked if Juan would fill in for a sick driver. Juan had found the occasion, a wedding, rather interesting, especially when the bride and groom forgot he was there and spent the ride to their wedding night exchanging gossip about the guests.

Vaguely Juan thought he was on the road to a dissertation topic, and kept driving occasionally. It afforded him glimpses into other lives, usually at dramatic moments. He enjoyed it. Until the night the Invisible Man rode in the back of his car.

"One of Councilman Ramon Carter's most interesting and popular customs is to let constituents fill in for him during City Council votes. Different people from his district get to cast votes personally on important city issues. The councilman feels this is important both symbolically and to keep citizens involved. So in the past year, the councilman from District 6 has worn this variety of faces."

Ace TV reporter Veronica Lewis lowered her microphone as the newscast went to video clips of various residents of District 6 – black, brown, pink, male, female, and indeterminate – sitting with council members. Veronica twirled her mic. She felt rather kicky, in a black short skirt and sleeveless blue tank top with a man's white dress shirt worn as a sort of jacket. Veronica had decided she should create her own style rather than look like everyone else on the tube. After all, she was a hot item at channel 6 since the scandals that she'd both unearthed and helped create had aired.

In fact, the station had decided it was time for her to make nice. They didn't want her to risk coming off as a vixen. Hence the glowing report on Councilman Ramon Carter. That, plus she'd heard great things about him.

Her camera came back on. Veronica expertly twirled the mic up close to her mouth and wrapped up. "Remarkably for a politician, Councilman Carter is so camera-shy he returned my calls for comments but said he didn't have time to appear on camera. Constituents and co-workers, however, have nothing but praise for his work ethic."

Cut to Mayor Howard Peak, who would say nice things about anybody on his way out, and a couple of constituents. Veronica yawned. Nice stuff was okay, but it wasn't nearly as much fun as gutting someone.

Councilman Carter's staffer Jack Jeffers called to fellow staffer Marty Brewster, "She's talking about him again! At least she's being nice, but still… If we have to get him on camera one of these days…"

The two of them talked freely about their boss even as they stood in his office. "Never mind," Marty said. "We've got to get him to the reception. Is the limo here?"

And so a few minutes later a small entourage tumbled toward the limousine driven by Juan Palomo. Jack Jeffers, in the lead, called, "This way, Councilman."

Juan held the door, several people got in the limo, then a couple more got out, one gave Juan directions and money, and for a minute the scene was nothing but bustle and confusion, until a staffer closed the door and said, "We'll meet you there."

So Juan drove. The curtain had been drawn in the back. He couldn't see how many people remained in his car. They were very quiet. In fact, he had the impression the passenger compartment was empty.

Well, this was his first time to drive a politician. They probably always seemed that way.

Young Gabe Grohman thought of himself as one of the well-to-do homeless. (This is the highest financial state a Grohman would ever claim. The word "wealthy" or, God forbid, "rich," would never pass his lips, except scornfully in reference to someone else. "Oh, he thinks he's rich as the Kennedys," they might say of some *nouveau* with real estate or, worse, dot.com money.)

Gabe was as comfortable as one could wish financially, but had no place to sleep. Traditionally a young man in his position wouldn't buy a house until he was ready to marry, and Gabe was not. Mostly in the nearly three years since college he had lived in his father's King William home, but since his father's death, staying there with his stepmother Evelyn had become impossible. He had an apartment downtown with a river view, which he had acquired mainly to have a place to take his married girl friend. They needed some place where she wouldn't be seen by their regular crowd, but the same things that kept those friends away kept Jessica from visiting often. She complained about the lack of parking and the downtown milieu.

Gabe wasn't really a downtown kind of guy, either. He had a bedroom in his grandmother's Olmos Park home, and ended up spending most evenings there out of inertia. So he and Miz Maddie were thrown together. Maddie seemed oddly cheerful these days, but the sight of her grandson moping around didn't help.

"What's the matter, Gabito?" No one had used this fake-Spanish nickname on him in quite a while, and the sound of it made Gabe smile. But he looked melancholy nevertheless.

Gabe didn't think he wanted to answer, but then heard himself speaking. "Sometimes it seems to me I'm having the same life Dad did. You know, working in the business, having friends, travelling. But I think he had more fun than I am."

Maddie Grohman agreed. In his best times, no one she'd ever known could match Jerry's zest for life. Gabe had quite obviously not inherited that trait (though otherwise he would have been disconcerted to know how much he resembled his father.)

And Maddie knew Gabe's problem. It was the problem of every bright young man from an old, moneyed family. Gabe hadn't chosen his own destiny. This was what chafed at him, though he didn't know it and Maddie didn't want to be the one to tell him.

"Gabe, I think you want a challenge. Your life seems too easy. But it will come. Every generation faces its own testing. Believe me."

Gabe looked at her curiously. "What was yours, Grandma?"

She smiled sadly. "My son is dead. My grandson's not enjoying life. I think this could be one now."

Gabe stood and held her arms briefly. "Don't worry about me. I just need, like you say, a project. What about you, Grandma? You need to stay young. Are you developing new interests? Or – new friends?"

His grandmother gave him a look. "Gabito, there may come a time when you are too subtle for me, but when that day comes it will be because I've gone dotty, and *every*one is too subtle for me. You're asking about Estela Valenzuela."

Gabe shrugged.

"I know I made you and Evelyn antagonistic to her, Gabe. That was a mistake. She's just a nice girl who knew your father. She doesn't want anything from us."

But maybe, Gabe thought, *I want something from her.* He turned away, hoping his grandmother hadn't read the thought.

"Just meet her, Gabito. You'll like her. You and Evelyn come to dinner."

"I haven't seen Evelyn in two weeks. We don't really talk now."

"Yes, she took the will reading hard. I hope she's okay."

Evelyn Grohman, widow of Jerry, daughter of generations of upright, rigid bluestockings, found herself in a low place. She stood blinking just inside the door of the bar near Travis Park downtown. Murkiness prevailed. The place was dim verging on dark, an odd phenomenon, since it was three o'clock in the afternoon. Evelyn looked back over her shoulder. Yes, sunlight still poured down outside.

Good. Evelyn wanted a dark spot, to match her mood. She walked resolutely to the bar and lounged against it, a studied vamp. "What does a girl have to do to get a drink around here?" she purred.

"Order one," the bartender said coolly.

Evelyn's eyes had begun to adjust to the dim lighting of the bar. The bartender, a tall, swarthy man looking over her head at a TV, stood waiting for her order.

"All right, big boy. I'll have a sloe gin fizz, and make it fast."

He turned his dead-eyed stare on Evelyn. She realized she'd committed a <u>faux pas</u> in the etiquette of slumming. She rapidly bypassed her second choice, a daiquiri. "Gin and tonic?"

The bartender turned away. Evelyn lounged so low along the bar she almost fell over. The place held half a dozen patrons in mid-afternoon. Only one other was a woman. Evelyn felt uneasy, but ready to confront her fear. For the last two weeks she had worked out at the Concord. She had jogged – well, walked fast around the neighborhood. She had deprived herself at meals. She had acted, in short, like a recently divorced woman instead of a widow.

Now Evelyn was tired of deprivation.

She turned to the man next to her at the bar, who had a blonde, braided ponytail halfway down his back, an earring in the ear facing her and, when he turned at Evelyn's tap on his arm, menace in his eye. But he had an attractive air of knowing his own mind, and he looked directly into Evelyn's eyes.

She gathered her courage. "Can I buy you a drink?"

The man looked amused. "Thanks, I have one."

Evelyn laughed. As the bartender delivered her drink she gulped it down, said, "Give my friend whatever he's having and I'll have another. Make it straight gin." Emboldened further, she returned the stranger's stare. She noticed that he'd grown more handsome while she'd downed her drink.

Evelyn said, "One is never enough. Now tell me everything but your name." She ran her hand along his tight forearm. She had never behaved this way before. It felt sleazy. In a thrilling sort of way. She had promised herself a new phase to her life.

"Let me guess," the man said, "you're in town for the floor products convention, and you decided while you're far from home to have an adventure."

"That's right," Evelyn said boldly. Her second drink came and she quaffed it quickly. It followed the two with which she'd fortified herself before leaving home. "For the first time. I want to be low. Wicked. Depravity 'R' Me."

"And so you came straight here. Where did you find me, at lowlifes.com?"

"Geez, what do you want, a blood test?"

"For starters. This isn't the 70s, you know." The man spoke to his companion on his other side. "Come on, Ted, let's get back. I want to look at those plans of yours in better light." Ted Flato leaned across, shook Evelyn's hand, said, "Didn't we meet at the Colemans'?" and the two men walked out, leaving their coffee cups on the bar.

Evelyn felt both relieved and disappointed. The depths of depravity had turned out to be embarrassingly shallow. "Geez," she said disgustedly. "Where's a girl supposed to go for sin?"

From the back of the barroom, a man stood up and came forward out of the shadows. He had long black hair, a moustache to match, a gypsy nose, and dark, dark eyes that penetrated the gloom and seemed to peer into Evelyn's soul. She gasped. She had never seen a man more sinister-looking.

"I believe I can help," he said in a deep voice. He took her hand. She let him. "Are you looking for adventure, my dear? Thrills? New experiences beyond your imagination?"

His voice took her. "Oh, yes," Evelyn breathed. "What's your name?"

"Call me Diablo. And follow me."

Gabe Grohman wandered dispiritedly through the Fiesta Carnival. He should be doing something with the in crowd. But seeing people he knew made him feel worse.

"Hey, sailor, want to spin 'til you puke?"

He was passing the cups ride, which made him sick just to watch. Gabe turned to decline the invitation from the seedy-looking, gum-cracking operator, then stared harder. "Oh, my God. Evelyn?"

Maddie Grohman had a granddaughter in Coronation this year. The Duchess of the Court of Swirling Splendor, the 19-year old sophomore at UT looked lovely, and appeared completely unflustered by the experience. Maddie wondered if she appreciated the occasion.

She would in future years. Sitting in the Municipal Auditorium, which breathed memories of so many symphony concerts, high school graduations, and Metallica blasts, Maddie remembered her own Coronation. Her year had been 1946, the first post-War crowning, when the nation and the city felt lucky and prosperous. Coronation had been more splendid than ever.

Maddie wasn't sure of what she'd been duchess, or the precise colors of her gown. But she remembered vividly her feelings: that life was new and wondrous and would always remain so. She could lift her chin and feel again the glow produced by a hundred simultaneous stares on her face and bare shoulders; feeling buoyed by their approval to the extent that she floated above the stage.

Suddenly, decades later, Maddie remembered one stare in particular, that of an unfamiliar man from out of town. He had watched her as if he knew something secret about her. At the ball she'd danced one dance with the man, and felt lightheaded afterward. But she'd danced most of her dances with Travis Grohman, whom she'd known all her life. A year later she'd married him.

Strange how feelings persisted long after memories of details. Maddie watched her granddaughter sweep across the stage, applauded heartily, and wished she could be there years from now when this night would mean most to the girl.

Estela checked the on-line attendance records again. She checked the parking records. She heard from her informal network of observers. Even her old friend Juan Palomo contributed a tidbit.

It couldn't be true. But she had a theory and she vowed to test it. Luckily, she had the perfect public opportunity.

"Ready?" her co-host, a beaming, white-ponytailed man in long shorts asked her hours later. Estela nodded, terrified, and they stepped out hand in hand. But when the applause and a hint of beer fumes hit her, she suddenly found herself in her element.

Estela strutted across the stage of the Empire Theater. She felt silly. She felt exposed. The latter feeling was not subjective. Estela was a last-minute replacement as Mistress of Ceremonies of Cornyation, and long-time mistress Brenda Ray had graciously loaned Estela her outfit, bought at a naughty store in San Francisco called Stormy Leather. It was a dominatrix costume, customized with Fiesta touches and, at Estela's insistence, modified to show a little less skin.

This was not Estela's first time on a runway, but it was the first time she'd stood in front of a crowd that cheered, stomped their feet, called her name, and bounced in and out of their seats. Estela understood now why more than one person had offered her pharmaceutical assistance in getting through this performance. (She'd declined.)

She raised her mic and yelled, "Why so quiet? You'd think this was a victory party for Suzanne Pierce."

The politically savvy crowd roared laughter. Councilwoman Pierce's name had become something of a joke all on its own since one revelation after another about her insider business connections had dropped her out of the lead in the mayor's race.

"Oh, look! She's here!" Estela pointed into the crowd.

Suzanne Pierce had been mad at the world for weeks, but she'd had these tickets and so she'd had a drink or four and come to see just how bad it could get. Spotted, she stood and raised one hand, curled into a fist, all except for one errant finger.

The crowd screamed approval. *Hmm*, thought Ms. Pierce, taking a deep bow and resuming her seat.

Onstage, Estela said, "And I see Councilman Ramon Carter in the crowd. Don't you ever go home?"

She pointed, the crowd cheered, but near the back of the theater, Carter's staffers Marty Brewster and Jack Jeffers grabbed each other. "Where? Where? You're supposed to be in charge of him tonight!" they accused each other.

Stalking across the stage, Estela was supposed to hand over her microphone to her co-host at this point. She should have been glad to do so and slink away to change into civvies. But the spotlight was on her, the crowd laughed at her jokes, and she began to understand how someone could get into this.

"*La Estrella!*" screamed a male voice. The crowd began to take up the cheer.

Gloom silted Gabe Grohman's soul exactly as oak pollen drifted down on cars and sidewalks, leaving a nasty greenish-yellow stain.

That was the shape of his mood these days: it gave rise to bad poetry. Fiesta was not a good time for a young man whose only current romantic attachment was to a married woman. Gabe could have dredged up a date, but felt too listless to begin a relationship that he only needed for a week or so. He had plenty to do. At 24, Gabe was a little too young to have been invited into the Cavaliers, but he was a member of the German club and the Order of the Alamo, both of which staged major events during Fiesta.

But Gabe felt left out. Everything had a sad air of nostalgia. He felt much too old for his age.

To make his depression completely insufferable, he attended the King William Fair. He had been years earlier when it had been a quaint little self-mocking neighborhood festivity, but like too much else the Fair had grown beyond its original proportions and purpose. Many King William residents made a point of being out of town on this Saturday.

He caught the tail end of the parade, laughed at the Duchess of Questionable Values, felt momentarily jolly, wandered and took in the sights and sounds and the stepping-on of feet. He came to a house on King William Street with a large wraparound porch. A party was going on. Through the windows Gabe saw people he knew. He smiled and waved and bounded up onto the porch. At the door, though, a burly man in a toga stopped him. "Sorry, sir, private party. Do you have the password?"

Through the wide front window Gabe suddenly caught a glimpse of Estela Valenzuela. She wore a garish cardboard tiara and a tacky outfit that she carried well. Gabe stared at her openmouthed. She was in. She was everywhere. He was out. How did she do this?

The burly man gently pushed him away.

But then came the most splendid and secret event of Fiesta, and Gabe stood very much on the inside here. The Queen's Ball. Most people in San Antonio hadn't even heard of it. Also called "the mini-Coronation," on the last Saturday of Fiesta the Ball echoed the Coronation and allowed its splendor to glimmer a little longer.

The Order of the Alamo hosted the event at the Menger Hotel. Gabe attended as a member of the Board of Directors and a former escort. He took his cousin Caroline, a family obligation but not an odious one. It saved Gabe the trouble of finding a real date, and allowed Caroline the opportunity (no one said this aloud) to make a social connection that might land her father a job that would allow him to return to S.A. from Dallas.

The partygoers looked elegant in black ties and long dresses. Most stopped off in the bar for a pre-event drink, and champagne began circulating early. Conviviality reigned. Gabe felt surrounded by old friends. One of those friends was Jim Ambrose, the husband of Gabe's girl friend, but even Jim seemed like a good guy tonight.

Just at sunset the lights around the pool went off and spotlights came out. The first duchess, 19, long-tressed, and beautiful if only for one night, emerged from a side door and walked beaming around the pool. Guests applauded. The crowd looked on indulgently, old veterans of the duchess wars, content to let younger models have their turn.

Other connections were made. It was common for the Queen's Ball to be followed shortly by an engagement announcement. (After all, coming out as a duchess meant an early retirement of sorts, so one could begin the next phase of one's life.) After each duchess took her turn in the spotlight she would disappear, reappear at a balcony above, and hang over long train over it, so that by the end of the event trains hung like elegant tapestries. Partygoers felt like knights and ladies, especially after another course of champagne.

Another, unspoken tradition prevailed at this event. Unmarried members of the Order brought dates. One could enhance one's prestige by bringing on one's arm a beauty no one had ever seen before. A lovely from out of town, or state, or beyond the zip code.

Gabe had declined to compete this year, but he stood in a cluster of young men around the bar and listened to their admiring comments. "Who's that girl with Alec Woods?" "Somebody said she's from California. Northern California." And that one with Denny, does she have a French accent?" "She's from Detroit." "You're kidding!" "Well, Grosse Pointe, actually." "Ah."

"And that girl in the corner, she's beautiful, where on earth - ?" "She graduated from Lee High School." "Lee? How on earth did George meet somebody like that?" "Fluke."

And then Chad McPlaster emerged from the hotel. Chad – spoiled heir, duffer, doughboy – had on his arm a beauty who drew every eye. Chad smiled as if he had died and gone to heaven

Gabe stepped away from the bar.

A murmur ran the room, until one man said it aloud, raising a glass: "*La Estrella!*" It was indeed Estela Valenzuela, looking striking in a simple ivory gown that left her shoulders bare and made the much more elaborate frocks around her look like circus costumes.

Gabe stared. She had invaded his final province. She had stolen the Ball. Effortlessly. Estela looked gracious but a tad confused. Gabe was even more galled to see that she didn't even realize what secret splendor she'd penetrated.

Gabe flushed hot, he burned cold. He watched the invader all night. She obviously made good impressions. People approached her out of curiosity, stayed to chat. What the hell could she have to say that was so interesting?

Finally around midnight he asked her for a dance. Estela's smile made her look seventeen. "I'd love to, Gabito."

He felt a shock – and another when she put her arm around his back, her hand light on the hollow above his spine. They fit so well, and moved so easily. He had never been much of a dancer before. He wasn't sure he *was* dancing.

Small talk: "How on earth did that doofus get you to come to this?"

"Chad?" She smiled. "He's sweet. We met at a party and he asked me."

"That's all it takes?"

She gave him a look that seemed reproachful. "Sometimes, Gabe."

They talked as they danced, he found himself mentioning his family, his father, and it didn't seem odd to him until later that Estela answered as if she knew them all. Talking to her, he felt as if he understood some things for the first time.

They only had the one dance. His cousin Caroline went home with a new friend, Estela left with her date, and Gabe left the party early, about 3 a.m. He walked through downtown San Antonio to his river-view apartment, completely unworried, his feet light on clouds of champagne and speculation.

At one point he thought he was lost. The street looked unfamiliar. It seemed to have become brick, or even cobblestones. Gabe approached an old-fashioned street lamp. For just a second, through his haze, he saw with absolute certainty the name of the street: "Milagro Lane."

Hot Mics

During Fiesta, the San Antonio mayor's race ran a poor third in popular interest, behind beer and *gorditas*. The politically obsessed who continued to watch the polls saw General A.E. "Hawk" Bintner's numbers twist and turn like a Carnival spin-and-whirl. He had the solid support of most business leaders, who liked his expressions of fiscal discipline. For the most part, the large military and retired military community professed support, although many of those privately planned to take this once-in-a-lifetime chance to vote *against* a commanding officer.

But to the average San Antonio voter, General Bintner's campaign promises to whip this town into shape held little allure, even less so during Fiesta. His numbers sagged. Then one news station captured footage of the general at NIOSA cracking a cascaron over the head of his aide, Major Margaret Weston. Bintner's numbers climbed. People liked a general who joined in the spirit.

Some viewers thought they saw in the *cascaron* incident between the general and his female aide a sign of sexual harassment. His numbers declined. Ah, voters.

Del Rivera, the football coach from MacArthur, also enjoyed business support, and a man who had taken his team to the state finals the previous fall had a great base of popularity. But dissension sprang from his own back yard.

At a pep rally for his candidacy, one Mac booster asked Rivera, with genuine perplexity, "You're a high school head football coach running for mayor. Why would you want that demotion in status?"

Another elbowed forward. "Forget that. I want to know if you're going to neglect coaching this team if you get this other part-time job."

"Uh . . ." the coach responded, unsure what answer would do him more damage.

Suzanne Pierce, the councilwoman and former leader in the polls, watched these scenes with disgust. These bozos had no business being mayor. That job was her destiny. It belonged to her by right. But it had been taken from her by publicized revelations of the conflicts between her representations of voters and business clients. And by that evil TV reporter Veronica Lewis: Pierce hadn't forgotten. Pierce never forgot anything. It was what made her a great lawyer and a terrible enemy.

She remained so obviously, constantly furious that Veronica noticed it. During a break at a city council meeting the TV reporter strolled toward the councilwoman. Veronica looked good and knew it, in tight black pants and a long-sleeved pink knit blouse shot through with silver threads like snail trails.

One more good story, maybe two, and Veronica could well be on her way to Houston or Miami or another big market. She smiled secretly at Suzanne Pierce's glare. Veronica's news director had given her a piece of advice she remembered: "If you know some newsmaker who doesn't like you, make them absolutely hate you. Sometimes they slip up that way."

Twirling her wireless microphone in her fingers like a baton, Veronica said, "You look distressed, councilwoman. Not getting enough coverage?"

"Cover this, fluffhead," Pierce snapped, covertly repeating the gesture she'd used to popular acclaim at Cornyation.

"Can I quote you on that?" Veronica laughed. She set down her mic on a nearby table and walked away. Quickly she huddled with her cameraman. "I left my mic hot. Can we pick up what she's saying?"

The councilman from District 8 sighed as he walked past Pierce on his way back to his seat. "I hate these open public forums."

"Well, you'd better listen to them," Pierce said, turning her back on the crowd. "Yeah, some of them are crazy. But after this election I might be one of those crazy people at the open microphone. I'm not going away. This city's not going to be done with me. I'm going to be auditing the books, I'm going to be following up rumors. I'm going to bring everybody down with me I can. You and the other fat cats who think they run this city better watch your backs."

Across the room, Veronica chortled. "Got that on tape? 'I might be one of these crazy people'? I think we've got our lead for tonight. Cool, calculating councilwoman definitively loses her cool. I love it."

As Pierce took her seat at the council table, prepared to resume being barraged by outraged citizens, she watched the delighted Veronica Lewis. Pierce's colleague from District 8 sat beside her. "What was that all about?" he asked in bewilderment.

Pierce made sure her microphone was turned off, and just to be sure covered it with her hand. "Sorry, Pete. The newshawk over there had left her microphone sitting beside us."

"So?"

Once again Pierce made absolutely sure she wasn't being overheard this time, and she smiled. "You don't think I'm stupid enough to say something in front of an open mic that I don't want people to hear, do you?"

Express-News headlines and lead:

PIERCE WINS MAYOR'S RACE
Secretly taped tirade wins support of H-TA/Kay Turner crowd

> In a surprising development, San Antonio voters, some of whom said they would like to have a devious insider on their side for a change, resurrected the political life of Suzanne Pierce....

Veronica Lewis watched the returns to the bitter end, growing glummer and glummer. "Well," her cameraman tried to console her, "the next mayor hates your guts. There's got to be something good in that."

Yes, dried-up sources, exclusive interviews to *other* reporters, and general exclusion from City Hall. Veronica saw her dreams of Houston turning into nightmares of Harlingen.

Up all night, and alone at last, Suzanne Pierce kept looking at those last numbers, the ones that gave her the race by half a percentage point. She smiled a slow, sly, sinfully sinister smile, and began making a list.

Excerpts from Rick Casey's column, May 9, 2001:

> "Suzanne Pierce's lunge-from-behind victory in the mayor's race drew nearly all the public attention and media interest. (And this columnist may be forgiven for hoping that Pierce's beginning her comeback by literally giving the finger to a TV newswoman is a harbinger of mayoral style to come.) But one of the council races carried some casual points of interest as well. Call it the stealth campaign.

"Councilman Ramon Carter won re-election decisively, with the kind of numbers most politicians dream of or pay for. And he did so, apparently, without making a single public appearance. In fact, in a sampling so random it would make throwing darts at a wall look scientific, when five of the councilman's constituents were asked to describe him, they came up with five very different descriptions. Hispanic respondents tended to think the councilman, based on his first name, Hispanic. Anglos voted for him in high proportion, possibly based on his last name.

"And, though Carter won more than 60 percent of the vote in his district, the most ringing endorsements any of these constituents had for him was, 'He didn't screw up anything real bad for the last two years.'

"In this day of term limits and the marginal competency those limits produce in our elected officials, that may just be the campaign slogan of the future. . . ."

Carter's staff, Marty Brewster, Jack Jeffers, and Leonard Bracero, didn't like the column mention, but remained quietly ecstatic about keeping their jobs for two more years. Until the morning of the press conference.

They didn't plan it, they certainly hadn't called one – they had never announced one press conference in the previous two years – but had one forced upon them the Thursday morning after the Casey column, as the three left City Hall together.

"Why aren't you three having lunch with the boss?" asked TV reporter Angela Vierville.

Marty Brewster was quick to respond. "The councilman doesn't eat lunch. He's much too busy working for his district."

Brad Messer, doing a live remote for KTSA, asked politely, "Could he just step out here for a few words with his devoted admirers?"

"Uh . . ." the staff responded in unison.

Fred Lozano had a cameraman, a microphone, and a visual aid. He held a pasteboard holding up five blown-up photographs where the staffers could see it. The five people represented in the photo lineup looked very different. One, in fact, was an African-American woman. "Could you just identify for your viewers which of these people is Councilman Carter?"

Jack Jeffers, who was young, African-American, and had once harbored political ambitions himself, was a speechwriter. He had a way with words. "Well . . ." he said slowly, thinking hard.

The Ware pair had hung around after their own radio show ended in order to see this. In a deep voice that sounded angry and amused at the same time, Ricci called out, "We'll make it easy for you. Just tell us what race Carter is."

"Or ethnic background," Trey clarified.

A calm, clear voice cut throught the clash. "Human," it said.

The reporters turned to see Estela Valenzuela striding into their midst. *"La Estrella,"* one murmured. The others merely said different versions of "What?"

Estella took a stand between the media and the councilman's staff, who watched her with equal curiosity. Cameras and microphones turned in her direction. Estela held her chin high. She wore a plain navy skirt, a white shirt with pleated front, and looked very professional. "Councilman Carter is of the human race," she repeated emphatically.

"That is as much as he wants said on the subject. He doesn't choose to trade on his ethnicity. He prefers not to create artificial divisions among his constituents or the people of this great city."

Estela looked at them sternly. "This is why Councilman Carter was re-elected so overwhelmingly. He deals in inclusiveness, not division. I have been studying his record and I have been very impressed."

"What's your role here?" asked Brad Messer. "Just a concerned citizen?"

"No." Estela pulled from her purse a large blue tee-shirt that said, "Keep Carter on Council," with his symbol, a mockingbird on the wing. "I've so admired Mr. Carter's record that I contacted him and, as of this week, I have joined his staff."

"You have?" one of the staff members said behind her. They looked at each other wonderingly. "He interviewed you personally?" Leonard Bracero asked.

"Yes." Estela turned to them with a straightforward look. "Didn't he tell you?"

"Uh, well . . . we've all been very busy. . . ."

Estela looked long and hard at Marty Brewster, who thought, *Uh oh*. Then the two joined forces to answer questions about their boss.

Veronica Lewis didn't join the media mob. She waited inside council chambers to speak to the mayor-elect. Trying to sound confident, Veronica held out her hand and said, "Congratulations, Ms. Pierce. Now that you're going to be mayor, I know that you will rise to the challenge, be a big person, and not . . ."

"Try to gut you?" answered Pierce, ignoring the outstretched hand. She laughed. "Honey, I've already done it. You just haven't felt the pain yet."

Express-News headlines:

FICTITIOUS PERSON ELECTED TO CITY COUNCIL

Non-Existent 'Ramon Carter' a Two-Year Incumbent

Voters Say They're Satisfied

H.T.A. Announces Slate of Fictitious Candidates

In the wake of the public revelation that newly re-elected City Councilman Ramon Carter did not technically exist, City Manager Helen Brechtel gathered Carter's staff in a conference room at City Hall. She deliberately chose one of the smaller rooms, so that she could breathe into their faces as she glared at them.

"Were you all insane? What were you thinking?"

Leonard Bracero, the councilman's community relations coordinator, showed some momentary spunk. "Why do you think we did anything?"

Bechtel's expression smoldered. "Either you perpetrated this fraud, or you haven't been smart enough to figure out that you've been working for no one for the last two years. Which way would you rather be known?"

The three veteran city staffers had never seen Bechtel so vibrant. She literally vibrated. They could barely see her, as if at any moment she might pass into another dimension. Which the staffers fervently hoped she would do.

Jack Jeffers, the speechwriter of the group, began a carefully-prepared speech. "The district has been well-represented for the last two years. If you match the councilman's votes to polling data, you will see that has voted more in-line with his constitutents' views than any other –"

"Of course you did what voters wanted!" Bechtel said harshly. "You were perpetrating a fraud. But how?"

"Let me describe a hypothetical situation," Jack answered. "Three veteran, well-trained and knowledgeable city staff people are attending a farewell party for their councilman, who's being forced out by term limits. They start to grumble at the thought of looking for new jobs or training some new bozo how City Council functions. One of them comes up with a really funny idea. 'Wouldn't it be great if we only had to do the councilman's job, not baby him along at the same time?'"

Bechtel folded her arms and said scathingly, "It was late at night by this time, I take it."

Marty Brewster spoke up. "It may be that alcohol played a role."

"I hope so," Bechtel said. "Because this is the kind of idiotic stunt people would expect from elected officials, not sober, hardworking professional staff. Well, it doesn't matter. You're all through. Be out of here in twenty minutes. I'm giving orders to security to shoot you all twenty-one minutes from now."

The youngest and most junior person in the room finally spoke up. "I don't think so," said Estela Valenzuela. Unlike the other staffers, she showed no sweat. Of course, she had only held this job about twenty hours, so had much less to lose than the others.

The city manager raised an eyebrow. "I don't even know what you're doing here."

"I'm working for District 6 Councilman Ramon Carter. Not for you. Check your municipal code."

"Carter doesn't exist."

"Prove that. Until there's a recall vote, we're all continuing to work for the district."

Bechtel glared. "I'm going to get to the bottom of this. There will be an investigation." She stalked out of the room.

Marty Brewster said to Jack Jeffers, "We're going to be investigated."

Leonard joined in. "By the City Attorney's Office."

"That means legal fees, hiring attorneys –"

"Probably in two or three years."

"After the statute of limitations expires."

There is no more secure job tenure than being investigated by a government agency. Smiles became general. The staffers became buoyant.

But Marty Brewster turned to Estela suspiciously. "I know why I'm here. I don't know what you're doing here."

Estela allowed herself a small smile. "Saving your jobs, apparently."

Veronica Lewis didn't fare nearly as well.

Her news director, Roger Boyd, didn't raise his voice. He just stared at her across his desk in the small office at KSAN-TV. Veronica sat slumped but angry. "You as good as endorsed him," Roger finally said.

"No. It was a news piece."

"The most glowing profile we gave to any candidate."

"I heard great things about him."

"Yes, Veronica, but in the news business we feel that an in-depth investigative report that fails to uncover that its subject doesn't actually exist is not Pulitzer material."

Veronica looked down. "I'm very sorry."

"Practice that line. Here's my idea. You make an on-air apology."

"Then pull out a knife and commit ritual hara-kiri?"

Roger considered. "I like the visual." Then he shook his head. "But now that you've told me about it, I foresee potential legal problems. Plus we could probably only use the footage once. No, my idea is that you go back to the minors. Do a stint in some training ground like Midland or Lubbock. They're nice places. I've flown over them a couple of times."

"I'd prefer the public disembowelment."

"Well, we'll keep your plan in the back of our minds. Not a word to anyone, though."

He held up a finger to his lips. Veronica left the office. She had been had, she knew. Someone had deliberately fed her good material about the fictitious Ramon Carter, providing Veronica with enough material to make a fool of herself once the truth was revealed. Veronica had a good idea who that person was – the next mayor of San Antonio. Possibly Carter's staffers as well.

Veronica seethed, but she remained outwardly calm. She had never been deep or devious, but she was determined. Her day would come, maybe after everyone had forgotten that she even had anything to get even for. Revenge is a dish best served cold. On a platter. With someone's head resting prominently in the center.

Gabe became a nightwalker. He wanted to see her again, Estela Valenzuela, but had no idea where to find her. Not in his usual Olmos Park/'09 haunts, he felt sure of that. Oh, she might turn up at his grandmother's house, but he didn't want to see her there. He wanted to find her in his own place, apart from his family, like the night when he'd danced one dance with her and afterwards thought he'd walked on Milagro Lane.

There was no such street. Gabe had scoured city maps and directories, even gone to the city government website. Milagro Lane: *nada*. But it meant miracle, and he'd felt rather miraculous the night he'd held her. He wanted to repeat the experience.

He went through his days at Grohman Enterprises, which ran out of remarkably modest offices high in the Tower Life Building. Truly, the business ran itself. Homebuilders bought stone and other materials, tenants in Grohman-owned buildings paid their rent, the cash flowed. At age 24, Gabe was still learning his way around. But he had learned this much: the Grohman family had been wealthy for generations and had invested well. On any given day, depending on stock values, the family was worth somewhere between 500 and 650 million. Not in a league with the Waltons, but pretty far off the street nevertheless. It would take an amazing level of incompetence to run that fortune into the ground in less than a century.

From the Tower Life to Gabe's riverview apartment was a walk of only a few blocks, and sometimes after dusk he extended that walk, melancholy and enjoying it. He kept an eye out for a certain face and otherwise enjoyed his romantic solitude.

Evenings found him often alone. He couldn't call his only romantic attachment, Jessica Ambrose, because her husband might answer the phone and even he might grow suspicious if that happened often. Gabe often took a long walk after dinner.

His address was on Losoya. One evening about 10 he walked idly along the river, then up the Commerce Street bridge and over to Market. In the small greensward across the street from the Convention Center, he encountered a lady in a dark blue dress, smoking a cigarette and letting her poodle play out its leash. She nodded. Gabe vaguely recognized that he had seen the woman before. Downtown residents saw each other – grocery-shopping at Walgreen's, in their cars searching for a secret space, walking.

With the notorious friendliness of a native San Antonian, Gabe said hello and stood under the trees with the lady. "Are we having a meeting?"

She gave him a cool look, then smiled slightly. "I'm here for the same reason you are."

That was interesting. So Estela Valenzuela attracted women as well? And did this one know that Estela would soon be passing by?

The lady inclined her head upwards. Gabe looked up at the grid of the Marriott, the larger one on the left. About halfway up, a shirtless man stood on one of the balconies, hands on the railing and inhaling deeply. From this distance the man looked young and fit and blond.

Behind him, a light appeared as an interior door opened, and a woman wearing only a towel joined the man on the balcony and leaned on his shoulder. The two laughed. One could say with confidence that the woman wore nothing but a towel, when it dropped to the balcony floor.

This was interesting. Like being at a drive-in porno theater. The lady beside Gabe wore a studious expression, like a reviewer. Gabe wondered if there was a downtown newsletter he didn't get.

She glanced at him, saw his surprise, and raised an eyebrow. "Surely you knew this is the best spot for seeing naked people? How long have you lived downtown?"

She walked on with her dog, leaving Gabe with a sudden sense of his own self-absorption. He had lived downtown for months without learning such significant news as that there were naked people to be seen. Truly, his interests were remarkably shallow.

A couple of days later Gabe dropped by his father's old house in King William. He still had clothes there, and was looking for a particular pair of tennis shorts as the weather warmed up. No one answered the door, so he let himself in. The house smelled musty. Evelyn must have let the live-in maid go.

Gabe got caught up in the nostalgia of exploring. It was a grand old house, with thick mahogany balustrades on the stairs, crystal chandeliers, and foot-wide moldings above the doors and at the tops of walls. A family should live here.

The doorbell rang, startling him. He was even more startled, but happily so, when he opened the door and saw Estela Valenzuela standing on the porch.

She looked surprised as well. "Gabe. I was – I didn't know you were here."

"You mean you weren't looking for me?"

"No. I wanted to ask your stepmother if I could look for – something I thought I left here."

When would that have been? Gabe wondered, then remembered. Estela had known his father.

But he was glad to see her, and said so. "Come in."

As she did, Estela stepped on an envelope. She picked it up and handed it to Gabe, because it bore his name. No stamp, no address, just Gabe's name.

"Somebody doesn't know I don't live here any more," he observed as he tore open the envelope. He read the short note quickly. "Hmm, that's funny."

"What is it?" Estela asked with some concern.

"Someone's kidnapped Evelyn." Gabe tapped the note on his hand, then brightened. "So. Got time for lunch?"

Evelyn in Sordid Splendor

A **few stories** above downtown San Antonio, Evelyn Grohman lay on her back looking at her reflection. Evelyn, 36-year-old widow of Jerry Grohman, outraged over being left only a life estate in his will, admitted to herself that she had gone a little nuts. But the result had been fun. She had spent Fiesta as a carnie worker, which was funny because she had never even been to Fiesta Carnival before.

The carnival had moved on and Evelyn had stayed with her new friend, who called himself Diablo and told her very little else about himself. He might have *been* the devil as far as Evelyn could tell. But a devil could have his place in a girl's life.

Evelyn's image reflecting back at her from the ceiling was interestingly fragmented. She wore bright blue harem pants and a filmy blouse in a peach color that didn't go with her hair (which was auburn this month). The mirrors above made her look cartoonishly hedonistic. The ceiling didn't hold a full-sized mirror, it was foot-square mirrors put together in a reflective mosaic. Installing a large mirror in the ceiling would been a major engineering enterprise, and the mirror-installers had performed their work clandestinely.

Evelyn lay in the bedroom of the penthouse suite above the old Alameda Theater. Local rumor had it that in the 70s the suite had been leased by two well-known businessmen, for afternoon use (not with each other, it should quickly be added). A few of their decorative touches remained, such as the mirrored ceiling. And in a corner of the wall where sunlight hit regularly, the paint had begun to fade and Evelyn, curious, had scratched it away further to reveal old red flocked wallpaper underneath. Red seemed to have been the dominant theme of the former decorating scheme.

Evelyn lay trying to figure out the placement of the mirrors. Of course, she used them to tuck stray hairs back into place, but she doubted that had been intended as their principal use. With her limited experience and imagination, Evelyn could only assume that a man could only get best use out of the mirrors if he were lying on his back. This suggested both wantonness and laziness, two qualities that both attracted Evelyn.

Enough lollygagging about. Evelyn bounded up. "Diablo?" she called.

A disembodied voice floated in from the living room. "Be back soon, my kitten. Just a little errand."

"What?" Evelyn hurried out, but only in time to see the elaborately-carved door of the suite closing. She didn't see, on the other side, Diablo rolling his eyes or his disgusted expression.

Evelyn hurried to catch up, or for a farewell kiss, but caught up short when she tried to turn the doorknob.

"Huh," she said, and called, "Wait, honey! You forgot to leave the key."

A few blocks away, the only member of Evelyn's family who knew she had been kidnapped sat at lunch. On a Thursday at noon El Mirador was crowded with people anticipating the weekend or just savoring soft chicken tacos. When Gabe Grohman and Estela Valenzuela walked in, Estela looked around and jokingly asked owner Julian Trevino, "Do you have a non-lawyer section?"

On the way to their table, Estela gave founder Mary Trevino a quick hug. In a back corner, celebrity CPA Leslie Beasley enjoyed puffed tacos with her daughter Emily. Leslie waved to Estela and called, "Loved the show!" Estela nodded modestly.

So once again, as at the Queen's Ball, Gabe didn't have Estela to himself. But then, he suddenly thought, he never would. After all, she had been his father's –

"Nngh!"

"What is it?" Estela asked, startled. So Gabe must have made the sound aloud. He'd thought it only a mental noise, to blot out the image that had started forming in his mind.

"Nothing, I'm fine. So tell me about you. How long have you been in San Antonio?"

Her expression said she knew that wasn't his question. Gabe just looked at her face. At first Estela seemed not as enchanting at lunch as by moonlight and champagne. A pretty girl, with skin as yet uncrinkled, and uniform in color except under her eyes, where two pale spots grew, as if she wore sunglasses while lying in the sun. Her eyes, he noticed again, were an unusual hazel color, brown predominating but with strong traces of green. Long lashes. Lovely cheekbones.

"I like your hair," he said suddenly.

Estela made a dismissive sound. "This is all I can do with it." She lifted a lock of thick black hair and let it fall heavily, straight as I-37. "Comanche hair. Unchanged for generations."

Gabe imagined reaching for her, imagined his hand in that hair. Then his imagined hand began to change into his father's hand.

"What?" Estela asked anxiously. "You know, I know a very good doctor who. . . ."

"It's all right." Gabe picked up a chip. Estela reciprocated and they clinked them together like wine glasses. They made a *tostada* toast.

"What about your stepmother?" Estela asked a minute later. "Aren't you going to try to ransom her?"

"I thought we might talk about that. Put our heads together." His voice faded for a moment, he managed not to make the yelping sound, but Estela looked at him as if he had.

Gabe smiled at her brightly.

Evelyn Grohman had so far enjoyed this confusing period of her life, which seemed to be continuing. She could hardly remember how it had begun. She had been angry at her late husband Jerry, at his whole family, and in fact at everyone who'd ever slighted her. In the first flush of her outrage, that had seemed like everyone she'd ever known.

Her stint as a worker at the Fiesta Carnival had been a blessing. With the other carnies she didn't have to put on her usual airs, or make the pretense to sophistication that sometimes made her time with her usual friends so hard to endure. Fueled by alcohol and other intoxicants of the senses, she had grown into a different person: looser, freer, more fun.

The good times had continued with her new friend Diablo after the carnival moved on. Late nights, wild rides, unfamiliar places: it left her head spinning, but in a good way.

Ending here. Evelyn knew she was in a penthouse suite, but didn't know exactly where. Growing bored while waiting for Diablo to return, she began to explore. She opened dresser drawers and closets, even the walk-in pantry in the kitchen. The suite seemed the kind of place that would have secret passages or hiding places, but Evelyn didn't find any. The place had an under-lived-in look, with only a few clothes hanging in the closet and almost no food in the kitchen.

Finally she realized how few windows there were to give away the location. Unbeknownst to Evelyn, she was on West Houston street in downtown San Antonio. The penthouse suite sat atop the Alameda Theater, a movie palace Evelyn had never frequented, of course, even when it had been open. In fact, she had never been on this part of Houston, at least not consciously. She and her companion had arrived here in the middle of the night, Evelyn half-asleep and seemingly half out of her mind.

She finally found a window that gave a narrow view downward. Looking down, she saw old mortared buildings, a few older model cars parked along the curb, and a building that said "El Tenampa Bar." From an unseen music store below, a song in Spanish filtered up to her ears. Not *La Vida Loca*, either.

Oh, my God, Evelyn thought. She was in Mexico.

From El Mirador, Gabe Grohman and Estela Valenzuela drove in Gabe's silver BMW. The car looked gray to Gabe, who suspected that the distinction between silver and gray was whether one had hired a marketing firm. He had always loved this car, but with Estela occupying the other leather bucket seat, it seemed ostentatious.

"Look," she said, "it has instructions. You didn't tell me that."

She held the note a kidnapper had left at Evelyn Grohman's King William home, the note Gabe had found just that morning. He had no idea how long Evelyn had been missing, or much concern. What was the worst that could happen?

Estela had turned over the note and found a phone number. "It says to call this number, 410...."

"That's Evelyn's cell phone number," Gabe said. "So I guess they really do have her."

"Or she's staged this herself."

"Why would she do that?"

"For attention. Money."

Gabe turned on Alamo and drove into King William. He said dismissively, "She has all the money she needs."

"Is there any such thing, for someone like Evelyn?"

Gabe glanced at Estela, wondering how she knew anything

about his stepmother. But of course: Gabe's father Jerry must have talked to Estela about his wife during their – times together. Gabe hastily tried to think of something else to take his mind off that subject.

He pulled into the parking lot of the Guenther House at the old Pioneer Flour Mills. As they got out, Estela gazed across the street at the Blue Star Art complex. "What is it?" Gabe asked. Estela only shook her head, looking distant.

Gabe took his own mobile phone with him as they walked into the gardens. He placed the call. The phone on the other end rang four times, he thought he was about to get voice mail, when a growling voice answered. "What?"

"Hello, this is Gabe Grohman. I'm calling about my stepmother Evelyn. I believe you have her." Gabe wasn't sure what tone to strike with a kidnapper, but felt he had just failed to find the correct one.

"About damned time!" the voice shouted. "Do you not care about this woman at all? Do you know what you've put her through? I was just about to say the hell with it and dump her body."

"Well, don't do that." Again, Gabe didn't feel he'd been tough enough. Deepening his own voice, he asked, "What do you want?"

Estela, watching him, saw Gabe grow more and more puzzled. Finally, with a noncommittal farewell, he ended the call.

"What does he want?" Estela asked.

"Information," Gabe said wonderingly. "He said I inherited all my father's papers, I can get the information for him, in exchange for Evelyn." Gabe shook his head. "This guy is in sad shape. He wants to give me somebody I don't really want in exchange for something I don't know. Did this guy come to the wrong place."

Estela Valenzuela went to see her old friend Juan Palomo at Lanier High School. She wanted to see for herself that he was actually teaching there.

Estela hadn't been inside Lanier in a few years. Either it had changed or she had. The campus still seemed spacious for a high school, featuring a large open mall area and a courtyard. Twenty-five years after its rebuilding, the school still seemed new. Estela passed unchallenged through the doors and past the administration offices. She could have been taken for a student, except that she wasn't wearing the uniform of khaki pants and white or blue shirt. She had a strong, swinging stride, but so did the few students she saw in the halls.

She found Juan in his own room having coffee. This last week of school, his free period really was free. Books had been collected, finals given. There would be no more pop quizzes or homework, primarily because the teachers didn't want to grade them.

Juan had his room decorated with quotes and posters from his political past. Photos of Bobby Kennedy, Martin Luther King, Jr., Henry Cisneros, and Bill Clinton adorned the walls unashamedly. At the age of 30, most of these were historical figures to Juan, but with his drooping moustache and round glasses he looked like a leftover 60s radical.

"Estela!" he greeted her joyfully, as if they hadn't met in years. In fact, they'd had lunch at the Malt House only a few weeks earlier, but hadn't really had a chance to catch up.

"I'd forgotten what this feels like," she said, after exchanging a quick embrace with him. Hugging a teacher in a classroom felt sinful. "This last week of school, the anticipation, dragging along and feeling exhilarated at the same time."

"Yes, and that's just the teachers," Juan observed. "So, Estela, are you here on a fact-finding mission? We're not in your non-existent city councilman's district."

"He's not non-existent, he's just low-profile," she smiled. "I just wanted to see you here. I still can't believe you. High school, Juan?"

"I wanted to make a difference." He shrugged, mocking himself. "This morning I went for the fences. Gave them my Cesar Chavez speech. You know, self-sacrifice, giving to the community. I didn't think they paid attention at all, but afterwards this one boy said, "Isn't there anything between working hard for forty years for nothing and having two hits and living with Puff Daddy. Can't you give us somebody between Chavez and J.Lo?"'

"It is possible to make contributions without making sacrifices."

"And how *is* your mother?" Juan asked.

Estela both smiled and sighed. "The same."

Juan studied her. "Maybe you, *Estrella*. You're a political star now. Maybe you can come be a role model for my classes. You're kind of a cross between Cesar and Jennifer." She rolled her eyes. Juan continued, "What are you up to now?"

"You know me. I don't plan anything, I just go with the inspiration. Milagro Lane."

He smiled at the reference, but continued to watch her intently. "I know how you used to be, Estela. I'm not sure I know you now."

Jerry Grohman walked into the offices of Grohman Enterprises to find a surprise. A large man in a western style sports coat threw wide his arms. Thick hair graying at the temples gave him a distinguished appearance that was done in by his goofy handlebar moustache.

"Uncle Jock! What are you doing here?"

Many wealthy south Texas families have one: the ranch uncle; the ranch brother. The family member who couldn't quite make it in town, couldn't accommodate his habits to civilization, and so ended up living on the family ranch. "Jock's in charge of the hunting operation," the Grohmans would say vaguely, meaning he could drink as much as he wanted, shoot cans, and sleep late.

The Employment Gap

Veronica Lewis morosely packed her one suitcase. The old bag had carried her through San Angelo State University, to news stints in Beaumont and Corpus Christi, here to San Antonio, and now they'd travel together downmarket. Veronica sniffled.

Her roommate came yawning out of the second bedroom of their northwest side garden home. "Z'up?"

Liv caught fads the way daycare babies catch colds. She had no immunity. The same age as Veronica, 28, Liv was a supervisor at the Gap store in Rivercenter, a responsibility she took very seriously. Liv lived her loyalty. Everything she owned said Gap. Her jeans said Gap, her tight green t-shirt said Gap, even her earrings. Her smile said gap. Yes: a small one between Liv's front teeth, a la David Letterman.

"My stint. My tenure." Seeing her roommate's uncomprehending look, Veronica explained, "My job is up, Liv. I'm fired."

"No way! Girl, you've been on the 'waves every night. You're busting major news. I hear people in the store talking about you!"

"Really?" Veronica brightened.

"Well, they talk about how you dress, but still. How can those dorks dump the hottest newsbabe in town?"

"He is. Roger. Last night I gave my on-air apology, today I'm going in to clean out my desk."

"'He'?" Liv grew a knowing look on her heart-shaped face. She took her roommate to the kitchen and sat her at their white-topped formica table. Liv pulled a chair out and sat in it obsequiously as if in front of a boss's desk. "Here's what you do, girlfriend. Follow my every move. You tell him you're sorry. You lean toward him. You need his help. What you need is guidance. A mentor. You know you can do better. Then, if you think the occasion calls for it, give him a little Sharon Stone action." Liv demonstrated, crossing her legs slowly. Since she wore a baby doll blue nightie that already displayed the frilly panties, the effect wasn't all that startling, but Veronica got the idea.

"That's horrible," she said. "Aren't we past that?"

"Only until there's a crisis," Liv said smugly. "And this is one. I'm not going to look for another roommate."

Veronica thought of another objection. "Then I'll still be working there, and he'll expect me to carry through."

Liv sighed. "Ronnie, Ronnie, Ronnie. Have you learned nothing from my example? That's why God invented lawsuits. It's called sexual harassment. He can't ask for that as a condition of employment."

Veronica shook her head. "This is icky, Liv. Either I do what I implicitly promise and I'm basically a hooker, or I don't and I'm – what?"

"Employed."

Veronica considered the proposition. Then she grimaced. "Wait, I forgot. This won't work from the premise. It's Roger."

Liv smirked. "He's a man, isn't he?"

"Not as you and I know the term. He's a news director. He's like the middle man between the workers and management. All he cares about is keeping his job and moving up. Ratings or embarrassing the station. That's it."

"Why didn't you say so? Then you tell him you hope to redeem yourself, so the whole thing doesn't reflect badly on him. After all, he's the one who brought you along, gave you the special assignments before you were ready to handle them. Management must understand that. But if between the two of you, you make it look like you planned this whole 'failure' just to set up a much bigger story, it'll be a triumph. But if you leave it will look like *he* screwed up."

Veronica sat back and marvelled at the roommate she often considered ditzy. "Liv, how do you think of these things?"

Liv smiled. "Girl, I've got a whole file. I've been 'fired'" – she made air quotes with her fingers – "from more jobs than you'll ever have. And I always kept the ones I wanted. So go out there and hustle."

A few minutes later Veronica left with a determined expression and a quicker step then she'd shown in days. When the door closed behind her, Liv shook her head. "The things a girl will do to hang onto a roommate who pays her share of the rent on time and doesn't have a boyfriend."

Gabe could barely hear the kidnapper's voice over the sound of Evelyn's moaning. "Don't you want to know what I'm doing to her?" the kidnapper growled.

"No! And could you please stop it while I'm on the line? I get the idea, just tell me what you want."

The moaning sound diminished. Gabe listened intently to his mobile phone as Estela Valenzuela kept a watchful eye on his changing expressions. They stood on the front porch of her small carriage house in King William.

"I have no idea," Gabe finally said. "All right, I'll do my best." He hung up wonderingly and said, "He wants to see leases. Very old leases."

In his puzzlement, Gabe didn't notice that Estela didn't reply, or that she turned away before he could see her face.

Diablo hung up the phone and returned his attentions to his "victim," Evelyn Grohman. She pouted at him, lifting one bare foot toward his face. "You missed a spot," she said.

He resumed his foot massage. Evelyn leaned back and sighed. She loved to hear him growl while he worked. It was such a sexy sound.

Jerry Grohman's office had sat mostly undisturbed since his death. Jerry, though nominally the CEO of Grohman Enterprises, had not been very involved in the company's day-to-day affairs. Managers continued to run things after his death. His office sat empty as if in tribute to him, honored by dust.

But now Jerry's son Gabe sifted through the papers, with his Uncle Jock looking over his shoulder. Gabe went into the old wooden filing cabinets, then deeper into the building for older documents. "Where do we keep our archives?" he asked the secretary Mrs. Olsen, who knew everything. Lisa Olsen, thirty-something and divorced, blonde, tiny-waisted, a jogger, looked as if she'd been hired for decorative purposes, but anyone who spent five minutes at Grohman Enterprises knew her as the driving force who kept the business going. (Uncle Jock, who never had spent five minutes in the office, eyed her appreciatively.)

"In a warehouse near downtown," she answered Gabe's question at once. "That's funny, your father asked me the same thing before he . . ."

Gabe jerked quickly around. "Did he order anything?"

"As a matter of fact, he did. I ordered a box for him just a couple of months ago. One of the earliest boxes. From the 1880's, I think."

"Where is it?"

"He sent it back to the warehouse."

Gabe took the secretary's arms. "Mrs. Olsen, did he keep anything?"

"I see some urgency in your question, Gabe, and I wish I could help you, but I couldn't read your father's mind. Why don't you ask your grandmother? He would have told her, wouldn't he?"

He might well have, but as a matter of fact, Gabe had been avoiding his grandmother lately.

Uncle Jock said, "You run along and look for your papers, son. I'll keep an eye on things here." He beamed at Mrs. Olsen. Gabe didn't want to leave Jock here to paw through his father's office. Mrs. Olsen, on the other hand, he didn't worry about. If Jock's smile tilted one millimeter more toward a leer, he was going to sustain an injury.

Madeleine ("Miz Maddie") Grohman, surveyed her elegant but rather crowded Olmos Park living room, put her hands on her hips, and said, "Nothing has worked right around here since Rosa left."

Rosa had been the Grohman family maid for decades, her departure still much mourned more than a year after the fact. Now Rosa had returned to her small house near Goliad Road on the south side to dote on her grandchildren, tend her garden, and thrive on what few maids in San Antonio ever acquired: a pension. She still returned for formal occasions when no one else would do, but Maddie had had to replace her with a series of lesser beings who just could not get things right, at least in Miz Maddie's view.

A visitor to the home would have been hard-pressed to say what wasn't "working" at the moment, but Miz Maddie saw problems everywhere: a fringe hanging crookedly on a chair back, the photos on the mantelpiece rearranged, a stray corner of a piece of sheet music sticking out of the piano seat.

As Maddie went about fixing things, she suddenly wondered whether she was getting old, to be worried about such trivial matters. But then she remembered she'd been the same way as a little girl, and felt reassured.

The doorbell rang. It was a solemn old tone, almost like a church bell, a soothing sound that reassured even as it announced an intruder. Miz Maddie was expecting no one.

She opened the door herself, not trusting the maid to get that right, either. A toad in a black suit stood on the doorstep.

No, on second look it was a man, but one with a broad face that got even broader the further one's eyes dropped down it, giving him that toad-like appearance. When he smiled, the effect increased.

"Mrs. Madeleine Grohman? I'm sorry to intrude myself into your life, my dear lady. I hope I've waited a decent enough interval after your son's untimely passing."

"Thank you. Waited for what?"

"May I come in?"

Maddie waved him inside. The man seemed vaguely oily and ominous, but not physically threatening. He removed his black fedora, revealing a gleaming scalp lovingly tended by a few combed-across black hairs. "May I assume that you are in charge of Grohman Enterprises now that your son Gerald is no longer – ah – fulfilling those responsibilities?"

"I suppose so," Maddie said, still puzzled. "It's a family business, we don't have stockholders to report to. Were you dealing with Jerry on some matter?"

"A rather large matter." The man set the briefcase he carried on a chair and removed two pages of densely-packed words. "This is a letter of intent from your son to me. While not a contract, it is enforceable."

"Intent to do what?"

"Why, to sell Grohman Enterprises."

Madeleine Grohman gaped at the stranger. If the man had punched her in the stomach, he could not have gotten her attention more forcefully. The odious little man – as she had suddenly begun to think of him – held in his hand a letter which he said represented her late son Jerry's offer to sell the business that the Grohman family had owned and run for generations.

"Obviously there's been a mistake," Miz Maddie said. She was glad to hear her voice sound firm. She knew from having been told several times over the decades that even at a time like this, when she felt hollowed out inside, her face would not betray her. When struck by a blow such as this, the only thing that seemed to happen to her countenance was that her eyelids grew heavier, as if she were losing interest. "And who in the world are you?"

"Pardon me, please. My name is Claude Duquesne." The black-suited, broad-faced man, holding the letter in one hand and his hat in the other, found himself unable to extend a hand for shaking, to Miz

Maddie's relief. Before he could shift things to free a hand, she took the letter from him and turned aside to read it.

"This sounds like just an offer, the first round of a negotiation," she said, though her heart sank at the letter's language.

"No, my dear lady, it is a firm offer, and quite enforceable, I assure you."

"What's the proposed sale price?"

"Forty-eight million dollars."

Maddie whirled back to stare at the man in horror. This was not possible. Even in his younger, wilder days, even drunk to the verge of passing out, Jerry would never have entertained such an offer. Forty-eight million dollars was a fire sale price. Grohman Enterprises was worth at least four times that. It could have lost several major assets and still been valued at more than this ridiculous price.

Carefully invested, forty-eight million dollars might produce an income of three or four million dollars a year. Not remotely sufficient for the needs of the extended Grohmann family.

More importantly, in every generation at least half a dozen Grohmans or Grohman in-laws worked in the family business. If that business were gone, no one would have a place to work. They could live off investments, clip coupons – and devote themselves to bad habits. Within two generations, the family would all be wastrels and lunatics.

Surely Jerry had understood this. Grohman Enterprises wasn't just a company. It was an extension of the family, the representation of the Grohman name and reputation to the public. Even in dark times such as the Depression and Democratically-controlled Congresses, no one had ever thought of selling out.

Certainly not for a lousy forty-eight mil.

"I don't understand. Who are you? Beyond your name."

The toad-like man bowed, so that lamplight reflected off his shiny scalp. "I represent a consortium of interests, Mrs. Grohman. We are investors, nothing more."

Meaning they would pick the company clean and let it go. "Obviously you reached my son during a weak moment. . . ."

"No, ma'am, as a matter of fact, he approached us."

Maddie's mind reeled. She finished reading the letter, and sure enough it firmly offered to sell Grohman Enterprises to the interests this Duquesne represented, for a price of forty-eight million dollars. The signature was undoubtedly that of her dead son.

"I'm sorry, but we must withdraw that offer. Jerry did not have the approval of the board."

The man was shaking his head, kindly but firmly. "I'm afraid that's not possible, Mrs. Grohman."

Maddie thought again of her reckless son, who had died in a car wreck only two months ago. Had his death been a suicide? Had he for some reason been in such dire straits that he could no longer carry on? Or had he been afraid of her – of his mother finding out that he planned to sell the family heritage?

These thoughts of Jerry were powerful enough to conjure him. Suddenly emerging from the shadows at the end of the long hall, the ghost of Jerry Grohman came striding. He was dressed as Jerry the businessman had appeared on his best days, in a three-piece gray pinstripe suit that made his slightly padded frame look svelte. But the clothes were disarrayed, Jerry's collar open and his tie pulled askew. When the ghost saw Claude Duquesne talking to his mother, and taking a letter back from her, Jerry began to look even more disordered. His face contorted horribly, in a way no human face could do, as he began to run down the hall. Jerry opened his mouth so wide it seemed he could swallow the intruder, and screamed a horrible banshee yell. He leaped, hands extended like claws.

And fell through Duquesne, hitting the floor on his far side and skidding several feet. Jerry pushed himself up, looking dazed and broken.

Claude Duquesne shivered briefly. "You do get strange drafts in these old places, don't you? Well, shall we begin to talk particulars?"

The man known as Diablo had gypsy features, a callous nose, and dark eyes that more than one woman had described as "mysterious." But after three weeks with Evelyn Grohman on his hands, he'd begun to feel a lot less mysterious.

As a kidnapping victim she was very demanding, the more so because she didn't know she'd been kidnapped. He had to drive uptown to the Central Market to buy her food, pay her constant compliments, and once in a bold, daring escapade had taken her shopping at Annie Gogglyn's in the heart of Alamo Heights. Evelyn had bought a short black skirt and tight electric blue top that would have looked charming on someone half her age – well, maybe a third her age.

He had painted her toenails, massaged her entire pudgy body, and lavished on her physical attentions he didn't care to contemplate. If he had ever before treated another woman this way, he would probably be happily married now, with four kids. Except that he couldn't stand it. No matter what he did, Evelyn purred and smiled and thought of more he could do. If he hadn't been so intent on not committing a crime, he would have killed her by now.

Thus the shopping expedition on her home turf, where she'd probably been seen by someone she knew. At any rate, the clerks would remember the sight of Evelyn in her teenager-intended purchases. Diablo planned to get the ransom he demanded without ever actually committing the crime. The Grohman family might call it kidnapping. Evelyn would remember it only as a very extended first date.

Accordingly, one weekday late afternoon he took Evelyn for a drink at the Esquire Bar. This represented a safely daring adventure. The old Bexar County Courthouse stood staunchly only a block away. Probably any number of lawyers negotiating or whining to a judge within its confines would have recognized Evelyn. The offices nearby undoubtedly held '09 types who knew her family. But few of them would venture inside the Esquire. The venerable old bar came with a force field that repelled people with too obviously high a credit rating.

They entered from bright May sunlight into a different sort of glare, of neon signs and watchful eyes. Evelyn walked daintily to the bar and asked for the no smoking section. The bartender laughed and pointed back outside.

The long wooden bar itself was famous, at one time the longest bar in Texas. Some of its patrons seemed to be the longest bar residents, as well. More than a dozen men, varying in age but not in expression, sat in frozen postures of self-contemplation. They didn't speak, in fact barely moved, yet somehow the beers in front of them were drained. It was rather Zen, in a south Texas kind of way.

Evelyn looked around happily. The dour looks of the inhabitants aside, the room itself had an old-fashioned elegance, with a hammered copper ceiling high above, crown molding, and – what seemed to be a theme of her life lately – red flocked wallpaper.

Diablo settled Evelyn at the bar, ordered beers and shots for both of them, and stood tall beside her. Evelyn laid an appreciative hand on his chest. "It's been fun," she smiled, and added demurely, "But I really do need to be getting home soon."

"Soon?"

"Well, you know. July. Or thereabouts."

Diablo shuddered invisibly. He took her hand with great, feigned sincerity. "Evelyn, do you know what you and I have in common? We've both been cheated by the Grohman family."

"Yes!" She slapped her hand on the bar, then seemed to hear exactly what he'd said. "Really? They cheated you too?"

"It's a complicated story. But I want to help you. You deserve so much more than the crumbs they've left you."

"You are absolutely right!"

He leaned close to her ear, his breath tickling the tendrils of hair at her neck. "Evelyn, if you'll help, we can correct these injustices." She turned to him wide-eyed, and he nodded knowingly. "Excuse me a moment, my dear."

He retreated to the far end of the room, where a tiny balcony overlooked a little-used stretch of the Riverwalk. Diablo took out Evelyn's cell phone and made a call. When it was answered he growled, "Gabe Grohman? Your time has run out…. Sure, you'll see her again. Which piece do you want first?"

Back at the bar, Evelyn happily contemplated the idea of spying on her in-laws for her new friend. It sounded exciting. She had wondered how she was going to fill her days. Then a hand brushed against her. Evelyn turned to snap that she wasn't a piece of meat, but stopped at sight of a man of about forty, distinguished in a youthful way, wearing an elegant blue suit and sporting a bright smile under a little sandy moustache.

"I'm so sorry, dear. Somebody bumped me. Horridly crowded in here, isn't it?"

Instinctively, Evelyn knew exactly what he meant: that there weren't enough of their kind inside the Esquire. She gave him her hand and her name.

"Charmed," he said. "I'm Chester Worthington Dilmore the Fifth. But they call me –"

"Cinco," Evelyn said.

"Yes." He smiled again. "Do you know me?"

"Not personally." Evelyn only knew his type. It was a type she liked. He stank of money. Not shiny new money, either, but money buried in vaults and bonds, dusty with antiquity.

She decided she'd been slumming long enough.

Milagro Lane Explained

Gabe Grohman wiped sweat from his forehead, leaving a streak of dust. This section of the warehouse a mile or so south of downtown was supposed to be climate-controlled, but the air-conditioning today wasn't keeping up with the confined heat. As Gabe wrestled boxes around he had discarded his suit coat, then rolled up his white shirtsleeves. He looked thoroughly disheveled.

The boxes that held old Grohman Enterprises documents were the size of filing cabinets, with three storage compartments in each. Gabe discovered that his ancestors had retained a great volume of records, some of them obviously relevant to the family business, others not so apparently. All the receipts from the building of the house in Olmos Park remained together neatly filed. One Alphonse Grohman had served as the general contractor and apparently held a tight grip on the financial reins. Building the house in 1910, including labor, had cost just shy of $20,000.

Gabe found other records, but not the ones for which he searched. Evelyn's kidnapper had said he wanted deeds and lease documents showing the Grohman family's dealings with the city of San Antonio in the 1880s. Gabe found his way into that decade, but not to precisely what he sought. As he read invoices and memos it seemed to him that his ancestors whispered in his ear. He had a vision of a lane opening, a lane lined with grim-faced men and conscientious women. All their eyes turned toward him....

The vision cleared. In its place stood Estela Valenzuela, in the doorway of the room. Gabe immediately sensed his own sweatiness and felt the dust on his arms and face. Estela looked cool as a March sunrise, in a blue halter top with her long hair falling freely to her bare shoulders.

"Maybe I could help," she offered.

"Why?"

She stepped into the room and looked uncharacteristically shy. "I was helping your father, Gabe, did you know that? Right before his accident. He was looking for documents from the 1880s."

Gabe's head jerked toward her. "Did he find them?"

"Some. But they weren't where they were supposed to be. Even the public records are missing from the Bexar County archives."

Gabe breathed shallowly in the dusty heat. "Why did he ask you to help?"

"I'm a finder, that's what I do." Estela smiled modestly. "Kind of a job I invented myself." She took clips from her pocket and efficiently pinned her hair back. She knelt and leafed through one of the large boxes.

Gabe knelt beside her. "Estela, I want to ask you about something."

"Yes?" Her green-flecked brown eyes seemed to grow bigger as she saw his earnestness.

But then Gabe found his nerve failing. He wanted to ask about Estela and his father, but there surrounded by Grohman ghosts, he couldn't. Instead he said, "Where's Milagro Lane?"

"How have you heard of that?" Estela asked, startled.

"It's not on any map. I've looked for it. It's not an old street name that's been changed, either. At least I don't think so. But the night I met you, the night we danced at the Queen's Ball. . . . When I was walking home I thought I saw a sign. I thought I walked on Milagro Lane."

"You were there?" Estela studied Gabe for the first time as if there might be more than his appearance revealed. He looked at her so curiously she had to begin explaining.

"It's not a place, Gabe. It's . . . a street of mind. I think my mother invented the expression. She's an artist."

Gabe quickly made a connection. "Your mother is Luz Valenzuela?"

"Yes. She invented her name, too. The perfect name for an artist, don't you think? Anyway, some days I'd come home and she'd be lying on the couch looking like she'd been eating bon bons and watching *telenovelas* all day, but she'd say, 'I'm exhausted. I spent three hours on *Milagro* Lane today.'"

Gabe began somehow to feel cooler. He pictured the house, the room, the couch as Estela spoke. She appeared to grow younger. "I don't . . ." he said.

"It's like being in the zone, but more than that, a place of insight. Of inspiration. At least that's what I understand. Once in a great while when she said it I'd go into her studio and find something extraordinary. It really seemed like she'd gone to another place and brought it back."

"Why '*Milagro*'?"

"Because Mom said it was always a miracle when art happened." Estela laughed wryly. "Some of her friends said it was a miracle if any work got done in that house." She looked at Gabe wonderingly. "And you were there. You saw it. I'm her daughter and I've never been there. Your father never got there, either."

Gabe had such mixed feelings he couldn't speak. Estela continued to study his face, and for the first time in his life Gabe felt himself worth studying.

Gabe and Estela stared into each other's eyes. Gabe saw deep brown mystery, intershot with flashes of green, like comets of emotion. Estela saw pale blue puzzlement.

Then Gabe's expression changed to shamed curiosity. "Estela, I have to ask you something."

She looked open to suggestion. Gabe continued, "Were you and my – Did you – ?" He started over, more roundaboutly. "You said you were working for my father on this project?"

"Yes, he asked me to help him find these lease documents."

"Why? I mean, why you?"

"I told you, Gabe, I'm a finder. Finding things is what I do. I made up the job myself. Started as favors for friends, then I finished college, someone who knew my work hired me for a bigger project, next thing I know it turned into a business. Your father was looking for something so he asked me to help."

"But how did he know you? Did he hear about your work?" That couldn't have been all, Gabe thought. Estela wouldn't have come to Jerry Grohman's funeral wearing a red dress (at the request of the deceased) if they'd had nothing more than a business relationship.

"Oh, I'd known Jerry for years. Years ago here, then we met a few times in San Francisco. He'd come out there when I was in college. On business, he said."

Gabe thought it very possible that the Grohman family business interests extended as far as the west coast, but doubted they'd needed the supervision of the company's CEO. Looking at Estela, a slight flush of heat turning her skin reddish and her eyes lively, her shoulders almost bare in a blue tanktop, he could imagine traveling two thousand miles just to see her.

Gabe's voice croaked a little when he spoke again. "Why didn't he tell anyone else in the family he was looking for something?"

"I don't know Gabe. You would have had to ask Jerry." She put her hand on his arm. "Now you need a flash of insight. Maybe you'll figure it out the next time you're on *Milagro* Lane."

Gabe felt flattered that Estela thought he had the capacity to go there again. And feeling her hand on him, he did feel inspired.

"I don't think there's any point looking here any more, Gabe. Your father and I already searched these boxes pretty thoroughly."

Mention of her working with his father cooled Gabe's attraction. He wondered if he'd ever be able to hear Estela mention Jerry without the remark's sounding – to Gabe – like a double entendre. And her revelation that his father had been looking for something important made Gabe wonder again if his death had been the accident everyone thought.

"Where are you going, then?" he asked. "Maybe we could –"

"I've got a job now, remember? I work for Ramon Carter."

"The non-existent city councilman?" Gabe asked derisively.

Estela stood up. "Oh, he exists, Gabe. Here." She laid her hand over her heart, smiling wryly.

"Why did you take a job like that, anyway?" Gabe stood up, dusted off his hands on his pants, and followed Estela outside.

Estela turned to him. "Don't you know, Gabe? To help with this search. We're looking for city records. Where better to work than for the city?"

Outside, the sunlight hit them. Jerry said, "I've got this family thing to go to, anyway."

"Really?" Estela sounded surprised, which in turn surprised Gabe. Did she expect to know all the family business, just because she'd had a "relationship" with one member of that family?

He wished he'd met her under other circumstances. As Estela gave him a little wave and walked off, glancing back once, he thought she wished the same. Or was that only his suddenly-active imagination? Until recently, he hadn't known he'd been cursed with such an ability.

Evelyn Grohman, after her chance meeting with Chester Worthington Dilmore V – "Cinco" to his friends, of whom Evelyn assumed he had many – quickly struck up a friendship. Cinco gave her a ride to her King William home. That quickly, Evelyn forgot her adventures with her new friend Diablo. But Diablo, watching her go, did not remotely forget Evelyn.

Evelyn enjoyed the ride and the conversation. She liked looking at Cinco, too. Sandy-haired down to the backs of his hands, with a fair complexion, Cinco was just the right size for a man. Not heavy, not deviantly thin. And they knew people in common.

As they drove up to her house, Cinco turned to Evelyn with a charming smile and said, "You must come to dinner one of these days. I'd like you to meet my partner."

Oh, dear. Evelyn had just enough sophistication to know that "partner" had a specific definition. It meant homosexual. Or at best it meant some long-term commitment not sanctioned by court or church, but a commitment nevertheless. Damn. Wouldn't you know?

"We have a little enterprise going," Cinco said modestly. "Something rather special, actually."

Evelyn perked up. Oh yes. "Partner" had some business meaning, too. Extending her hand, she said, "I'd love to."

Madeleine Grohman sat in the plush, old-fashioned office of her old family lawyer. Javier Gustado in fact wasn't old – mid-fifties – but he had a great deal and variety of legal experience, and the Grohmans had relied on his advice for years. Javier had begun his career at the City Attorney's Office in the 1970s, gone out on his own before that decade ended, then joined a small firm that through his industry and contacts had grown into a very respected mid-sized one, with Javier's name near the top of the letterhead.

He had helped the Grohman family out of bad contracts, bad personal relationships, two or three family members out of some very bad habits. But the family had never presented him with such a problem as Miz Maddie had laid on his desk that morning.

"I have to tell you, Maddie, it looks valid to me. There are certain requirements of a binding letter of intent, and I see them all here. Offer to sell, a set price, clearly defined assets, even witnesses to the signature."

"But it can't happen, Javier! Sell Grohman Enterprises? Not in my lifetime."

Miz Maddie had had a day to gain her composure, since the visit by the odious little man who'd given her this letter. Her hands had stopped trembling, her famous resolve had surged to the foreground. When a 74-year-old person vowed that something would not happen in her lifetime, some might not have thought that so formidable a waiting period. But this morning Miz Maddie looked her old steely self, as if she'd be around for decades yet.

Javier Gustado had thick brown hair gone nicely gray and wavy at the temples, a forehead that folded impressively when he frowned, and a moustache that he had grown precisely for stroking at times like these, making him look thoughtful.

"Maybe if we can show he was deceived, we can void this. Why on earth would Jerry have made this offer?"

Maddie shook her head. "I haven't a clue."

The ghost of her son, pacing the floor behind Maddie, had been desperately trying to give her one, but with no luck. He went and sat in the other visitor's chair, stared back and forth between his mother and her lawyer, and suddenly said, "Boogabooga!"

Nothing. No response at all. Was there no one left among the living that Jerry could reach?

Estela Valenzuela enjoyed her new job as aide to a councilman who never appeared. She had government hours: sometimes long hours on a weekend, sometimes short ones during the week. The boss never complained. Estela got her job done: dealing with constituent complaints, issuing press releases, interfering with city staff.

The primary perk of lower-level government work is feeling like an insider. Plus, sometimes Estela was privy to some interesting scenes. Such as this one: She stood at a hallway juncture looking down two hallways. Down one came the new mayor of San Antonio, Suzanne Pierce, only in office a week but already breathing more fire then her predecessor had in four years. And coming up the other corridor was Veronica Lewis, disgraced TV reporter, returning for the first time to City Hall not in triumph but in fact rather sneakily. Obviously she had hoped to slip in unobtrusively. Estela faded back and watched the two women approach the corner from opposite directions.

They almost bumped heads, then recognized each other with unmatching shrieks. Veronica's was an *Eek* of dismay. Mayor Pierce's sounded more as if she'd stepped in something.

She recovered first. "What the hell are you doing here? I thought you'd been reassigned to Cotulla, or Tierra del Fuego."

"No, just a little vacation," Veronica said. She made a face of apology and regret. "And I've been demoted. I'm not on camera any more. Just a researcher."

"Well, at least San Antonio's been spared something," Pierce said scathingly. "What are you researching?"

"Actually," Veronica said, producing a notepad, "I'm responding to a great many inquiries concerning how you're going to make a living for the next two years. You had a six-figure income from your law firm, but you've resigned from there now. Being mayor of San Antonio pays considerably less. How will you put bread on the table?"

Suzanne Pierce avoided the question. "Whence came these many inquiries?"

"'Whence'?" Veronica said, wincing.

"Yes, whence. From where. Who's asking?"

"Oh." Veronica smiled brightly. "From all quadrants of the city, Your Honor. From the many, many quadrants of the city."

Suzanne Pierce rolled her eyes. She looked at Veronica's outfit, a short purple skirt, and a small white blouse that gave the illusion – or maybe not illusion – of having translucent streaks throughout. Disgustedly, she said, "I see you're not planning to appear on videotape again any time soon. Except maybe in pornography."

Veronica smiled. "Thank you. My roommate helped me pick it out."

The mayor of San Antonio began to develop an extremely grudging respect for Veronica, whose nitwit routine may have been only an act, but a deeply committed one. She was easy to dislike but damned difficult to insult.

From her shadowed corner, Estela Valenzuela looked on and thought, *God, I love this job.*

The entire Grohman clan didn't gather very often. Generally it took a funeral or wedding to bring them together. But on this morning in June, many of them had met for a civic occasion.

The city had arranged to have a cabin that had been built by the original Grohman immigrants moved from its location on the

Guadalupe River near Seguin, to HemisFair Park in downtown San Antonio. This effort continued the city's effort to create a historical park to draw people to the less-used areas of the park. Eventually plans called for the area to include re-creations of the first City Hall and courthouse and there was even talk of having actors portray historical figures. (Politicians become interesting and even beloved once they are safely long dead.)

The Grohmans, as they had with many other enterprises, were getting in on the ground floor. Their old cabin now sat, apparently as solidly as ever, less than a city block from Durango Street and the federal courthouse. Many of the family, led by Miz Maddie, had gathered to witness its dedication and the placement of a plaque.

Gabe Grohman arrived late, dusty and beguiled from his meeting with Estela Valenzuela. The first person Gabe saw was his brother Duke, which made Gabe's heart fill with remorse. Duke was Gabe's half-brother actually, and so much younger that he had never been a part of Gabe's life. But that was all the more reason that Gabe should have stepped in and drawn the boy closer after their father's death.

Duke was 11, the same age Gabe had been when he'd lost his father – to divorce, not death, but it had felt almost the same at the time. No one knew better than Gabe what young Duke must be feeling these days. In the days after the funeral Gabe had spent extra time with the boy, called him every day and dropped by a few times, but then he'd been diverted by life and never had the heart-to-heart talk he'd planned.

At the park, Gabe walked through the small crowd and put his arm around his brother's shoulder. The boy was thin and blond and winsome, but with a wicked gleam in his eye when excited about a project. Gabe wondered again why the family had given the boy a dog's nickname. Gabe had always refused to use it, calling him instead by his name, Preston.

"How are you, Pres?" he asked softly, bending close.

"Better than you, dog breath," the boy snapped.

Now Gabe remembered why he'd spent so little time with young Preston as the boy was growing up. He was a jerk.

The cabin stood remarkably well-preserved. It was built of cedar logs stacked atop each other, cut to fit snugly with mud plastered in the crevices. Wind would have seeped through, but that would have been a good thing in the summer. In winter all the beds would have been pulled closer to the stone fireplace. There was only one door, no windows, which would have been hard to cut and have opened the place to mosquitoes. The ceiling was very low by modern standards. A kitchen table with spindly ladderback chairs, and a wooden bedstead, were the only furniture that remained. Miz Maddie gave the place a critical inspection.

"After the family started doing better financially the place had a hardwood floor, but the city wanted to make it look more authentic with this swept-dirt floor." She sounded as if she spoke from personal memories. Looking around, she said, "Can you believe people lived like this?"

"Without maids, you mean?" said Rosa Perez.

Rosa had been Miz Maddie's maid for decades. In retirement now for a year, she occasionally allowed herself to be drawn back for family occasions, at which times she was always treated like a long-unseen foreign relative. Rosa was short, slight, but very sturdy. Her curly hair remained mostly brown, but with a dusting of gray that made it look like an aura illuminating her head. She still seemed constantly busy, even when standing still. Rosa smiled as she spoke, and Maddie hugged her quickly.

There was another Grohman family home that had been donated to the city. It was now one of the highlights of the King William tour, a two-story stone mansion built during the 1880s, when the family was harvesting stone from city-owned property, digging the holes that had later become Sunken Gardens and the zoo. So in only 40 years the family had gone from this one-room hovel to relative splendor. But those 40 years had been a person's life expectancy during the time when people had lived in this cabin. Miz Maddie looked around the room, folded her arms, and let her eyes go moist. Rosa, noticing, touched her old employer's arm briefly in passing.

Outside, Gabe decided he'd do better with his little brother when he could get him alone. He chatted with various relatives, some of whom he hadn't seen in months.

Jessica Ambrose also worked the crowd. She grew a secret smile when she saw Gabe, and she slowly approached him from behind, wondering if anyone noticed. Sometimes – this was one of those times – Jessica thought being the mistress was so cool. It felt exactly as if she were a secret member of the Grohman family, which gave her an extra family in addition to her own. God knows she could use that at times.

Jessica was here officially because her husband Jim's company had moved the cabin. He took part in the ceremony, grinning like an idiot and chatting with the city manager as if they were old friends. Besides, Jessica was entitled to be here on her own, as an old friend of the family – friendlier to some family members than others, of course.

She moved up behind Gabe where no one could see and gently stroked the back of his neck. His reaction was gratifying. He turned quickly, his eyes widened at sight of Jessica, and he actually blushed, which made her smile. How cute.

Now Gabe remembered why he used to miss so many of these family occasions. Guilt everywhere he looked.

When Gabe felt the cool, light touch of fingers on the back of his neck, he couldn't think of a single relative who would touch him that way. He turned quickly to find Jessica Ambrose giving him a look that was the sly equivalent of her touch.

"Hello, Mr. Grohman," she said in a husky voice.

Gabe started to turn away, then remembered that he could speak to Jessica in public. In private he could do much more, and had, but no one could know that.

"Hello, Mrs. Ambrose," Gabe said with an attempt at irony. Jessica, blond and well-kept and slinky in a summery green dress, stepped close in the crowd as if she couldn't hear him, and touched his leg with hers.

Looking over her shoulder, Gabe said heartily, "Hi, Jim!"

Jim Ambrose, tanned and athletic-looking, came up and put his arm around her. Taking her husband's hand, Jessica smiled slyly at Gabe.

"Isn't this great?" Jim said expansively. "Can you believe your folks lived like this, Gabe?" He waved at the old one-room log cabin, moved intact from its original location. Gabe turned to look at it. The cabin did look awfully primitive.

"Everybody did, I think," Gabe said.

Uncle Jock, rugged and sun-browned, explained to Gabe's cousin Helen why he couldn't get to town very often. "I try to get away from the ranch, but those horses expect to see me every day. The hands tell me that if I'm gone for more than a day they get irritable and off their feed. Even the deer seem more restless, they say."

"And we hate to drag you away from them," Helen said graciously, turning away.

People passed through the interior of the cabin, noting its rusticity and making jokes about its lack of comforts. "How did they live without air conditioning?" one cousin asked, as if the Grohmans of 1840 had had a choice.

Only Miz Maddie and her retired maid Rosa remained inside. The place seemed to whisper to Maddie, and Rosa seemed to hear whatever passed through her old employer's head.

As Gabe had said, nearly everyone whose family went back a few generations in Texas had ancestors who had lived in such hovels. The cabin was close, low, and dark. The people who'd built this cabin and walked, slept, and eaten on its dirt floor had remained part of the natural world. Outdoor Texas couldn't be ignored the way it could be in a modern home.

Maddie didn't think about the discomfort. She thought of how close this family must have remained, bound together by hard work, common goals, and living in the same room.

"Some poor lady spent her whole life here," she sighed.

"No, ma'am," Rosa said. She knew the family history better than most family members. "By the 1850s they'd moved into a house in Seguin and opened a general store."

"Even so," Maddie sighed. "Think of them here. Think of all we owe them."

Rosa, whose family had lived in not much nicer accommodations than this much more recently, had five grandchildren who had graduated from high school, a feat she had never come close to accomplishing. In many ways Rosa felt more in common with the long-ago generations of the Grohman family than with the current crop. She answered, "You owe them to live as well as possible. That's what they wanted for you."

The old wooden bedstead in the corner had a mattress stuffed with corn shucks. A coverlet had been tossed on top. Without saying a word, the two women pulled the old bed out from the wall and began making it. Miz Maddie fluffed up its pillow.

Outside, a new arrival caused a commotion in the crowd. A pewter-colored Jaguar pulled up to the red curb. A sandy-haired, smiling man whom no one recognized hopped out of the driver's seat, called, "Cheers!" to the crowd, and opened the passenger door. Evelyn Grohman, wearing an ivory tea dress and more jewelry than looked comfortable in San Antonio in June, stepped out, smiling demurely and trying very hard to keep from laughing aloud.

"Hello, everyone!" she called cheerily.

The crowd moved toward her. Gabe, who had tried unsuccessfully to rescue Evelyn from her supposed kidnapping, hid his shock. He put his arm around his eleven-year-old half-brother's shoulders and said, "Look, Preston. Your mom's back."

The boy, usually known as Duke, gave her a casual glance and said, "Yeah. Looks like she's put on a few pounds."

Actually, it looked as if Evelyn had picked up about 170 pounds, in the person of the well-dressed, fortyish man on her arm. Obviously delighted, Evelyn introduced everyone to Chester Worthington Dilmore V – "Cinco."

Gabe felt a strange twinge – not jealousy but something very like it – at sight of his father's widow in the company of a new man.

He would have felt even worse if he could have seen Evelyn's recent masculine company. Across the park, looking at the scene through binoculars, the man known as Diablo muttered in his moustache and smiled.

"We Have to Talk"

When Evelyn Grohman, whom no one in the family had seen in weeks, arrived at the gathering in HemisFair Park, the crowd gravitated toward her. Jessica Ambrose pretended to do so, pressing up against the back of the person in front of her as if the force of the crowd had driven her onto him. But then she held that position.

When Gabe Grohman turned and saw Jessica's face inches from his, and felt her front pressed against his back, alarm swept through him. And not merely because Jessica's husband Jim stood a few feet away in the crowd. No, Jessica's proprietary smile worried him more than the physical threat of Jim Ambrose.

The crowd parted around them. Gabe drew her aside and whispered earnestly, "Jessica, we have to talk."

In the history of romantic relationships, there may have been more ominous words than "We have to talk," but they would have involved actual death threats. Jessica, only twenty-four and once-married, but wise in the ways of her crowd, knew very well that when a man wanted to talk, trouble lurked in the neighborhood. Because men don't want to talk. If for some reason a woman wants to inspire fear in the man with whom she's romantically involved (Jessica had such urges occasionally), she tells him to talk to her. Then, of course, he babbles about baseball, or what he had for lunch, or any topic, anything at all, rather than Something Important.

So when Gabe said he wanted to talk, Jessica felt a shift in her perfect world beginning. But she kept her intuition to herself, smiled intimately, and said softly, "Of course, darling. Your place or yours?"

She laughed at her own joke. Gabe didn't. He squeezed her hand very briefly, said, "I'll send you an e-mail, okay?" and walked away.

Yes, it was bad. He had held her hand in public, even if only for a moment. Jessica's eyes narrowed as she watched Gabe depart. She muttered, "I swear, if you kiss me off in an e-mail, I'll have your —"

"What's that, dear?" A strong arm went around her waist.

Jessica said to her husband, "I was just wondering if there's any place around here where we could get sweetbreads for lunch? Why don't we try the Palm?"

The cabin had been dedicated, the historical plaque hung, the occasion marked. The Grohman family and friends began to break down into smaller groups, some of which hadn't spoken to each other in years. Visitors to HemisFair park mingled with the group. Across the way, the man known as Diablo saw his chance to join the crowd.

Gabe made his way to his stepmother Evelyn. He took her arm, the most affectionate gesture he'd ever show her.

"Evelyn, are you all right?"

She laughed. "I'm wonderful, Gabito. Have you met Cinco?"

Gabe nodded to the new boyfriend and took Evelyn aside. Indeed, she looked younger than her 36 years, lighthearted and happy as a teenager who'd snagged a date with the most popular boy in school. Gabe said with concern, "Evelyn, I thought you . . . Are you sure you're all right?"

He didn't want to upset her by reminding her that she'd recently been kidnapped, which from her expression would have been news to Evelyn. Again she insisted on her wonderfulness and walked away.

Diablo, a dark shadow in the bright morning sunlight, passed behind Evelyn. "Remember, my sweet. Vengeance for old wrongs."

Evelyn didn't quite get his meaning, but she thought of Diablo affectionately. Already she felt nostalgic over her days with him. She turned and gave him a conspiratorial wink.

Diablo passed on, well satisfied. That is, until he saw Gabe Grohman. Diablo still had use for Evelyn. For Gabe he had none. Gabe Grohman may never have set eyes on Diablo, but Diablo hated him passionately. As he had Gabe's father. That hatred had not been consumed by Jerry's death.

Veronica Lewis walked softly and carried a big notebook. Slipping down the corridors of City Hall, she wore white capris and a dark red sleeveless top. She hoped this gave her a light-hearted, touristy look that diminished suspicion.

It was five-thirty in the afternoon of a summer Thursday. Not only had the secretaries gone home, so had most of the politicians and staffers. If not home then to receptions or constituent meetings. Veronica thought it a good time for anyone remaining in the building to be making stealthy calls, and in turn for her to overhear them.

She remained curious about how Suzanne Pierce would make a living in the notoriously low-paid job of mayor, especially given the lifestyle she'd enjoyed as a partner in a major law firm.

Walking softly into the mayor's reception area, Veronica indeed heard a low voice. The voice was saying something about money, leases, city-owned property. Veronica crept closer to the open door of the mayor's inner office. The woman's voice grew louder and said, "Oh, Henry, it would take at least a hundred thousand for me to overcome my ethical objections to a plan like that."

Veronica scribbled the quote in her notebook and leaned around the doorjamb to confirm the speaker's identity . . . only to come face to face with Estela Valenzuela, grinning mischievously.

"Got you," she said.

Veronica put away her notebook and sighed. "You are the sneakiest person in this building."

"Present company excepted," Estela observed.

"Oh, thanks." Veronica had a sudden thought. "You know, the mayor's trying to get rid of you at the first opportunity. And she hates me. You and I might be able to do each other some good."

Estela watched her. Veronica noted that Estela was very dressed up for City Hall, in a red dress. After a moment, Estela nodded. "Let's see how we get along. I'm on my way to a party. Want to be my date?"

Veronica had had no idea, but she was a reporter. "Sure," she said quickly.

And they went out arm in arm, Estela beginning to hum an unfamiliar tune. Well, it's kinky, Veronica thought, but is it news?

Part II

But Is It Art?

But Is It Art?

"You never get a crowd this good-looking at one of my openings," Ramos Ramos observed wistfully, looking around the central gallery of the San Antonio Museum of Art.

"You can remember back that far?" Jaime Jones answered. He couldn't help himself. He loved Ramos, but a straight line was a straight line.

The two moved easily in the throng attending the reception for the exhibition of Linda Pace's "The Red Project." It was a mixed group, the usual art crowd, languid and casually dressed, mingling with well-off socialites. These two groups often intersected anyway, but never more so than here, where a well-known arts patroness had become the artist.

Jaime, an artist beginning to enjoy some acclaim himself, had dragged his heels about coming, but Ramos Ramos had insisted. "This will be the greatest display of insincere kissing-up in San Antonio this year. How can you miss it?"

Most local artists never got an exhibit at the art museum, and many grumbled at the attention afforded this first-time effort. But of course no one would complain to the artist herself, one of the most generous financial contributors to visual arts in the city. As one artist said from the far side of the room, "If Linda Pace comes in here and props up her canvas, who's going to tell her to get it the hell out of here?"

Jaime and Ramos studied the very large rectangle to which Pace had affixed many, many "found" objects, all red. Plastic cups, Viewmasters, a Teletubby, rubber monster hands: toys, mementos, souvenirs, trash. All undeniably red. "What do you think?" Ramos asked. Jaime shrugged. "Interesting. But does having a giant vat of Superglue make you an artist?"

"I know. Other people have garage sales – Uh oh, it's our turn. Linda, darling! Let me just say one word: stunning. Can't take my eyes off it. I know people hate to hear their work described as interesting, but this is an epic achievement in interestingness."

The artist, in a black dress with a black and white scarf, as if in contrast to her work, wore a slight smile and took the flattery completely in stride, perhaps even with a grain of salt. She turned to Jaime, who saw it was his turn and said, "I'm too overcome to speak."

They moved on to make way for others. Ramos said, "'Overcome,' that was good. What did you think of mine?"

"I'm sure it's one of the leading entries. Oh, look who's here. But of course, it wouldn't be an event without *La Estrella*. But this is a new twist."

"So to speak," Ramos added. Because Estela Valenzuela had just made an entrance, not only wearing her red dress but arm in arm with TV reporter Veronica Lewis, who appeared a little uncomfortable but put on a brave front.

Estela never did anything just for effect. If she had done so here, she would have been disappointed. This was the arts crowd. Two women arriving together caused not a ripple in this group, which included same-sex couples and indeterminate-sex couples. Estela did find to her surprise that she felt immediately at home. She had grown up with these people. One flamboyant man with a silver goatee exclaimed over her, saying, "I remember when you were tiny, Estela. I remember you before you were a wicked gleam in your mother's eye." He would have been dismayed at how conventional he sounded.

She hugged Jaime and Ramos, made catty chitchat with other artists, and received compliments over having grown up. Estela felt warmly embraced. It wasn't until she stood in front of the eight-foot-by-eight-foot "Red," though, that she felt something deeper.

Like nearly everyone who stood there, Estela's first thought was that she could have done this herself, given enough time and leisure. But she continued to stare, following tiny paths like trickling streams through the objects. She lost all expression, and didn't move except for her hands, which began to twitch.

"What do you think?" asked Linda Pace, who hadn't asked anyone else's opinion. "It makes me think of my mother," Estela said in a hollow voice. Pace felt sincerely complimented for the first time that evening.

Estela's hands continued to move. For the first time in a long while, she wanted to hold a brush.

Gabe Grohman had never finished going through his father's desk at Grohman Enterprises. No one had. That evening, still possessed by his searching urge, he finished the job. In a bottom drawer, shoved to the back and hidden under papers, he found his father's diary.

Not really a diary. Jerry Grohman hadn't been the type to keep a journal. It was a desk calendar from 1995, one with plenty of spaces for writing on the dates. Jerry had made notes to himself. They became notes to Gabe, who leafed through it hastily. The year 1995 seemed both remote and recent. It was the year Gabe had gone away to college. He looked through the summer months, trying to find some reference to himself, some indication that his father had thought about him when he'd been on the cusp of growing up.

On the date of July 2nd, Gabe came across two words that hit him so hard he sat down on the floor in the dimly lit office. No description of an event, and nothing to indicate his father's feelings, but nevertheless Gabe felt struck. The words were: "Estela's birthday."

Gabe turned off lights in the offices and carried the diary to his car, intending o read it more thoroughly at home. It was nine o'clock at night, the sun had finally gone down. Gabe's BMW was the last car left in the small parking lot of the office near the Quarry Market. But Gabe was not the last person.

As he put his key in the door lock, Gabe felt more than heard a presence behind him. He turned and was immediately enfolded in black. Someone had thrown a cloth bag over his head. As Gabe struggled to free himself and to breathe, he felt a sharp pain to the back of his head, followed by a burst of light.

Someone had hit him with something like a baseball bat. Gabe slumped to the dirty ground beside his car. The diary slipped from his fingers.

When Gabe woke, he was surrounded by family. It was only his Uncle Jock, but nevertheless Gabe felt surrounded, as his beefy, sun-burned uncle hovered inches away from him.

"Are you all right, son?"

The classic question one male asks another. Gabe lay on the oil-stained parking lot of Grohman Enterprises, half under his own car, with a lump the size of half a tennis ball on the side of his head, but Uncle Jock had to ask if he was all right. Meaning, *Shake it off. Be a man. Please don't tell me I have to do something for you.*

No wonder Jock had become the ranch uncle, the one informally exiled from town, the relative who couldn't quite function in society.

"I'm okay," Gabe said. The classic male response. Actually, it wasn't too bad, lying on the pavement. There was something soft under his head. When he turned he saw it was a cloth bag, probably the one that his unknown attacker had pulled over Gabe's head before bashing it.

"The diary!" Gabe said. Gabe tried to look and feel all around him for his father's 1995 desk calendar that he had found just before the attack.

"It's gone," Uncle Jock said kindly.

"What is?" Gabe felt very confused. Concussion will do that.

"Whatever you're looking for. It's just you here on the asphalt, boy. I came back because I wasn't sure I'd locked up. Good thing I did."

"What time is it?"

"Close on midnight. I'd be going out to check the stock if I was at the ranch. Sometimes this time of night, when the breeze shifts, they get awful restless. I remember one time…"

"Uncle Jock?"

"Sure, boy, what is it?"

"Can I faint now?"

"Man's gotta do what a man's gotta do."

Before Gabe heard the end of this touching sentiment, he had acquiesced to his own request. He fell back into unconsciousness hoping he would awake to a place less dense with male relatives. Also soft. Soft would be nice. . . .

Gabe achieved his wish. He awoke on the soft bosom of Estela Valenzuela.

Figuratively speaking. Gabe lay somewhere, and Estela was bending over him, adjusting his pillows. As Gabe began to regain consciousness, his flickering vision took in the sight of her near him, made something else of her white sleeveless blouse, and his subconscious began to create a dream that made him not want to wake up.

But he did, in time to clutch her hand as she withdrew. "Don't go," he said.

"You're awake." She smiled at him. She had a beautiful smile. He hadn't noticed before. In fact, he wasn't sure he'd ever seen her smile. "I was worried about you," she added. Her concern touched him deeply.

Gabe began to stroke her hand.

"Estela," he said softly. "I've been afraid to tell you this. I don't even think I'd realized it. But I know it now. I love you, Estela."

Estela felt shocked. She'd been aware of Gabe's admiring stare, she knew she had an effect on him the night they'd danced at the Queen's Ball. She had felt his interest but had no idea of its depth. It had been quite a while since anyone had told Estela she was loved.

A young maid, about Estela's age, passed by behind her and whispered in Spanish, "He just told me the same thing."

Just as Gabe began to wonder where he was, he recognized the scratchy brocade on which he lay. He was on his grandmother's sofa. Gabe sat up abruptly.

A large, florid man in a *guyabera* approached. "There you are, son." The doctor took Gabe's wrist. He showed no emotion over what the pulse told him. "You've got to take it easy," he advised.

Dr. Zell was retired, but Miz Maddie didn't seem to know that. He would still make a house call for her, because Maddie had always been his favorite patient, he usually got to see some drama on his visits, and she poured a delicious port wine.

The doctor examined Gabe's pupils and his head. He talked softly but forcefully. "You've had a mild concussion, son. Listen to me. Concussion has an effect on people. It – heightens emotions. You'll find yourself crying over dog food commercials. Take things easy for the next couple of weeks. Don't make any long-term commitments."

He gave Gabe a significant look

Estela Valenzuela sat carefully next to Gabe on the scratchy brocaded couch in a side parlor of his grandmother's house. The house was large enough to boast both front and side parlors, this one small and seldom used. It had seemed the safest place to put Gabe when he'd been brought in unconscious. The room itself was wildly over-furnished, with old chairs, portraits, an upright piano, and two fringed floor lamps. When Miz Maddie could no longer stand an item, but couldn't bring herself to dispose of it, she would say, "Take it to the side parlor." Furnishing purgatory, one step from the Salvation Army.

The room felt stuffy to Estela, overfilled with furniture and emotion. Gabe had just told her he loved her. Of course, he had said the same things to the maid and the doctor. Dr. Zell had told him he had a concussion that would make him more susceptible to his emotions. He still had dried tears on his cheeks as he held Estela's hand.

"Why are you here?" he asked.

"I heard you were hurt. Your grandmother called, I thought she might need help."

"But shouldn't you be with friends? Your family?"

"What do you mean?"

From the pocket of his khaki pants Gabe drew out a small object wrapped in Kleenex. He pressed it into her hand. "Happy birthday, Estela," he said simply.

Estela sat amazed. She had thought almost no one knew. She hadn't received a card or a gift. Her grandmother had called and invited her to dinner, but otherwise, at around noon on July 2nd, her birthday had so far gone unobserved. Except by this relative stranger.

"How did you know?" she asked wonderingly.

He didn't answer her. "I hope you like it. I didn't have time to shop." Gabe had only found out the date of Estela's birthday about fifteen hours earlier, just before being hit on the head and spending the remaining interval unconscious. Bur somewhere in those hours of darkness he had made a decision.

Estela unwrapped the tissue and inhaled a deep breath.

For Jerry Grohman, life had been much better when he'd been alive. He'd been at the peak of his game and his form, able to buy anything that caught his fancy, be anywhere in the world within a day. He could affect lives at the touch of a few buttons. Granted, he hadn't been as close as he would have liked to his children, and his love life hadn't been all he could have wished, but he had opportunities, he could make changes.

Now, a ghost, he could go places but not affect anything. He could walk into any movie in town but couldn't have popcorn. Everyone's secrets were open to him, but he had no one to tell. He could spy on the sex lives of the rich and famous, or the young and limber, but that grew quickly frustrating, given his own lack of physical being.

Jerry felt pretty sure that he'd been left on this plane of existence to perform a mission, and he even had a good idea what that mission was: to save the family fortune, or name, or honor. But he had discovered his extreme limitations in this regard. He had tried communicating with his mother, his son, and Estela, all to no avail. And a ghost without living allies had very little chance of changing the course of events.

When he dropped in on any of his family, he could only watch as everything he'd left behind went to hell. His mother, having found out he had put the family business up for sale, would probably have him dug up and reburied in some anonymous pauper's grave. His 11 year old son Preston, known as "Duke," was turning more mean-spirited every day. His widow Evelyn was getting herself into some kind of trouble, though Jerry was vague on details. As in the last few years of his marriage, he couldn't stand to be around Evelyn for more than a few minutes at a time.

And now the young woman he cared about most in the world was staring into the eyes of his son Gabe, which was not remotely what Jerry had intended. They had grabbed hands by accident but held them together on purpose. Gabe's hands twitched slightly. He adjusted himself on the couch in a way his father recognized.

As for Estela, it had been quite some time since Jerry had seen a woman looking into his eyes with love, or at least the awakening of that kind of interest, but if memory served, that's how Estela looked now. Her eyes scanned across Gabe's face, back and forth, up and down. Her hand clenched. Her chest swelled with breath. (Actually, Jerry felt guilty even noticing that detail.)

Gabe also had the look of a young man in love: slightly stupid, as if he'd just been hit in the head. (Oh, that's right, he had. And his father hadn't been able to save him from that, either.) His dry lips parted. He was about to speak.

Jerry did not want to hear it. Whatever declaration his son was about to make, Jerry would rather be elsewhere. He decided to go drop in on the Clintons. For a lifelong Republican, their current home life was an endless source of entertainment.

He popped out of existence with less impact than an exploding soap bubble.

On the couch in his grandmother's little-used parlor, Gabe leaned slowly toward Estela. Slowly enough to give her time to pull back, or exclaim that he was making a mistake. She didn't. In fact, she leaned toward him. Their lips met very slowly, so slowly neither of them could say when the contact was complete. The gentle impact seemed to continue, grow deeper. New avenues of lip became accessible.

The moment seemed to go on a long time before they broke apart. Gabe felt the need to say something complimentary. "Wow" seemed to lack subtlety, while "Thank you" might make him seem servile. Instead he said, "I've never done that before."

"You haven't?" Estela said, gazing at him in surprise. "Well, you're pretty good, for a beginner."

"No, I mean – just –" Gabe couldn't explain, but it had felt like the first time.

Estela leaned toward him again. This kiss was briefer, because Gabe suddenly became anxious to move. "Let's get out of here. I hear my grandmother coming."

They went out the front door quickly, tiptoeing like thieves. One of them even giggled like a teenager. Once they stood outside in the bright sunlight, they stared at each other. "Did you need to go somewhere?" Estela said.

They couldn't stay here, and Gabe couldn't take her to his stepmother's house. They just drove for a while, apparently just chatting but actually looking for a place to be. Gabe drove to his downtown apartment, but saw Jessica Ambrose's car parked at the meter. Jessica had a key to his apartment.

"What's the matter?" Estela asked.

"Nothing, nothing. How abojut if we go to your house?"

Gabe drove into King William. Estela showed him the way. They walked up to her door, smiling at each other. After Estela let them inside, Gabe touched her arm.

And the phone rang.

Veronica Lewis was a reporter. She spent her days listening to thieves, liars, pornographers, egomaniacs, drunkards, and lechers of every stripe. Then she had to leave the newsroom and find news.

Which seemed to be in short supply lately. Roger the news director was on a tear. "How come KSAT had this 'Cruising Girls' story and we didn't?" he yelled to the room at large.

"Gee, Roge," anchorwoman Denise Twirl whined. "It's not like it was breaking news."

"Sex sells!" Roger screamed, a vein standing out in his neck. "Sex sells, and I want some!"

Veronica bent low at her desk. Since being demoted to off-air researcher, she had even more pressure to dig up stories. Hastily, she checked her usual sources, but neither the newspaper nor talk radio had anything interesting. She made a call.

"Hello?" The voice on the other end, obviously speaking on a cell phone, sounded peeved.

So Veronica peeved right back. "Well, hello. Thank you very much for a lovely evening, and let's do it again some time."

"Veronica?" Estela Valenzuela said.

"The same. You ask me out on a date, you take me to an art exhibit apparently to show me off, and then you run off when you make a better connection. I can only assume…"

"I'm sorry," Estela said. "We had kind of a family emergency. And gosh, Veronica, I had no idea. I mean, it's been a while since I took an attractive young lady like yourself out, so I had no idea your expectations included —"

"All right, all right," Veronica snapped. "Don't flatter yourself. I'm not that desperate. Although check back with me next week. Actually, I had a boyfriend, here at the station, but when I got demoted he said we should postpone the announcement."

"The announcement of what?"

"That we were, you know, doing it. Kind of a sort of, you know, engagement thing."

"People announce that now?"

"But anyway," Veronica said petulantly, slapping one hand into the other palm as if Estela could see her, "my point is, my ego was already a little fragile, and you . . ."

"Veronica, I'm sorry. How can I make it up to you?"

"Glad you asked. Actually, I could use a story, and what with the way you're always sneaking around City Hall, I thought maybe you could help."

Estela paused. Victoria heard some kind of interference over the line. She waited, tapping a pencil on a notepad.

"Actually, I could use a favor, too," Estela said. "And it might turn into a story. Look into this for me when you can." Estela told her in as few words as possible. Veronica made a half a note, yawning.

"Fine, fine, fine. And my payback is – ?"

A long pause was followed by a change in Estela's voice. "Veronica, I'm going to tell you, but you cannot quote me, not even as an informed source. Are you ready? I know you're checking into Suzanne Pierce's finances. Maybe you should look into her love life instead."

"Ooh," Veronica said. "That's kind of icky. And it's not even a sweeps month. I'd rather stick to how she's making a living."

"Maybe," Estela said very slowly, "it's the same story."

Veronica sat up so alertly everyone in the newsroom turned to stare. "Are you serious? Are you calling the mayor of San Antonio a – ?"

"No, I'm not," Estela said. "But remember where you heard it first. Goodbye, Veronica."

"Would you please not answer if it rings again?" Gabe asked Estela as she hung up the phone. He was having enough trouble working up his nerve to try to kiss her again, without the constant interruptions to her attention.

"All right," Estela said, and smiled as the phone rang again. She also smiled at Gabe's discomfiture, because she knew exactly what he was thinking. She wasn't opposed to the project herself, but enjoyed seeing him strive to achieve it.

"But if I don't answer, someone might just drop by. I mean, this is my neighborhood, it's a very friendly place, and today is my birthday."

Gabe stood perfectly still in the living room of Estela's rented carriage house in King William, wondering how to get her away from everyone else on earth who knew her. Thinking along the ends of the ends of the earth, his other problem resurfaced, that of finding the documents his father had taken out of storage just before he died. Gabe had searched the office, the storehouse, most of his father's house....

"Estela," he said in a strange, hollow voice, "You saw Dad the week before he died, didn't you? Did he go anywhere in particular, or talk about any place?"

"I don't know, Gabe. I only saw him once. And he only said one strange thing. He was going to get some of Joe's fish. Who the heck is Joe?"

Gabe smiled. "Where on earth are you from? And how fast can you pack?"

As they travelled south, Gabe and Estela ran through a range of emotions. She began to have second thoughts about the suddenness of this trip. Gabe began to wonder who this young woman was. They didn't have a lovers' quarrel, which should traditionally be saved until after becoming lovers, but they did grow a little uneasy around each other.

Earlier, standing in Estela's living room while she changed clothes, Gabe pictured that process, so that by the time she emerged he felt himself transparent with desire. Meanwhile, as Estela changed, she imagined him imagining her, thought about what she was doing, and emerged from the bedroom with a glow herself. In the car, their hands crept together. But as they contined driving through the flat, uneventful countryside, a strange moodiness overtook Gabe.

When Estela asked about the fish again, he said, "Joe's fish is a dish served exclusively at one of Dad's favorite restaurants. I would have said his very favorite, except now I know I didn't know all his favorite things. Maybe some place he took you was his favorite."

Estela said quietly, "He was very proud of you, Gabe. He used to talk about you all the time. I remember him talking about you winning a medal for swimming."

"I quit the swim team when I was eleven," Gabe said. Which was the year his parents had gotten divorced and Jerry, apparently, had started spending even more time with Estela and her mother. Gabe fell silent for many miles. But as they neared the coast he came out of it. A smile began to play on his lips. He started surfing the radio stations listening for the Beach Boys. Estela saw his mood lighten and covered his hand with hers again.

They got out of the car on the ferry crossing to Port Aransas, and watched the waves and smelled the salt air. "This is one of the craziest things I've ever done," Estela said. Gabe felt flattered that she had done it with him.

On the island, he drove straight to the Seafood and Spaghetti Works. The restaurant's geodesic dome was nearly hidden now by later additions, but veterans who had been coming here since it opened in 1979 still remembered it as round and as home. Gabe and Estela sat upstairs. He felt proprietary as he made suggestions about the menu. Estela gazed around at the kites hanging from the ceiling and felt happy for Gabe's happiness.

It was dark by the time they finished dinner. Gabe drove some ways down the beach and parked, and they walked on the sand. Estela, wearing shorts, simply discarded her sandals. Gabe rolled up his pants and left his shoes and socks in the car.

They strolled, walked in the waves, saw sandcastles slowly turning to melted slums, and bumped shoulders. Something about the salty air and the sea spray made Gabe bolder, or Estela more receptive. They came to a stop with no one else nearby, the night soft with stars. Gabe said, "I'm sorry I kissed you back at my grandmother's house."

"Why?" Estela exclaimed, feeling insulted.

"Because everyone should have their first kiss on the beach." He leaned toward her.

Later Gabe drove to a nearby condo complex, the Pelican. Not one of the newer, huger places, the Pelican was nicely aged.

"You made a reservation?" Estela asked, again feeling slightly insulted. Had Gabe been so sure of her?

"No. This is my family's place. We've had it for years."

They held hands going up the stairs, and Gabe almost felt like carrying her over the threshold. "Let's not overdo it," he told himself. His concussion was probably still playing on his feelings. But he did stop to kiss her again. Estela put her arms around his neck. They pressed against each other. Nothing seems to work as well for speeding romance as the nearness of the ocean.

Gabe found his key and opened the door, but didn't turn on the light. He didn't have to. The lights were already on.

"That's funny."

"Oh, look," his grandmother exclaimed, coming around the corner from the living room and smiling at them both. "Now it's a party!"

Island of Lost Time

Estela and Gabe had just enjoyed a slow building of intimacy: a long drive of shared thoughts, a romantic dinner, an even lovelier stroll on the beach, a long moonlit kiss, all building to a crescendo of walking into the Grohman family condo and finding it inhabited by Grohmans. Foremost among them Madeleine Grohman, which made Gabe want to run screaming back to the mainland. He'd always had a feeling that his grandmother could read his mind, and at this moment he thought a convenience store clerk could have glanced at him with Estela and known what he was thinking.

Even the way the matriarch smiled at Estela made him think she was onto him. Estela put up a better front than Gabe, smiling shyly and saying, "Gabe wanted me to see the family home away from home."

"Yes," he said quickly, "but we just need to pick up a few things and be heading back."

"Nonsense," Maddie Grohman said. "You have to stay here with us tonight."

Yep. She knew.

Madeleine Grohman, who never travelled alone, had invited several family members who had other plans, until she'd come to Evelyn and Evelyn's 11-year-old son Preston. Evelyn was finding herself bored rattling around the old house in King William, and Preston was even more bored in the summer, which made him unbearable to be around. Evelyn had gladly taken the offer of the beach trip. Maybe young Preston (known as "Duke" within the family) would find it fun, or at least Evelyn would have someone else to help her cope with him.

So Gabe and Estela walked into a party of people who looked to them for entertainment. The evening passed every slowly, with Gabe thinking of excuses to get away and get his grandmother's expression shooting them all down before he could even open his mouth. He sought Estela's eyes, but when he caught them they both felt observed, and looked away.

Time dragged until bedtime. Gabe protested again that he and Estela had to be on their way, but his grandmother quieted him with a look. The condo had three bedrooms. Maddie had already taken the master, Evelyn and Duke each had another, and Miz Maddie simply added the newcomers. Divided by gender.

"Think I'll take a last stroll on the beach," Gabe announced. But Estela, with the others watching, was too embarrassed to join him. So Gabe walked by himself, returning to the condo sandy and grumpy. Maddie was the only one up, so Gabe went to bed beside his half brother. "What's new, Duke?"

"Killer Vibes," the boy said quickly. "The video game of the century. But I can't get it."

"Didn't you just get the Playstation 2?"

"Yeah, but now this new game you can only play on Gameboy Advance, and Mom won't let me get it. She says only one new thing a year. Why do they have to keep coming up with new stuff?"

Poor Preston. Only eleven years old, and he already had future fatigue. Gabe, unsympathetic, lay waiting for the kid to go to sleep.

Nights seem darker at the coast. Some time in the middle of this one, Gabe made his way carefully out of the small bedroom into the large living room of the condo. Looking through the plate glass windows, he saw what he had most hoped to see, a figure on the balcony. Gratefully, he opened the door and stepped out. He tiptoed toward her, until she turned and Gabe almost shrieked.

"What's the matter, child?" his grandmother asked. "Miss your own bed?"

The beach gave Maddie Grohman a sense of rejuvenation. The waves rolled in as if they could bring back lost scenes and people, even other places. Sitting out on the balcony, breathing that life-filled air, Maddie felt like doing something she hadn't done in years.

After she'd scared the wits – as well, she hoped, as certain inappropriate urges – out of her grandson, she waited on the balcony until she was certain everyone else was safely asleep. By then Maddie knew she would never be able to sleep herself. Uncharacteristically, she gave in to a reckless impulse, walking out on the boardwalk in her sandals and coverup. She had the night to herself. The stars were very bright, but the moon was only a sliver. When she topped the dunes, the gulf provided its own illumination, the white crests atop the waves shining.

The beach stretched wide and quiet, except for the steady insistence of the waves. She thought of the first Indians to find this place, the sense of isolation it must have produced. The night was dark enough to inspire the same feeling in her. At 4 o'clock In the morning, she saw no other human being. Maddie left her sandals and walked along barefoot, feeling younger with every step. Finally, after looking around carefully, she left her clothes on the beach and plunged headlong into the waves

Well, no, she didn't. After all, she was 74 years old and much too dignified ever to be naked except when absolutely required.

But the idea of taking that wicked swim had crossed her mind, which distinguished this night from many thousands of others.

As it turned out, it was a very good thing she hadn't doffed her clothes, since a stranger stood at the edge of the dunes back near the boardwalk, watching Madeleine Grohman and waiting for her.

In the summer, Port Aransas is more or less a suburb of San Antonio. Vacationers from S.A. almost expect to run into someone from home. However, not at 4 o'clock in the morning on the beach.

As Madeleine Grohman returned from her very late walk on the beach, she was tired but felt her senses heightened by the darkness, the waves, the constant assault of smells. As she neared the boardwalk leading back to her condo complex, she sensed more than saw the man waiting. In the same way, she knew she didn't know the man.

"Hello, ma'am," he called politely while she was some distance away, as if he didn't want to frighten her. Maddie felt she had no choice but to walk on toward him. He stepped aside so as not to block the entrance to the boardwalk, another gesture of sensitivity.

"I hardly know whether to say good evening or good morning," Maddie said lightly.

"A transitional time," the man agreed in a pleasant voice. "The times of day I love most. I hate to miss any, especially these days."

That was Maddie's first clue that the man was roughly her own age. That was a novelty. At 74, Maddie saw her oldest friends more and more rarely, and everyone else on earth seemed younger than she. She didn't realize except in occasional moments like this the comfort of being with a contemporary, even a stranger. Unconsciously, she relaxed.

"Are you staying here, Mr. . . ."

"Groppe. Stefan Groppe. When I was young, I let people call me Steve, but now I insist on my own name. No, ma'am, I have a little place down the beach. Bought it years ago when people could afford places in Port Aransas. I live in San Antonio."

They made very minor chitchat, geographical in nature. The man had thick hair still mostly black, a moustache, and eyes so dark she couldn't see them in the night. "It's late even for so pleasant a meeting," Maddie said. "Good night, Mr. Groppe."

"He raised two fingers to his forehead in salute. "Good night, Mrs. Grohman."

Ten yards up the boardwalk, Maddie had the distinct idea she hadn't told the man her name. She looked back and saw him still waiting. She had the sudden impression the man knew even more about her – perhaps even what she'd thought of doing when she imagined herself alone on the beach.

By the afternoon of his first full day, Gabe refused to go to the beach again. He already had a bachelor burn – a swatch of sunburn across the center of his back, the place a person cannot reach without assistance. He hadn't had the nerve to ask Estela to rub sunblock there, and didn't want to be touched by any of his relatives.

Estela, on the other hand, had turned golden after one morning on the beach, with glints of highlights in her dark hair. Gabe would have given a great deal for the opportunity to rub lotion on her smooth brown skin. But not here with his relatives, especially his grandmother, looking on.

So when the gang returned to the beach in the afternoon, Gabe stayed in the condo, wearing a garish blue and yellow Hawaiian shirt and a pout. Gabe hadn't packed in San Antonio, so he now wore clothes from the condo's closets, outfits left behind here by at least three generations of his family, who generally left their taste in San Antonio when they came to the beach.

Wearing the old clothes reminded Gabe of one of his reasons for coming here. He found the key to the family closet and began to explore.

Estela strolled the beach alone. She wore a royal blue two-piece swimsuit and a straw sunhat, though no man who saw her would have remembered the latter article. Estela's bathing suit – okay, bikini, she had to admit it – was as conservatively cut as she had been able to find, but that still showed enough flesh that when she appeared in it, Evelyn Grohman said, "My," with the obvious envy that is the most sincere compliment one woman pays another, and young Duke made no attempt not to stare.

And Gabe hadn't come to the beach this afternoon, so Estela walked alone. And came across an old friend.

In the summer it seems that half the people in San Antonio go to Port Aransas, so a visitor there who doesn't come across a hometown acquaintance must be a recluse. Estela shouldn't have been surprised to find Juan Palomo.

The 30-year-old teacher wore a Panama hat that made him look like Leon Redbone, and a years-out-of-date baggie swimsuit. He sat on a towel alone, and waved casually as Estela appeared. "So you're a member of the Grohman familhy now," he said as she sat beside him.

"Are you spying on me?"

"No," he joked, "there's a website. I'm following your adventures online. Hell, Estela, it's Port A. You're not being secretive." He added, "What would your mother think?"

"There's never any telling what she will think, and I don't plan to ask her. And you won't either," she added quickly.

Juan shrugged.

Back at the condo, Gabe reached the back wall inside the closet, behind the rain slickers. His hands found a panel there. He wondered if anyone even knew the small cabinet was there, and who had been the last person to open it.

Once he opened the small enclosure, though, he knew: his father had been here. Papers fell into his hands.

He made his way out into the light and almost at once realized what he'd discovered. "I've got them!" he shouted.

"He seems like a very nice fellow," Evelyn Grohman was saying to her one-time mother-in-law Miz Maddie. "But very slow to make his move, if you know what I mean."

Evelyn sat on the beach under a very large yellow umbrella. She worried more about freckles than about cancer. Evelyn found herself talking freely, something she hadn't often done to the matriarch of the family. But Evelyn had a lot to talk about and not much choice in audiences. She'd never had close women friends. In her experience women tended to envy or belittle her. Women, in Evelyn's estimation, were not much good for anything. The feeling seemed to be mutual.

She continued describing her new friend Cinco. "Maybe he's just not interested," she concluded, waiting for the expected compliment from Miz Maddie.

"Maybe he's just being sensitive," Maddie offered.

"What do you mean?"

"Your recent bereavement, Evelyn," Maddie said pointedly.

"Oh." Evelyn considered that idea. When trying to figure out why a man did something, sensitivity was never Evelyn's first guess. "I think he just doesn't see me often enough," she concluded. "We need to run into each other more often."

"Maybe he's here at the beach," Miz Maddie joked, and laughed to herself to see Evelyn crane her neck and stare up and down the sand.

"Did you come out here to find yourself?" Estela asked Juan Palomo. Juan had been a friend of Estela's mother when Estela was growing up, she thought of him as a sort of uncle. And she teased him the way one does a favorite uncle. "Decide what you're going to do this coming year?"

Juan had spent the past school year teaching government at Lanier High School, but Estela thought of it as a stopgap measure. In the old days Juan had been very ambitious.

"You know what I've been doing, lying here on the beach?" he replied thoughtfully. "Besides roasting? I've been missing school. Yes, Lanier. It's weird. I was as eager for school to be over as any of the kids. I had big plans for what I'd do this summer. Now... I'm wondering what's happening to my kids. Whether this one boy raised the money to get to college. Whether this other girl is still reading as much. The thing about teaching is, something significant happened every day. Either I felt like I reached somebody, or at the end of the day I saw an opportunity I'd missed, so I looked forward to trying again the next day. I didn't see a lot of big results, but . . ."

"Your year made a difference," Estela said. She lounged back on her elbows, her face hidden by her sunhat, so that she became a length of brown flesh interrupted by brief bands of royal blue swimsuit. But Juan stared out at the gulf, where the waves poured relentlessly in, one after another, unstoppable, lulling in their constancy.

"Maybe it did," he said thoughtfully. Then he reached over and tipped back Estela's hat so that he could look into her brown eyes, which had the same greenish sparkles as the waves. "What are you doing, helping me find my vocation?"

Estela grinned. "That's what I do, I'm a finder."

"And what is it you want, Estela? Not to be some spoiled 09er, I hope."

"That is far, far away," she said.

She stood and said goodbye and walked slowly away. Juan, though he usually thought of her like a little sister or a niece, couldn't help noticing that she'd grown since the last time he'd seen her in a bathing suit. Her hips had learned an interesting rhythm, too. Or maybe the waves beside her gave that illusion.

Afternoons last forever at the beach. The sun seems thumbtacked to the top of the sky. It can hang there until eight, nine o'clock at night. No wonder alcoholism seems so prevalent in the sunny climes. Who can wait until sundown to start drinking? And once that rule goes by the board, it's only a couple of steps to drinking all day.

Gabe sat in the condo and studied the old leases he'd found hidden away there. He waited to share his discovery with Estela. And waited. Five o'clock came and no one returned from the beach. Gabe decided he could have a gin and tonic. A strong one. Still no one appeared. As he continued to think about Estela, it seemed he and she grew more intimate – in her absence. Gabe did all the work for her.

Finally he took a walk. A short one, because the sun beat down on his unprotected head. He returned to the condo with sunspots dancing inside his eyelids and the gin having gone straight to his head. And to discover that his exercise had been rewarded. Outside the hall bathroom, the blue bikini lay on the floor. From inside the bathroom came the sound of the shower.

Actually, he had something to tell her. Actually, it was rather urgent. Gabe would just let her know. And if she decided the news was important enough to hop out of the shower, that would be her decision.

He entered the steamy bathroom. The shower beat down behind the translucent curtain, through which a feminine form showed. "Guess what I've got!" Gabe called.

The water shut off. The curtain opened. Her body was round and pink and inviting.

Pink? "Why, whatever have you got, Gabito?" Evelyn said with a smile.

Gabe shrieked. He turned back to the doorway. Estela, having changed in the other bathroom, pushed open the bathroom door to drop her bathing suit in the sink. Gabe caught her eyes. Estela looked past him at his naked stepmother.

He shrieked again.

Estela's having found Gabe in the bathroom, where his naked stepmother was just emerging from the shower, made for an interesting evening. Evelyn would try to catch Gabe's eye, and when she did Evelyn would pretend to be flustered, Gabe would actually blush, and Estela would stare at both of them as if their family comprised something she wouldn't want to watch on cable-TV, let alone participate in.

Immediately after the incident, while Evelyn was dressing and before the others came back, Gabe had tried to explain to Estela. "I'm sorry. I didn't know Evelyn was in the shower. I thought it was you!"

"So you were trying to peek in on me in the shower, not your stepmother. Oh, well, Gabe, all is forgiven."

"I came to show you what I found. I found what we came here looking for."

But before he could explain further, they were inundated by kids. As if there weren't family enough, Gabe's older sister Marilyn arrived with her three young children. After three hours in the car, they bounced around like animated cartoon versions of themselves. They were so delighted to see their grandmother and cousin Duke that they immediately asked if they could spend the night here. Their mother consented even more quickly. A critical observer might have thought the whole exchange had a rehearsed quality.

Marilyn had announced that she was staying at the Sandcastle, a few condos down the block. A couple of hundred yards and a heaven of solitude away. Gabe took his sister aside.

"Listen, uh, Marilyn, I know you'll be worried if you can't stay here with the kids. So you can have my place, and I'll get Estela out of the way, and we can kind of housesit your place at the Sandcastle for you. I hate to leave Grandma, but . . ."

Marilyn had the most teeth of anyone in the family, and she showed them all whenever she smiled at her little brother. "That's sweet, Gabe, but you know the last time I spent the night under a different roof from my children?"

"Last weekend?"

"That's right, and it was lovely, and I plan to do it again tonight. Why else do you think Ed and I came down here while Grandma was here?"

So Marilyn made her escape, the condo seemed filled with children, and the evening dragged. Gabe had spent part of the afternoon trying to find another place to stay, but it was Fourth of July week in Port Aransas. Nothing – but nothing – was available. To get a few feet of space on the sand he would have needed a reservation.

Miz Maddie seemed in a pensive mood. After dark she went out on the balcony alone. Later Gabe followed. His grandmother stood at the railing gazing out toward the Gulf. "What's the matter, Grandma?"

She had actually been remembering the man she'd met on the early-morning beach, the stranger who had seemed somehow not a stranger. She kept picturing him until he seemed tantalizingly familiar, particularly his dark eyes, watching her. But she wouldn't tell Gabe that. "Thinking of all the people I've seen on this beach. All the years. You'd think they'd be stored somewhere, wouldn't you?"

He went and held her. She was a tough old lady, she always held the family together, and no one ever gave much thought to what Maddie might need. Poor Grandma, he thought, always stuck in the past – not realizing in the least that his grandmother still had as long a view of the future as he had. Maybe longer, since she had no short-term plans for seduction to block her vision.

But there would be no seduction that night, by anyone. The children all wanted to sleep together in the living room of the condo, off which all the bedroom doors opened. By dark children lay scattered around the place like landmines – almost as dangerous to any midnight creeper with the bad luck to step on one.

So Gabe slept alone, restlessly and sometimes wakefully. During the night he had a revelation about himself, Estela, and his father. It woke him early, before sunrise, and wouldn't let him go back to sleep.

In the pre-dawn darkness he pulled on a semi-dry bathing suit and T-shirt and slipped out the front door of the condominium, discovering that they'd forgotten to lock it overnight. Barefoot, he walked the boardwalk to the beach. The dry, white sand was cool underfoot. The constant breeze from the water ruffled his hair. Like so much else, Gabe realized, he'd taken this place for granted. In the early morning loneliness, he saw it fresh: the eternal renewal, the constant struggle for life, the stench of death. This year there was more seaweed washing up on the beach than they'd ever seen. It lay in rotting piles above the tideline. The water itself was the dirty green of the Gulf, but in the dimness it looked clean and new, star-laden.

Gabe realized that a full moon had risen. It cast enough light that ahead, on the edge of the sea, he saw a man and a woman. They wore bathing suits, the woman's a one-piece white that emphasized her long, black hair and brown skin. The man and woman were adults, but young in the way they frolicked and laughed. Gabe tried to draw closer, to get a better look at them, but as he did so the light subtly changed. The man turned and dived into the water.

The woman turned to Gabe, but she was no longer the same woman. Her white bathing suit had become a short white robe. As she came closer, her features resolved into Estela Valenzuela's. She stared at Gabe, who wore the strangest expression. "My God, it's happened again, hasn't it?" she said. "You were on Milagro Lane. What did you see, Gabe?"

Near-dawn began to lighten the sky as Estela stared at Gabe. Still, the starlight reflected off the wavecaps provided the major illumination, as Gabe tried to describe his recent vision. "Didn't you see them, the man and the woman?" he asked. "You must have, the moon was so bright."

"There is no moon, Gabe," Estela said, shaking her head.

Gabe looked around and saw that she was right. But a moment earlier.... "I saw a woman who looked like you," he said slowly, "and a man who looked like – my father." He hadn't realized it until he said it.

Estela understood this vision, but didn't think sharing her knowledge would reassure Gabe. She thought he'd seen an actual historical occasion, and was deeply envious.

"What are you doing out here?" he asked.

"I couldn't sleep."

"Without me," Gabe said, taking her arm. They began to walk.

"I've slept every night of my life without you, Gabe. No, it was sharing a bed with Evelyn."

"She didn't want to talk, did she?" Gabe sounded alarmed.

"No, she fell right to sleep. She must have a very clear conscience. But I think she feels love-deprived." Estela hesitated, then said it: "She snuggles."

Gabe said nothing for several more steps. "Stop that," Estela said.

"What?"

"Imagining your stepmother snuggling up against me. You're turning it pornographic!"

"I was not. It sounds sweet. You and Evelyn in bed together. Nearly naked. Hot summer night. One of you moaning softly in her sleep..."

Estela punched his arm. "Okay," Gabe surrendered. "Now I'm just imagining you."

"That's better."

Even this early, they weren't alone on the most heavily populated portion of one of the most popular beaches in Texas. A fisherman stood out in the surf fifty yards away. Two joggers ran by. Crabs scuttled by. Sea gulls had called an early morning conference, stood chatting together, and eyed the humans suspiciously.

But the darkness gave privacy. When Estela and Gabe stopped again they felt all alone. They kissed with the water lapping at their feet. The kiss was tender and sweet and should have been allowed to continue for three days. But inevitably other things intruded, including Gabe's thoughts. In a minute he became aware of what they were wearing. Gabe wore a swimsuit and T-shirt, Estela a short white robe over, presumably, her bathing suit. This was a moment when these entanglements should simply fall away, leaving them to make love on the beach, or in the sky. In real life, he had to decide whether he should do something. Slip a hand down her back, or under her robe. Was it too early in the relationship? Would he offend her?

There should be a signal to tell a man these things. Color-changing ears would be nice. Okay, her ear's turned red: it's all right to fondle. Nope, still only pink: hold off.

They broke apart for a moment, then resumed. Estela's hands moved from Gabe's arms to his back. Okay: permission granted.

But then she turned and resumed walking, taking his hand. Well, that was an advance. Hand-holding is seldom the pinnacle of a man's romantic ambition, but it does seem intimate.

"I think my father wanted you and me to get together," Gabe said. That was the realization he'd had during the night. Estela looked at him perplexedly. "He mentioned Joe's fish to you. That wouldn't mean anything to you, but he knew it would mean Port Aransas to me. And this is where he hid the leases he knew I needed to find."

Estela said gently, "If he wanted us to meet, he had plenty of opportunities he didn't take. And he just happened to mention Joe's fish. He didn't know he was going to die."

"No, I'm sure," Gabe said happily. "That's why he asked you to wear a red dress to his funeral, so we'd notice you and meet."

Estela had doubts about this theory, but it seemed to make Gabe happy, so she didn't contradict again. "What do the leases show?"

"I'm not sure. They show that the Grohman family leased city-owned property from San Antonio from 1881 to 1884, to quarry the stone out of it. But we already knew that."

With a little research, Gabe could have discovered the problem there. In fact, a family historian could have told him right away. He would have his chance. His grandmother waited for them, back at the boardwalk.

Veronica Lewis rode the waves. Up and down, up and down. It was very restful. Better than water aerobics (on which she'd done a story, with great tape); the water did all the work. She closed her eyes and drifted, forgetting the newsroom, the mayor who hated her, her broken-off relationship with her sort-of boyfriend. She spread her arms and legs and tried to become one with the water.

Her hand brushed another human being. Another one swam into her right leg. Yet another came up under her left leg, almost somersaulting her backwards. Veronica sighed, opened her eyes, and gave up the isolated-Pacific-beach fantasy.

Veronica rode in the wave pool at Lost Lagoon in Seaworld. Fifty other people floated and screamed and jumped within twenty feet of her. But this was the only vacation Veronica could afford, in both time and money: one day at Seaworld, and she probably wouldn't have gone for that if there hadn't been such a good coupon in the *Express-News*.

She was also afraid of being off the job for more than a day, because it might become permanent, given her tenuous status there. In fact, she wouldn't have come to Seaworld except for hope of finding a story. She had asked around to see if she could uncover more details of Deborah Daniels' bumping her head on a waterslide and then throwing her anchor weight around. There were great rumors around the newsrooms in town that she had reduced a couple of teenage lifeguards to tears.

But no one here was talking. They were clammed up tighter than – Veronica couldn't think of an analogy. Sitting in the shallow water, she wondered if the station would like just a fun-type summer vacation piece. A woman walked slowly by along the edge of the water, obviously pleased with her leopard-print thong bikini, which had apparently been purchased in a store equipped with specially-designed rear-view mirrors – or no mirrors at all. Jessica framed the woman's rear end with the pretend-camera of her fingers, thinking, "Women Who Should Never Wear Thongs, and the Men Who Buy Them For Them." Film at 10. She could definitely get some footage here.

But if Veronica was really going to work her way back to on-air status, it wouldn't be through skin-and-fluff features pieces. She needed to uncover some hard news – which meant she needed to work her way out of Mayor Suzanne Pierce's doghouse. That, or uncover some major dirt on Pierce.

Veronica remembered some advice her mentor had once given her. Well, he wasn't really a mentor so much as he was a grumpy, grumbling middle-aged newswriter, half-drunk much of the time, who occasionally put his arm around Veronica so that his hand dangled at her breast while he dispensed what passed for wisdom in the news business.

"Make friends with 'em," he'd advised once, about the newsmakers that they covered. "You'd be surprised – a lot of those rich, powerful types don't have any friends. At least not any they trust. That's why models marry rock stars: because they're both rich and famous so they don't think one's sucking up to the other. You can do the same thing with politicians and scum like that. They think you're famous too, so you're on an equal footing. You can make friends. Then you'll really be in tight."

"Does that work?" Veronica had asked, wide-eyed but moving her shoulders to shift his hand away from the good stuff.

"Not usually," the mentor had burped. "But sometimes if they see you getting friendly they think they can use you, and sometimes that helps too."

Sitting in the shallow float pool, Veronica pondered this wisdom. "... use me," she muttered aloud. The man next to her eyed her appreciatively. Veronica stood up and walked out, aware of looking thin and long-limbed in her blue polka dot bikini. Yes, the station might go for some footage from here. And maybe she could do the on-air reporting in her swimsuit. Another excuse for putting more skin into the news, and that was what the news director was always screaming for. Up close among all these near-naked bodies, the effect wasn't so much sexy as nasty. But in TV news that amounted to the same thing.

Veronica remembered the advice Estela Valenzuela had given her, to look into the mayor's love life. Estela had said that would also amount to investigating the mayor's sources of income, which sounded nasty enough to interest Roger the news director. So it was make friends with the mayor or spy on her, but at any rate to make her produce news.

Madeleine Grohman watched Gabe and Estela Valenzuela stroll up the dawn-lighted beach toward her as she stood at the end of the boardwalk. Maddie could tell just when the young couple spotted her, because their hands pulled apart. Maddie liked Estela very much, and she wanted only the best for her grandson. She felt even more responsible for him since his father had died. Maddie didn't want to spoil their fun. But that was, after all, the elder generation's duty.

When they came close she smiled at them both. "Hello, Estela, my dear. Gabe, we have to talk."

For Love or Money – or Both

Deciding to implement her new idea immediately, reporter Veronica Lewis hurried away from Seaworld and drove to City Hall, not even changing out of her polka dot bikini, just throwing a translucent cover-up over it. It was a late Friday afternoon in July, probably no one would be at City Hall anyway. Sure enough, she had her pick of parking spaces, and an appreciative security guard let her in through the basement entrance. Veronica hurried upstairs toward the mayor's office.

She would follow her old mentor's advice and try to make friends. And she would use Estela Valenzuela's tip about the mayor's love life and financial life being one and the same, but not in the way Estela had hinted. Veronica would warn Mayor Suzanne Pierce that someone was trying to dig up dirt on her. Pierce would be grateful. She and Veronica would become friendly. News would surely follow.

The receptionist's office was empty. "Mayor!" Veronica called, flinging open the inner door. "Mayor! I've got to warn you...."

The door swung open to reveal Mayor Suzanne Pierce sitting on her desk, wearing a broad, loose smile and a white blouse open one button lower than was strictly businesslike. A man in a suit stood close by, returning her smile. They clinked martini glasses.

On the desk near them lay something Veronica was certain she recognized: a check.

Recovering quickly, the man came forward, hand extended. "Hello?"

"I'm so sorry," Veronica said. "I thought I needed to talk to the mayor right away. I'm Veronica Lewis, I...."

"She used to be a TV reporter," the mayor said scathingly, "and now she's fallen even lower."

"Charmed," said the man, blond and 40 and overly debonair. "And you have impeccable credentials for the job, if I may say so without being politically incorrect. Chester Worthington Dilmore V. Please. Call me Cinco." He took her hand as if at a cotillion.

"Uh..." Veronica said suavely, giving Suzanne Pierce a bewildered look.

Pierce didn't appear to have moved, but both her martini glass and the check on her desk had disappeared. She glared at Veronica, clearly wishing she would too.

Madeleine Grohman had actually come to the early-morning beach hoping to see again the dark-eyed man from yesterday morning. His stare had haunted her dreams. Instead she found her grandson Gabe strolling hand in hand with Estela Valenzuela. Maddie had mixed feelings. Estela seemed a very sweet girl, but after all, what did they know of her or her family – of whom she seemed to have none?

So while Maddie didn't want to spoil Gabe's fun, she did find this a good time to let him in on the family crisis. Estela understood being dismissed, and walked on up the boardwalk to the condo. Gabe stared after her, which Maddie, taking a glance at the girl's figure illuminated through her cover-up by the rising sun, could understand.

But business called. "Gabe," she said, "We have a family problem of, I'm afraid, extraordinary proportions. It's time to gather the clan. I need to stay here for a few more days, out of sight. But you can go home and get started." She looked intently into his innocent blue eyes.

"Can you help me, Gabito?"

Back at the condo, Estela found Evelyn Grohman not only awake but in a cheerful mood. Gabe's bursting in on her in the shower the day before had boosted Evelyn's spirits enormously. Nothing made her happier than feeling wanted. Watching her bounce around in her baby doll nightie, Estela hadn't the heart to tell her that Gabe had thought it was Estela in the shower.

Gabe came in a few minutes later, looking pale – a difficult feat to pull off in Port Aransas in July. "What is it?" Estela asked in some alarm.

Evelyn, meanwhile, gave him a coy look and wiggled out of the room.

"The family has an even bigger problem than I thought," Gabe said. "Grandma was just telling me about it. Someone's filed a lawsuit to force the sale of Grohman Enterprises. They say Dad promised to sell to them."

Estela stared. They had seemed closer to solving the mystery of Jerry Grohman's death once Gabe had found the old leases here in Port A. This new problem took her completely by surprise.

"That's not the worst of it," Gabe said. His hands shook as he took Estela's.

"My God, Gabe, what is it?"

A high, girlish voice trilled from the other room. "No one come in here now. I'm not decent."

Gabe said, "Grandma asked me to give Evelyn a ride home to San Antonio."

The things you see when you don't have a cameraman, reporter Veronica Lewis thought. She stood in Mayor Suzanne Pierce's office and felt quite certain she had just seen a martini glass in the mayor's hand and a check on her desk. But in the moments she'd been distracted by the mayor's companion introducing himself, both had disappeared. And Veronica had no videotaped proof.

Veronica felt decidedly unsexy standing in City Hall in her blue polka dot bikini and thin coverup. Instead it seemed like one of those dreams in which she'd forgotten to get dressed and then had to appear on camera or at a formal party.

The mayor, in fact, projected more carnal interest just through that one extra undone button on her white blouse. But by the time Pierce walked around her desk and sat behind it, she was buttoned up tight again. The woman was a magician. Veronica even began to doubt the accuracy of her own memories. She was the perfect television reporter: if there was no tape of an event, it hadn't happened.

The companion, Chester Worthington Dilmore V, took Veronica's arm and unsubtly but charmingly steered her out. "Goodbye, your Honor," he called breezily to the mayor. "Now tell me all about the television news business, my dear. It sounds fascinating...."

The interior of Gabe's silver BMW had never before felt so confining. The trunk was stuffed to capacity with his stepmother's luggage, and the passenger compartment filled to overflowing with Evelyn's presence. She chatted, she laughed airily, she waved her arms, her hand brushing Gabe's ear or arm. Evelyn wore a short skirt and simple white blouse, and imagined Gabe sneaking peeks at her. The idea cheered Evelyn, who loved attention more than chocolate.

She made Gabe's skin crawl. He flinched away from her every time she moved. He drove over the white line of the highway. And he tried desperately to catch Estela's eyes in the rearview mirror.

Estela sat in the back seat with 11-year-old Preston. Estela wondered if she should call him that or use his family nickname, Duke. Maybe she could ask how he'd come to be called Duke. She could ask when school was starting.

Actually, her conversational gambits were purely theoretical, since Preston sat playing his Gameboy and listening to Blink-182 on the earphones of his portable CD player. He might as well not have been in the car – or this world – at all.

His deceased father, too, was beginning to find Duke maddening. The ghost of Jerry Grohman also sat in the back seat on he other side of his young son, trying to catch his attention. Jerry felt quite certain that Duke had heard Jerry speak to him early that morning. This made Duke the only living human Jerry had been able to reach. But ever since that episode, Duke had had some device attached to his ears. Trying to reach him was becoming infuriating.

So both the dead and the living sat in the back seat on either side of the lad, and fumed.

Gabe stopped at an Exxon station at Mathis, managed to interest everyone in the restrooms or candy, and managed not very subtly to slip Estela into the front seat and Evelyn into the back. He travelled up the highway more comfortably from that point on, though he still couldn't talk to Estela about any of the several subjects that he wanted. He did, however, tiptoe his fingers across the seat and touch her hand. She smiled, behind her sunglasses.

Evelyn, left to her own devices, reproached herself for teasing Gabe. She felt sure there was nothing illegal about intimacy with a stepson who bore none of her blood, but it certainly seemed inappropriate. Her friends – if she had any – would snicker. Besides, Evelyn had already married into the Grohman family once. No point in overdoing it.

And marriage was her goal. Evelyn had been a widow for four months now, and had grown weary of life on her own. Right there in the car she decided: time to end the mourning period and return to the world.

Mayor Suzanne Pierce gave her company time to exit the building, then hurried down through City Hall and grabbed a cab. Feeling tipsy on a double martini and a big contribution toward "retiring her campaign debt," she told the driver, "The Maloney party, and step on it. It's at the Presidio restaurant."

The cab driver, who had recently dropped out of college to find himself, kept himself pharmaceutically alert on these night shifts. His drug of choice made him chatty but not bright. Eyeing his ride in the rearview mirror but not recognizing her eminence, he said, "Running late, lady?"

Pierce crossed her legs and said airily, "The party can't start til the entertainment arrives."

The cabbie, continuing to stare at his passenger rather than the street, gave his most ingratiating smile and said, "You coming out of the cake, sweetie?"

Pierce gave him a smile like Mack the Knife chatting up a sailor. "No, but I might put something in it. Like maybe your severed head."

The cab driver maintained a respectful silence the rest of the short trip. The hairs standing up on the back of his neck kept him alert and respectful.

Gabe drove up to the house in King William where Evelyn and Duke lived. Gabe parked his BMW in the driveway and gazed fondly at the house for many reasons: His father had lived here and Gabe had spent many happy hours in the house. It was a beautiful old two-story Victorian mansion with a wide front porch and gingerbread trim, a house that would please any beholder's eye. But mainly Gabe looked at the house so happily because Evelyn would be getting out here. As would young Duke, leaving Gabe alone with Estela Valenzuela. Gabe had been pursuing that goal in vain for days. In fact, he had begun to feel that his whole youth had been spent in pursuit of time alone with Estela.

Evelyn looked at the house much less happily. To her it represented the past, which had never intrigued her, and isolation from her friends in '09. But during the ride back from the coast Evelyn had made up her mind to do something about that. She looked at the house with determination.

Then she stepped out lightly and closed the car door behind her. Gabe rolled down his window. Evelyn leaned in, very close to him, though Gabe shied away as much as space would permit.

"Gabe, I have a lot of work to do. I want you to do me a favor."

"Anything," Gabe said promptly. Anything that meant driving away and leaving her here.

"Keep your brother for a few days, would you? I need him out of the house, he hasn't seen much of you since Jerry died, and I think he needs a man's influence. Besides, I'm moving and he'll be underfoot. And he's all packed already, his clothes are in the trunk. Thanks, Gabito."

Evelyn said all this in a rush, and walked quickly away. "Wait, wait!" Gabe called, but to no avail. Gabe looked helplessly from Estela to the 11-year-old boy in the backseat.

"Well, you know, between his CD player and his Gameboy, Duke doesn't even know what's going on around him anyway."

He looked hopefully at Estela. She stared back, unconvinced.

"That's right," came a young voice from the back seat. "Go ahead and kiss her."

So Gabe took Estela home, a few blocks away, and escorted her to her front door, feeling about 16 years old. She allowed him to kiss her goodbye, both aware of the boy ogling them from the car. When the kiss ended Gabe looked unhappy. "This is becoming less and less of a big experience, isn't it, this kissing thing?" he asked.

"Maybe," Estela said, putting her hands on his shoulders, "we should have a date. You know, like a normal night out together, instead of a trip to the beach or me interpreting your hallucinations for you."

Gabe stared at her strangely. "And I took you for such an unconventional girl," he said.

A few days later Pauline Rhinehart Byrnes popped into her bridge club shouting delightedly. This was very unusual behavior for Pauline, a respectable married lady of a certain age (meaning uncertain, since she hadn't let it be known for decades). Her husband Frank had respectably made his money in oil in the 60s, and the Byrneses belonged to the proper clubs and supported the right charities. They had seen their four children through college and into marriage, all appropriate ones. Pauline loved her children more than lunch at the Argyle, and her grandchildren were young gods and goddesses. Her youngest daughter Evelyn had made an especially fine marriage, into one of the oldest families in San Antonio.

(Digression: How can one family be older than another? Did we come down from the trees at different times? No, in this case "old" means well-established. In other words, it's not the family that's old; it's their money. The family had been lucky enough to have a clever, moneymaking ancestor earlier in the centuries than most families. That was true of the Grohmans, who had made their money in the mid-1800s, and hadn't produced enough scoundrels or addicts in the meantime to dissipate the fortune.

(Or "old" can mean long-resident in the area, or in other words no one had had the curiosity or gumption to leave in a long time. By this standard, Eskimos and Australian aborigines must be the oldest families on the planet – and quite choosy about accepting new members.)

(Digression ended.) The sight of Evelyn Grohman's respectable mother giggling like a schoolgirl caught the other ladies' attention. Mrs. Bynres rushed into the sun parlor of the house on Mandalay shouting, "My baby's coming home! My baby's coming home!"

The other women gathered around to offer congratulations. The newest member, the wife of a retired ambassador who had spent most of her life out of the country, saw the delight on her new friend's face and imagined a long-postponed reunion.

"That's wonderful, dear. Where has she been living? New York? France?"

Pauline sighed contentedly. "King William," she said.

77 Candles

When you have a birthday in the higher digits, both your friends and your enemies cheer. When legendary trial lawyer Pat Maloney turned 77, his friends decided to throw a party. (What his enemies did is not recorded, though he had outlived many of them, a victory in itself.) Normally this would be a private family occasion, but Maloney was turning 77, which seemed a significant pair of digits, and an old family friend had decided a big celebration was called for. So on a Friday summer evening the restaurant on the Riverwalk level of the Presidio building filled with people, including friends, relations, and politicos of every stripe.

Actually one stripe predominated. Gabe Quintanilla, county chair of the Democratic party, looked very pleased, standing as he was near ground zero of his party's financial base. A lot of his people were in attendance, as old friends of the honoree's.

Marty Brewster worked the crowd. The staff aide for Ramon Carter, the city councilman whose very existence was a matter of debate, had to appear in his place on many occasions. This was a fun one, but also a working evening for Marty. Twenty-eight, thin, nervous, she passed through the crowd in black slacks and her all-purpose spangly blouse. She waved to many faces in the crowd: city councilpeople, judges, lawyers, and lots and lots of nuns and priests. (Pat Maloney had for decades hosted and subsidized the Catholic church in San Antonio. Whether this was atonement for sins or a simple matter of faith was between him and his confessor.)

The guest of honor, not moving far from the center table, had a continuous knot of well-wishers. Marty made her way slowly through them and finally grasped his hand. Maloney's glasses magnified his eyes as he stared at her with his perpetual twinkle. In an earlier, much shorter incarnation, he had probably been a leprechaun.

"Sir, on this splendid occasion of this great anniversary of your birth, Councilman Ramon Carter has personally ordered me to convey his very best wishes. And wants you to know that he proposed the city proclamation in your honor."

The old Irishman, lawyer, raconteur and former world-class drinker gave her a knowing grin. Amid the uproar he held her hand

and said, "I only supported your boss because I knew early on that he didn't really exist."

Marty had handled this question a lot. Doing her impression of Rafiki the baboon from Lion King (at which she'd gotten rather good in recent months), she put her hand over her heart and said, "Oh, he lives, sir. He lives here."

"That's a good place for a politician," Pat Maloney said. "Too many of them live here." He patted his wallet, which was, indeed, a goal for many office-seekers. On the other hand, some cynics might have thought he was referring to his pocket. Over the years he'd been thought to have quite a collection of politicos in his pocket.

At that point someone cleared his throat at the microphone. Guests at the gala included the mayor and three former mayors, Phil Hardberger, the highest ranking judge in the region, and some of the most successful plaintiff's lawyers in Texas, including Frank Herrera of San Antonio and Joe Jamail of Houston. Assigning speaking order became a delicate task. God won out, and Archbishop Flores went first.

Smiling and joking, the Archbishop praised Maloney's many contributions to the church. But then he asked the packed crowd to lift their hands in Maloney's direction and pray for his health.

The room went silent, except for the murmur of prayer. Marty Brewster raised her arm by reflection, the way she said the pledge of allegiance when occasion demanded. But as she stood among all the friends, something happened. She looked at Pat Maloney, thought of the many people who had reviled his name over the years, but of the many here and elsewhere who obviously loved him. "He must have done something right," she muttered.

A voice at her shoulder said, "There are lots of priests here, Marty. Have anything to confess?"

Marty turned and saw Estela Valenzuela watching her closely. When Marty had no immediate answer, Estela said, "I try to get forgiven in advance. When I'm just thinking about doing something, I go to confession."

Marty whispered back, "Does that work? Will they do that?"

Estela grinned. "No, but it's fun to hear them explain why they can't. And sometimes I get a sort of hypothetical forgiveness. 'Okay, Estela, come back to me afterwards, and if it wasn't too bad. . . .'"

She laughed gaily. Marty wondered at her happiness.

"By the way," Estela added, apparently an afterthought. "Gabe Grohman just came across some old leases between his company and the city. Where would the originals be stored?"

"Beats me. Why would I know something like that?"

Before Estela could reply, she realized people were watching. If the archbishop had to shush her, would her hopes of heaven be lessened? Rather than test the theory, she shut up and closed her eyes, joining in the blessing of hope.

August. If the entire cast of "Riverdance," naked but for dance shoes, had clogged down the street at the same time a potential raincloud hovered in the sky, San Antonians would gaze upward. There could be no rarer or more beautiful event in August than a hint of rain.

The pace slowed. Air conditioners worked harder than people. Sunlight beat down, making outdoor public spaces look like a war zone. People might pass through the parks and plazas, but they ducked for cover as if from mortar fire. Travelers waiting for buses stood back under trees. A shade salesman would have gotten rich in a week.

Here and there throughout the city, though, a bustling energy prevailed. It took a great incentive to inspire work in this atmosphere, but some people felt sufficient motivation.

Evelyn Grohman was one. She rushed around the yard and rooms of her King William house, urging the moving men to faster activity. Now that Evelyn had decided to return to her roots, she wanted the deed accomplished quickly. A great anticipation had begun to stir in her. She felt like a girl going off to college.

No "For Sale" sign stood in the yard. Evelyn's late husband Jerry had left her only a life estate in this house; she couldn't sell. She had found a lovely house in Terrell Hills, only three blocks from her parents, and hoped to rent this place for enough to make the mortgage payments. Evelyn had no idea of the value of the two-story, 95-year-old Victorian manse on Adams Street. To her it was just home, and too old-fashioned for her taste. But she had a realtor friend come give her advice. As the professional walked through, noting the wide staircase with carved balustrade, the transoms over the doors, the hardwood floors, and original chandeliers, a gleam came into her eye – a gleam richer than that shining from the foot-tall molding around the ceilings.

"My dear, we will find a very special tenant for this place."

Gabe Grohman returned to the office, his young half-brother Duke in tow. Evelyn had unceremoniously dumped responsibility for her son on Gabe, and Gabe didn't want to act as if this were a burden. Not in front of the boy. After only one evening in Duke's company, Gabe had begun to suspect that the reason for the boy's perpetually surly attitude was that Duke had no one's complete attention.

So Gabe acted as if a visit to the office of Grohman Enterprises was a treat. When they pulled into the parking lot near the Quarry Market, the boy looked at it listlessly and said, "Will I have to work here some day?"

"You can do anything you want," Gabe said automatically, repeating the fable that adults tell children. But in the age of George W. Bush, even an 11-year-old knew that some careers were a matter of destiny rather than choice. Duke rolled his eyes.

"Actually," Gabe said more gloomily as he remembered his mission here, "you should probably strike out on your own when you're older, Duke. Make your own way."

He didn't add that Grohman Enterprises, which had flourished under six generations of family management, might not be around for Duke's adulthood.

"Hello, Mrs. Olsen," he said heartily. The athletic, attractive blonde secretary who ran the office with great efficiency as long as management kept out of her way smiled at him.

"Welcome back, Gabe. How was your vacation?"

Gabe's memory rapidly flashed back over finding the old city leases in Port Aransas, kissing Estela Valenzuela with water lapping at their feet, then hearing his grandmother's portentous news, and he couldn't characterize the experience.

"Like a week at the beach, Mrs. Olsen. You remember Duke, don't you? Mrs. Olsen, I'm looking for some records of quarrying activity from the 1880s. We wouldn't have those ledgers here, would we? Would they be in storage?"

"Actually, I think your father got those out a few months ago. Want me to see if I can turn them up?"

"You're amazing as always, Mrs. Olsen."

A few minutes later she had him installed in his father's old office with a stack of ledgers. The books held a meticulous chronicling of financial dealings of Grohman Enterprises throughout the 1880s. The ink had faded, but the numbers remained so precisely-written and well-aligned that Gabe could imagine the force of the man who had written them more than a hundred years ago. He must have been a Grohman.

"Can I help?"

Gabe thought Mrs. Olsen had safely distracted young Duke, but the boy peeked around the office door, obviously bored. Gabe started to give him an excuse and steer him away – the way Gabe himself had always been treated at that age – then thought, "Why not?" and waved him in.

He divided the pile of books. "What are we looking for?" Duke looked uncharacteristically pleased and energetic.

"I'm not sure," Gabe said. "Something to show our dealings with the city in the 1880s. Probably 1881 to '84." That had been the years the Grohman family had leased city land to quarry out its stone.

"Okay." Duke went happily about the project. Gabe wanted to tousle his hair.

Shortly Gabe lost himself in the books, which represented more than numbers. He could picture his family at work: both hard labor and the meticulous task of recording the work. The books also showed the family branching out. Sometimes the writer would jot down notes of business ideas, even family appointments. Gabe began to feel the workings of a head that had been in the grave a long time.

"Is this something?" Duke asked.

Gabe went to look at his brother's ledger, doubtful he'd found anything. Standing over the boy's shoulder, he began turning pages. A moment later young Duke said, "Gabe?" Gabe had turned as stiff as the stone his family had dug out of city-owned land.

Evelyn Grohman and her mother Mrs. Byrnes wandered through the house in King William. The moving men had almost emptied it out, giving the old house a nostalgic, abandoned feel. Evelyn looked forward to going "home" to Terrell Hills, being closer to her social set and her new romantic interest, but she couldn't help noticing sites, empty now, where special occasions had occurred: Jerry kissing her by the mantelpiece, the mark on the wall where her son Duke had rammed his Razor into it.

"It'll be so lovely having you home," Mrs. Byrnes said, patting her arm. "I'm already planning the homecoming party." She glanced out the window, where a few strollers had stopped to watch moving day. One wore a bandanna on his head, another a big straw hat like a gardener. Across the street a woman pushed a baby stroller.

"It's a lovely house," Mrs. Byrnes said, "but frankly I'm surprised you've stayed here so long with these people. I'll be in the car."

"It'll be nice to go home," Evelyn said vacantly. Then, as she heard the front door close behind her mother, a crease appeared on her forehead. What had her mother meant by "these people"? Artists? Gays? Hispanics?

True, Evelyn's neighbors in King William were more colorful than the people with whom she'd grown up, but no more eccentric. Evelyn hadn't exactly felt at home here, so close to the city's center, but not because of the people.

Drug-users? Writers? Restauranteurs?

Evelyn had never thought of her mother as narrow-minded, and Mrs. Byrnes would certainly never offer a politically incorrect opinion in public. But as the remark continued to nag at Evelyn, she wondered if she was making a mistake leaving King William. She felt a moment's regret.

Waiters? Artisans? Democrats?

Evelyn's tiny world-view grew just a little. She was glad for her sojourn in King William.

On the other hand, the shopping left a lot to be desired. Evelyn smiled, squared her shoulders, and walked out.

One of the King William residents who'd seen Evelyn moving out was Estela Valenzuela. She hurried home and called Grohman Enterprises. "Gabe," she said when he came on the line, "we've got a problem."

"How did you know?" he asked, his voice a little hollow.

"I saw it! What are you talking about?"

Gabe started to answer truthfully, My family stole several thousand tons of stone from the city of San Antonio about a hundred years ago. Then he decided to keep this worry to himself for a while.

Estela hastily explained Evelyn's departure. "Gabe, you can't let strangers rent that place! Your father kept records there. He hid things. I'll bet there are still documents in the attic. From the way Evelyn was moving, they might be lying around in the hall."

"She'd never rent the place to me," Gabe said. "And frankly I wouldn't want Evelyn to be my landlady. She'd think she could drop in any time..." He didn't have to explain further.

"I'll find somebody," Estela said.

She hung up the phone in the living room of her rented carriage house, and looked around the cozy room. Estela certainly couldn't afford that near-mansion Evelyn was leaving behind. Who did she know, outside the Grohman family, who had money?

"La Estrella," a voice trilled from her front window. A moment later her front door opened. Two men stood there, one thin and pale, the other sleek and brown. "Telegram!" said the latter, pretending to open an envelope. "Oh my God, it's margarita time, and we're late."

The two smiled at her. Estela smiled back. "Jaime Jones and Ramos Ramos," she said. "The millionaire artists."

The two men looked at each other, baffled. "Us?"

Calling from his father's old office, Gabe coughed delicately into the phone, trying to give an off-hand effect. On the other end of the line Javier Gustado, the Grohman family lawyer, sat up more alertly.

"I just have – kind of a hypothetical question. Some friends and I were talking –"

"I've been expecting this call, Gabe. How much does she want?"

"Who? Oh, no. Nothing like that." Gabe laughed, feeling both embarrassed and vaguely flattered. "No, here's the thing, Mr. Gustado..."

Quickly he sketched the dilemma, making it as anonymous as possible. When he finished, Gustado pondered and said, "So this hypothetical company kept taking city property after their lease expired, a long time ago? Well, yeah, the city's got a bad statute of limitations problem there."

"That's what I thought," Gabe said, greatly relieved.

"Unless there was fraud."

"Fraud?"

"You know, like that King Ranch lawsuit that's still going on about something that happened in the 1800s, because one side claims the other forged a document or something. So in your imaginary case, if somebody from this company stole the contract from the city or otherwise did something to keep the city from finding out what they were doing, the city might have a damned good case."

Gabe thought of the original leases Estela said were missing from the city archives. The leases Gabe had found hidden in his family's condo in Port Aransas. In a secret compartment, yet. Could some average citizen – or, say, 12 of them – construe that as fraud?

"That's not a problem, is it?" Javier said. "In your hypothetical world?"

"Jessica," Gabe said again, "we have to talk."

"Of course, darling," Jessica Ambrose answered in that languid, knowing voice that used to entice him so strongly. "We never have talked enough, have we?"

"I'll pick you up. You know, at the –"

"Of course Gabe. Noonish?"

At that hour, Gabe cruised slowly through the parking lot of the Quarry Market, near Bed, Bath and Beyond. It was a good meeting spot, near Gabe's office, and no one who saw Jessica's car parked at the Quarry all day would find it odd. Jessica spotted him and smiled broadly. After quick glances around, she hopped into his leather bucket seat, settling in as if at the head of her own dining room table. Jessica took off her sunglasses and winked at him.

God, she was lovely. And that wicked gleam in her eye still affected him like the first sip of a martini. But he wasn't here for that. He was here to break up.

Gabe took 281 toward downtown, then switched over to 35 South. Jessica saw a sign and asked, "Are we going to Laredo?" Jessica had been to Laredo. Mexico had shopping and bars. But Gabe was taking her some place she'd never been: the south side.

He exited at Southwest Military and Jessica thought it just amazing. It was as if there was a whole other city here. Some of the businesses had discovered it, too: she saw a Chuck E. Cheese, Hollywood Video. . . .

Gabe stopped just short of the famous Bud Jones restaurant, pulling into the adjoining parking lot. "Somebody told me about this place," he said. And he'd been fairly certain they wouldn't run into anyone they knew. So he and Jessica entered Don Pedro's, a south side landmark.

The large front room boasted a style that might be called neon hacienda. Inverted trenches in the high white ceiling added style, skylights provided light, and brightly-colored paintings of missions enlivened the walls. Gabe and Jessica blinked. All the other customers looked like regulars. Seated at a table, Gabe turned his attention to the menu.

"Wow, the regular plate includes a puffy taco. This is my new favorite place."

He would have gone on making small talk indefinitely, but Jessica took his hand on the tabletop. Her touch steeled his resolve. "Jessica, I want to talk."

Her hand clenched.

Gabe cleared his throat. Looking down, he quickly dived into the heart of his planned speech. "Jessica, what we've had together has been great. Some of the best times of my life. Really." He looked into her eyes, which had gone the gray of gunmetal. "But for too long now when we get together what you do is talk bad about Jim. I'm afraid we're doing damage to your marriage. And I wouldn't want that for the world. As long as I'm around I think you won't work at it. I'm not good for you."

"And so?" Ice in her tone. It's rare to get chilled in San Antonio in August. But Jessica did it for Gabe.

"So I think we should stop seeing each other. You know, in this way."

A long pause made him think he was going to get away clean. Then Jessica began talking in a low, hard voice. "Not a chance, my love. I gave it up for you, Gabe. My fidelity. I lost my faithfulness virginity to you. When I'm 80 years old, if I'm still, God help me, married to Jim, I will still have been an unfaithful wife. It doesn't heal."

Gabe looked up at her in surprise. Jessica looked remarkably unmarked, with her smooth white skin and resolute, full-lipped mouth. If she had worn a scarlet A, people would have taken it for a fashion accessory.

"Now you're telling me I have to go on being an adulteress but not have the adultery? The only fun in my life?"

Gabe said hesitantly, "Jessica, you're a beautiful woman. I'm sure if you want-"

"What are you suggesting now, that I be a serial adulteress? Not for little Jessica, thank you. You know what those women are like."

"I do?"

"Oh, Gabe, please. Monica Stillman? Bev Livingston? Hello?"

Actually, Gabe thought the women in question more fun than most of his crowd. Looking at Jessica, he saw no fun in her at all. But then her expression softened. She looked at him with concern.

"I know what this is about. It's about that Hispanic girl, isn't it? It's all right, Gabe. You're young and single. Have a good time."

Without an uncivil word, she had just insulted the hell out of Estela Valenzuela. They both knew it.

Jessica said firmly. "No, Gabe, you're not breaking up with me. It wouldn't be right. You and I belong together. Even your grandmother secretly approves."

"If I stop sleeping with you, you're going to tell my grandmother on me?"

Jessica smiled as if he'd been funny. "We'll be fine, Gabe. What are you having, the green enchiladas? You know you need to watch your cholesterol."

She released his hand. But that didn't mean she let go. Gabe stared at her in awe.

Jaime Jones and Ramos Ramos stood in the huge living room of Jerry Grohman's old house in King William. Ramos in his guayabera, shorts and sandals and Jaime in his multi-colored shirt and painter's pants, in the elegant old room, cried out for the caption, What's wrong with this picture?

Ramos stared up at the crown molding ten feet over his head. "Formidable!"

"This place is perfect for you," Estela said.

"This place is way too good for us," Jaime said.

"You don't understand. This is a career move. You're on the brink, Jaime. You too, Ramos. This is how you get the attention you deserve.

You have parties here. You get interviewed here. People will take you seriously."

Jaime put his hands on Estela's shoulders. "Thank you, Estela. You've touched me to the bottom of my heart. Plink! That was the sound of hitting bottom. Estela, you are full of something other than deep concern for my career. Give."

Estela sighed and appeared to come clean. "I love this house, Jaime. I don't want to see it lived in by strangers. Neither does Gabe. This place has magic."

Jaime smiled at her. "Have I got a deal for you. This place is too expensive for us. And too big. And I don't think Ramos and I are planning to have children. Are we?"

His partner said, "Well, who knows? Some day I might meet the right girl…"

"Not in the places you hang out. Here's the deal, Estela. We can only afford this place if we have a lodger. A tenant."

Estela stared at him. "What?"

"You love this place so much. What do you say, roomie?"

Stairway to Heaven

The extended Grohman clan had gathered at Miz Maddie's Olmos Park mansion to learn of a threat to the family fortune. They hadn't expected to face death as well.

The young cousin who first spotted the flames outside the bathroom window responded quickly. Unfortunately, the boy had a reputation. When the eight-year-old burst out of the bathroom screaming, "Fire!" at the top of his lungs, no one moved. In the den where most of the family congregated, the boy's mother sighed. "He just wants attention," she explained.

But in rolling her eyes she too caught a glimpse of the dancing flames, outside the back door. She dropped her glass and screamed, setting off panic.

The huge old house was built of brick, it wouldn't surrender to fire easily. But someone had broken a window and poured gasoline inside. It ran in a narrow river through the parlor and down the front hallway to the door. Maddie used the front parlor to store furniture she could no longer stand to look at daily. The old pieces – horsehair sofa, overstuffed armchair, brittle plant stands – caught fire quickly, almost eagerly, a furniture mass suicide. The fire rolled cheerily out into the hall, blocking escape from the front door.

The arsonist had started another fire just outside the french doors that provided the exit to outside from the den. Plants, redwood patio furniture, and the deck itself burned, cutting off escape through that exit.

Uncle Jock, the least useful Grohman in any social situation, unexpectedly behaved heroically when action was called for. Setting down his bourbon, he dashed across the room, past bewildered, frightened adults, and reached the game table where 76-year-old Marsh Grohman played 42 with three children.

"Excuse me, Uncle Marsh. Watch out, kids!" Jock grabbed the heavy game table, heaved it overhead, and hurled it through the broad picture window. Glass shattered, setting off more screams.

Making sure no heavy pieces still hung from the frame, Jock grabbed all three children. "Come on, kids. I've got the kids!" he yelled.

He stepped carefully through the open window frame. To his left, the fire burned. Skirting it, Jock made his way down the sloping lawn to the pool. Without hesitation, he threw the children into the shallow end. "Have fun, kids!" he yelled, and headed back for more.

Artists Ramos Ramos and Jaime Jones had just moved into Jerry and Evelyn Grohman's old house in King William. Deciding to snoop around a little, they had immediately made a find: a cache of old canceled checks from Jerry Grohman to Luz Valenzuela, each check carefully marked "child support."

"Whoa," Jaime said, immediately getting the implications.

Ramos' mind was on another track. "This is why Luz always lived better than the rest of us starving artists." He went off into a brief fantasy about having a rich person's child, until his partner dug an elbow in his ribs. "Gabe's father paying child support to Estela's mother. This means Gabe and Estela . . ."

"Wow," Ramos said. "But aren't they, like, an item? Do you think they've already – ?" Then he gave a tolerant shrug. "Hey, maybe she already knows. I wouldn't have thought Estela was that kinky, personally, but to each . . ."

"She doesn't know!" Jaime found himself outraged at the suggestion. He, like many people in the artistic community who had watched Estela grow up, felt protective toward her. In spite of her unconventional upbringing, there remained a purity about Estela that anyone with a nurturing instinct wanted to preserve. Miz Maddie had seen it. Now Jaime Jones felt the same protective urge.

Ramos shrugged. "It's none of our business."

"Of course it is! We can't let this happen. It's genetically unsafe. It would kill both their families. Besides, it's just . . ."

"Icky," Ramos suggested. Both men nodded.

"This is an act of providence that she's coming to live with us. It's the hand of fate. We have to protect her. We have to become her *duenas*."

"What's a *duena*?"

Ramos' education in Hispanic culture, present and past, continued as his partner explained. "It's a governess. Sort of a maid and watchdog all in one."

"Cool. Does this job come with a costume?" Ramos reacted to the look his partner gave him. "Hey, I like costumes. Oh, like you don't."

"Listen . . ."

"Hi, guys!" Estela Valenzuela strolled in. She wore a white peasant blouse that ended just above her waistband, showing a narrow strip of taut, brown abdomen, and cut-off jean shorts that made her legs look long. "Where should I put my stuff?"

Ramos looked her up and down. "The bedroom right next to ours," he said.

Jock Grohman kept returning to the house, leading relatives to safety. He instructed his brother-in-law to turn on a hose, and formed a bucket brigade from the pool to the burning patio. The next day's news story would call him a hero, and so would his family. But he couldn't be everywhere.

Miz Maddie was in the kitchen with Rosa when she first smelled smoke. Maddie ran out into the den, saw that everyone looked relatively safe, and bolted back. Running faster than she had in decades, she darted up a narrow back staircase to the second floor.

Old houses and old people are particularly vulnerable to fire. The destroyer of memories. Maddie loved her house, but she could let it go. Some few precious things, though, she refused to live without.

Behind her, Rosa called her name and followed her. On the second floor they walked into hell.

Fire climbs. That is its imperative. Smoke, too, seeks the sky. The old parlor lay just below the main staircase of the house. Thick black clouds climbed the stairs and poured out into the second floor hallway. Flames began to lick up the banister and the old carpet runner. On the second floor the sparks found houseplants, carpet, curtains. The fire took the second story for its own.

But Maddie plunged toward it, into her bedroom. Smoke thickened. She coughed and waved her arms futilely. Rosa grabbed her arm, but to no avail.

Maddie ignored her jewelry box, grabbing a couple of old family photographs off the wall. "Take these!" she yelled, thrusting them into Rosa's hands.

Maddie went to the closet, reached up to a shelf, and took down a shoebox. "Come on!" she screamed.

But the smoke had grown too thick. She couldn't find Rosa. Or the door. Coughing, she held her shoebox tightly and groped blindly through the smoke.

Preston "Duke" Grohman found himself alone in the fire that engulfed his grandmother's house. During the big adult confab he had slipped away, upstairs where he wasn't supposed to go. Young Duke was a born snoop. He loved to spy through the house. His brother Gabe had a room here, where Preston had turned up a few interesting items in the past. He liked to pry through his grandmother's room, too.

So Preston didn't hear the first cries of "Fire!" By the time he sniffed something wrong, smoke poured up the staircase, trapping him. He retreated to a bedroom across the hall, hiding both from the fire and from the anger of any adult who might find him here. He heard people pass out in the hallway, and slunk back.

By the time he ventured out of the room, the hallway had filled with smoke. The boy immediately began choking. "Help," he tried to shout, but it came out a croak. Tears poured down his cheeks. He fell to the floor, unable to call out again.

"Here I am, son," said a familiar voice. A hand emerged from the smoke. Preston took it. The hand's grip was strong but cold. It raised gooseflesh all over his back, which helped bring him to alertness. He tried to peer through the smoke.

"Daddy?" he said.

"Come on, son," Jerry Grohman said. "Stay down on the ground. Crawl with me. This way."

"Are you taking me to heaven?" Duke asked wonderingly.

"I certainly hope not."

But even a ghost can't be everywhere at once. As the late Jerry Grohman tried to lead his son to safety, the two unknowingly passed the bedroom where Jerry's mother fell to her knees, unable to find the door through the smoke. And across town, Jerry's other son drove into the same sort of danger that had killed his father.

Driving his BMW sedately down Durango, past the old HemisFair grounds, Gabe experienced his usual welter of feelings. His family fortune appeared on the verge of extinction, through scandal and lawsuit. In his personal life, Gabe had tried to break up with his married girl friend and failed. Somehow Jessica had threatened him. Gabe still hadn't puzzled out how she had done that. The lady had a will harder than diamond.

Nevertheless, Gabe felt unexpectedly happy. He had just come from seeing Estela, and while holding her had realized for the first time that he loved her. Not only that he loved her, but that he had never been in love before. The feeling didn't push his other problems out of his mind, but robbed them of significance. He and Estela could be poor together. Having absolutely no experience of deprivation, Gabe found the prospect romantic.

He almost turned the car around and drove back to her. Had he done so, he might have noticed the small black sedan following him.

Instead he drove blithely on. Gabe was late for the big meeting at his grandmother's house, and he had information to share. He rose onto 281 and headed north. A few minutes later he took the Hildebrand exit and turned left, toward Devine Road. Along that short stretch of road, he began to feel disoriented. The landscape had subtly altered from the familiar. Stopped at the intersection, Gabe looked back. Shouldn't he still be able to see the expressway from here? He couldn't. Nor could he find the largest landmark, the tower of the new BAMC.

He turned onto Devine, which seemed narrower than he remembered. A couple of houses appeared to have gone missing. Gabe's arms tingled. He began to feel that he was somewhere else. Or somewhen else.

Was he travelling on Milagro Lane? He had found that street of strange inspiration before, even before Estela had explained its meaning to him. Milagro meant miracle, and anything could happen there.

At the intersection with Olmos Drive, instead of turning left toward his grandmother's house, instinct made Gabe turn right. He was driving across Olmos Basin. To his left, the white bulwark of the dam should have loomed, but he didn't see it. Instead he found himself driving on the top of the old dam. Gabe was 24 years old, he didn't remember this dam. It was a narrow, twisting roadway, hemmed in by stone walls. He began to feel trapped.

At one of these narrow turnings, he felt the first thud against his back bumper.

Veronica Lewis had an instinct for news. She could always find it on TV. Hit buttons at random on the remote control and up would pop CNN or a local news broadcast. She could do it blindfolded. Once she actually started working in the field of TV news, though, this talent did Veronica little good. Picky news directors much preferred stories that hadn't already aired on another station.

And she'd never been able to translate this ability into real life. Where was news to be found? Certain locations could usually be forced to yield a story – the courthouse, the police station – but news was a cunning prey. It could pop up anywhere.

As Veronica drove on 281 toward downtown, she saw smoke rising. It drew her attention, curling lazily into the air like a signal. Impulsively, Veronica exited and drove toward it.

Probably nothing. Burning trash, or leaves. She couldn't have the good fortune actually to stumble onto something newsworthy.

But as Veronica drove into Olmos Park the column of smoke grew thicker and blacker. Then she heard a siren.

She turned a corner and saw fire engulfing one of those beautiful old mansions. Neighbors had gathered on the street. This was no grass fire. It looked like a genuine tragedy.

Her luck was improving.

Luckily, Veronica had her videocamera. She always came equipped. Now if she could only find someone to point it at her.

While she waited, she took footage of the burning mansion. No other news crews had arrived, she had an exclusive. The fire had made strong headway through the old house. While she made tape and commentary, Veronica asked gathered neighbors who lived here. When she heard the name "Grohman," Veronica became even more excited. A relative newcomer to San Antonio, she still recognized the name of one of the oldest, wealthiest families in town. This was a story.

On the second floor of the house, windows faced the street. Behind one window, Veronica saw shadows move. Probably smoke.

But for just a moment she thought she saw a human form outlined behind the glass.

"Did anybody else see that?" she asked.

Evelyn Grohman had been in the powder room freshening up her makeup when the fire started. She returned to the den to find it full of smoke and void of people. Evelyn made her way to the broken window and out, where she saw most of the family gathered around the pool. Quickly she looked for one face and didn't find it.

"Preston?" she called.

No one answered. Evelyn turned and plunged back into the burning house.

The place had filled with smoke by now. Evelyn called her son's name again, thought she heard an answer, but was quickly overcome. She sank to the floor, calling feebly.

Young Preston, crawling through the relatively smoke-free kitchen, heard his mother's voice and called back. He started to turn that direction, but a voice only Preston could hear said, "Go on, son. I'll get her."

"Daddy?" Preston called, feeling terribly alone.

"Don't worry," the ghost answered. "I'll be back."

It was Arnold Shwarzenegger's line from "The Terminator," the last thing Jerry Grohman had said to Preston every night before the boy fell asleep. Smiling, with tears running down his face, Preston found the kitchen door and ran out into the bright, fresh air.

Evelyn felt herself lifted. To her amazement, she was being rescued by Cinco, her new love interest. He looked so blondly handsome, and lifted her so easily. Evelyn felt protected for the first time in a long while. "Where did you come from?" she asked wonderingly.

"Your imagination, my dear."

She opened her eyes. "Jock, you idiot! What are you doing? Put me down."

He did, unceremoniously, and scanned the crowd. "Where's mama?" he said, then called it more loudly. The whole clan began to search for Miz Maddie, without result.

The kitchen door on the side of the house opened again. Rosa came stumbling out, her face almost black with smoke and the effort to breathe. In the fresh air she collapsed. Quickly a crowd surrounded her. "She's upstairs," Rosa gasped. "Miz Maddie went upstairs. She was looking for something. I lost her."

"Mama!" Jock screamed, and lunged for the door. Everyone held him back, although one uncle said, "Ah, let him go." But smoke completely filled the house now. Jock wouldn't even have made it to the stairs.

Rosa's eyes opened wider, as she looked at the faces around her. "I was lost too," she said softly. "Someone led me out. Who was it?"

No one answered. But when Rosa came to young Preston, his bright eyes held a secret. Her gaze lingered on him the longest. "Oh, child," she said, and reached out her hand. Preston took it. Rosa seemed to learn something from the connection.

At the front of the house, Veronica Lewis said, "Here. Just point it and shoot. Hold this button down. It'll focus by itself. Make sure you keep it on me, right?"

"Yes, ma'am."

Veronica had found a 12-year-old boy to be her cameraman. When it comes to technology, always look for a 12-year-old. The boy seemed confident with the instrument. Veronica gave the camera a thumbs-up and began climbing.

She had found ornamental vines holding onto the brick. They seemed to lead right up to the bedroom window where she'd seen a shadow. The only questions were how strong the vines were and how hot the brick wall. Veronica touched her hand to it. Not too bad.

The vines held as she climbed. "Just like Spiderman," she said. Her career decision never to let her weight top 105 now looked awfully smart. On the other hand, her decorative white sandals with the three-inch cork soles were not designed for this. She caught a window ledge, then an ornamental sconce. She reached the brick ledge just below the second-floor window. The brick had grown much hotter, but she coped.

She looked down, hoping the cameraboy wasn't focusing exclusively on her rear end. That was one disadvantage of a twelve-year-old. She waved to the crowd. Take this, Danger Boy, she thought.

Veronica looked through the window and saw nothing but smoke. Nonetheless, she thought she'd found the right window. Perched precariously on the window ledge, she turned and saw that the firefighters had gotten their hose hooked up. "In here!" she screamed. "I see her!"

The powerful spray obligingly lurched toward her. Veronica leaned over closer to be sure she got into the shot, and the spray wavered and caught her. It hit Veronica full in the chest and knocked her back through the window.

She landed on the floor, drenched and furious. Fresh air poured into the room through the broken window. And Veronica found that she had fallen on someone.

The woman clutched something to her breast. Veronica tried to pull her up to the air from the window, but couldn't budge the woman.

She stuck her head out the window and called, "Hurry! I don't think she's breathing."

As she lay soaked on the floor of the smoke-filled bedroom, with Miz Maddie's inert body beside her, Veronica Lewis didn't know how lucky she was. The broken window downstairs had started a draft, and other open windows and doors created cross-currents, so that air came in through the broken window beside Veronica, rather than smoke billowing out. She could breathe, for the moment.

She pulled harder and got Miz Maddie up to the window, half-leaning out so she got some air. The old lady was hard to move because she wouldn't release the shoebox she held tight against her chest with both hands.

A ladder clattered against the brick wall beside them, and a firefighter came quickly up. He managed to get a sling contraption under the older woman and lift her as gently as possible out the window. "Are you all right?" he said tersely to Veronica, then let her fend for herself.

A sizable crowd had gathered below. At this culmination of the rescue, they cheered. Veronica stood atop the ladder and smiled and waved. Then she remembered she was being videotaped, and changed her response to a grim smile and a tight little salute. *Just doing my job, folks.*

This tape would need editing.

In the old house in King William, Estela Valenzuela stared at her new roommates. Jaime and Ramos had never been predictable, that was one reason she enjoyed their company. But today they seemed to be acting strange even by their own standards. She gave up trying to understand and said, "I'd better get going. Gabe wants me to drop by his grandmother's house. They're having a big family meeting."

"You're going like that?" Jaime said in obvious disapproval of her cut-off shorts. To his partner he whispered, "We need to get her to tone it down. We don't want her getting Gabe all hot and excited."

Ramos whispered back, "But if she goes to this big family thing looking trampy maybe they'll all disapprove and make him break up with her."

"That won't work. Then they'll just have some secret, back-door romance...."

"But we guard the back door!"

Estela stood staring at their consultation. "What are you two whispering about?"

"Nothing," they said in unison.

"I'm going to change," she said. "Okay, mámas?" She paused for a moment, looking pensive. "I think Gabe needs me there."

Gabe definitely needed her, but he would never make it to his grandmother's house today. He found himself crossing the old dam over Olmos Basin. Fog had settled around him, shrouding much of the landscape, and what Gabe could see seemed less familiar than it should.

He remembered Whitley Strieber's revelations about Olmos Basin being a hotbed of alien activity, and wondered whether he was about to be abducted. But that was no UFO behind him. It was a black sedan, and when Gabe slowed down it slammed into his back bumper again, pushing him into the old stone wall of the dam.

Gabe cried out and cursed and hit his accelerator. He sped off the end of the dam, turned right, then left at the next intersection, going in a big circle, trying to lose his pursuer.

Without success. The car stayed right on his tail. Gabe couldn't see the driver, and couldn't tell much about the car, except that it had a strong radiator guard. And good steering. It stayed right with him.

Looking back in the rearview mirror, he could only make out a silhouette in the other car, but thought he saw the driver's long hair swinging. Could it be Jessica Ambrose chasing him? Gabe almost pulled over to confront her, but the other driver clearly had no plans to negotiate.

Gabe drove down to the big circle between the Alamo Heights Pool and the nature trails. Realizing he could be trapped there, he spun around and started up the hill, back toward the dam. The BMW had powerful acceleration, he began to put more distance between him and his pursuer. Gabe grinned tightly.

He was doing almost 60 when he topped the hill, flying briefly into the air. Now he just had to make the turn onto the dam and he'd be safe. He could reach the family home and call…

Gabe had reckoned without his pursuer having a partner. Just as he slowed to start his turn, a second black sedan pulled out of the side street, right into his path. The car stopped there, twenty yards ahead.

Gabe yanked on the steering wheel and went over the curb. But this was where the residential area ended and went cosmic. Gabe's car hurtled down, then lost the ground altogether, flying through the air with tree limbs whipping by, until abruptly it slammed into a tree and fell.

The sound of his car horn drifted up from the lonely gorge of the Olmos Basin.

Once Rosa determined that Miz Maddie was alive, she started fussing at her. "Crazy *vieja!* What was so precious you had to go into a burning house for? Jewels? Confederate war bonds?"

She opened the shoebox. "Letters?"

Miz Maddie removed her oxygen mask to say hoarsely, "They're from my mother. Whenever I was out of town she'd write to me. When I was at camp or away at school. Even on my honeymoon. When I first got them they made me mad, I thought she was still trying to tell me what to do. But I read them again when I was older and I saw she was just trying to hold onto me."

She sank back onto the stretcher. So this box of paper had become Maddie's way of trying to keep her mother close, long after it was no longer possible. Rosa glanced through the envelopes. On many of them the ink had run, soaked by the firefighters' hoses. And Rosa's tears weren't helping. Rosa closed the box and handed it back to her old employer.

She looked at the building that had been the main Grohman home for four generations. From here it didn't look too bad, but Rosa knew better. Inside it was a shell, where smoke and fire had run wild.

But in memory Rosa could step back into that beautiful old home, and see it filled with happy people. Rending the veil to the past; holding onto the impossible, that was what life was about. And you couldn't do it with paper.

The ambulance closed its doors and took Miz Maddie away.

Members of the extended Grohman family moved slowly from the back yard to the front. Evelyn had her arm around her son Duke. Duke, too, had been given oxygen, since he had been one of the last people to get out of the house. He seemed fine, except that he kept looking around, scanning the faces near him as if he didn't recognize any of them. "Poor boy," Evelyn thought, "he's in shock."

Evelyn glanced across the street, then stared. The man called Diablo, with whom she'd shared a brief, passionate fling, stood on the other side of a small black car. When he saw Evelyn, he gave her a grim smile and a triumphant gesture. Then he stared at the ravaged Grohman house with obvious satisfaction. Finally he ducked into the car and it drove out of sight.

Evelyn's hand flew to her mouth. If Diablo had been here watching all the time, why hadn't he joined in the rescue efforts? But then she thought, "Maybe he had. Maybe he had called for the fire truck." Evelyn decided to break the habit of a lifetime and try to think the best of people.

A man broke through the knot of onlookers and came striding toward her. His hair flared blondly in the sunlight, and his blue polo shirt brought out the color of his eyes. Compared to the bedraggled, coughing people around him, Chester Worthington Dilmore V looked like a young emperor walking triumphantly across a battlefield.

"Cinco! What are you doing here?"

"I heard about the fire on the radio and rushed over to see if you were okay. My dear, what peril! Are you all right?"

"I'm fine." Evelyn accepted his quick embrace, while still staring at him. "You know what happened, Cinco? I was inside, I passed out.

Then I dreamed you rescued me."

"You did? How tremendously flattering. I only wish it could have been true."

He hugged her again, which felt very comforting to Evelyn. But still she looked at him with puzzlement.

Others around her shared that expression. The survivors were in their second lives now, everything seemed fresh and new.

Jock Grohman stood with an aged relative. In fact, a small cluster stood around him. Jock's actions had been the most surprising aspect of the fire. He had sprung quickly into action, getting most of the family out safely. Relatives now patted his back and gave him re-evaluating gazes.

They all looked up at the house, which stood, but was clearly gutted inside. Jock looked grim and angry. "It'll be all right," he said. "We'll rebuild it. It'll be better than ever. We won't let this stop us."

An aunt said, "What will we use for money, Jock?"

Several of them nodded, remembering Maddie's announcement of the financial disaster that had befallen the family, just before this physical catastrophe.

"We'll get it done," Jock said implacably. "We've done it before, haven't we? The family didn't come over from the old country with a fortune, did we?"

Some of his determination trickled outward, causing lifted chins and straighter postures. Then Jock turned to the man beside him and said, "By the way, Uncle Marsh, where is the old country? I never got straight on that. I mean, they're all pretty old over there, aren't they?"

Uncle Marsh stared at him, reappraising his reappraisal.

They all heard the squeal of tires. By the time they turned to look, Estela Valenzuela was running toward them, ignoring yellow tape and the police officer who tried to stop her. One glance at the old house told her what had happened. "Where's Gabe?" she called to his family.

"Gabe?" They all echoed the name. "He never got here," one answered.

"Thank God," Estela said. "I was afraid something had happened to him."

Off in Olmos Basin, Gabe's car horn stopped, and an eerie silence descended over the basin.

Part III

Elsewhen

Elsewhen

Veronica Lewis clutched a microphone and stared earnestly into the camera. She wore a black smudge across her cheek and her hair in disarray. Just before going on the air, she had checked her appearance in a car's side mirror and thought she looked terribly dashing.

"Luckily the tragedy here in Olmos Park resulted in no loss of life, as far as we know now. Two survivors have been taken away in ambulances, however."

In her earpiece, the noon anchor back at the station said, "In fact, Veronica, we've been told that you yourself were responsible for rescuing one of those people. Is that correct?"

"Yes, Carl, I did what I could. Before the firefighters arrived I thought I saw someone behind a second story window, and I climbed up to try to get her out. With a great deal of help from the fire team, we were successful."

Veronica could recount this with unassuming modesty, since she knew that while she spoke the station would be running the footage of her climbing the front of the house and going in through a window to find Madeleine Grohman.

Veronica re-ran the event in her mind, as well. She'd only seen a splendid opportunity to get herself back on-air, but looking back at the gutted mansion she suddenly realized that she had actually saved a life.

When the camera's red light blinked on again, Veronica appeared uncharacteristically sober. "It's always a tragedy when a home is destroyed, but as one family member said to me, 'It's only a building.' This is a time to be thankful. Back to you, Carl."

Estela Valenzuela circulated through the crowd asking if any of them had heard from Gabe. None had. Estela called his mobile phone and got only a recording of Gabe's cheerful-sounding voice inviting her to leave a message. She did, but had a strange feeling it wouldn't be received.

No one noticed her growing anxiety except the ghost of Jerry Grohman. Jerry always took a special interest in Estela, but this time he was more concerned about his son. He concentrated, let his mind spread outward, then abruptly blinked away.

Babes in Playland

Down in the Olmos Basin, Gabe lay unconscious in his car, which had flown through the air, crashed into a tree, and dropped into the dense brush of the basin. The car couldn't be seen from any road.

Slowly Gabe came to himself. Lights flashed, drawing his attention. Then his other senses came into play. He heard gaudy music, laughter, the lighthearted screams of young women. He smelled cotton candy and the sweat of a summer crowd. Gabe seemed to be whirling. He saw that the flashing lights revolved. Brightly painted horses circled on a carousel. Gabe recognized the carousel. Until recently it had stood in Brackenridge Park, near the train station.

But he wasn't in Brackenridge Park now. Gabe walked on densely packed dirt, past booths trying to grab his pocket change. "Three balls for a quarter!" called the barker from one booth. Behind him three wooden milk bottles stood in a pyramid that looked deceptively easy to bring down.

Down at the end of the midway, a roller coaster dipped and swooped. Its wheels clattered over wooden ties. The coaster looked short and harmless to Gabe, nowhere near as heart-wrenching as the Rattler or the Steel Eel. But the people riding screamed in appreciation, and a line of people waited to take their place.

Where in the world was he? The place seemed both unknown and oddly familiar. To his left stood a two-story funhouse. Inside it, Gabe saw people groping through a maze of mirrors and glass. Others walked across a swaying bridge, and when one girl reached the end a blast of air lifted her skirt, making her scream.

"Come on, Jerry! You coming or not?"

Jerry? Was his father here? But of course not; Gabe's father was nowhere. But a teenaged boy down the midway waved his arm, and seemed to be looking right at Gabe. Gabe looked over his shoulder. There was a crowd behind him, but no one who seemed to be responding to the boy's call.

In a mirror outside the funhouse, Gabe caught sight of his reflection. It looked like him, but younger and different. After a long stare, Gabe recognized his father's face. But it was impossibly youthful, maybe 17 years old.

Where was he? Gabe looked behind him and saw the backward sign of the amusement park: "Playland Park."

The only Playland Gabe knew was a barren ruin just off Broadway. This lively place couldn't be it.

A hand grabbed his arm. "Come on, Jerry, this place is deadsville. Let's find the girls."

The boy was obviously talking to him. He frowned and said, "What's with you, Jerry? You didn't buy some bad acid from somebody here, did you? Come on, man, you know better than that."

Gabe allowed himself to be led. Passing the amusements booths again, he found a swarthy, dark-eyed man in one of the booths staring at him. When Gabe looked his way, the man smiled, but continued his scrutiny. Gabe couldn't place him.

He looked back at the face of the boy with him, which seemed familiar. But who was he? And for that matter, who was Gabe? And where was he?

Gabe Grohman did a quick review of his life, trying to decide whether he was in heaven or hell. Playland Park seemed to be a little of both. Gabe stared at the Tilt-a-Whirl, two large canisters that spun as they turned in large circles, at the bumper cars where pre-adolescent boys let loose their aggression, and at the booths where people tried to throw small hoops around Coke bottles or knock over solid wooden milk bottles with a softball. Like everything in hell, each feat looked easier than it was.

But his worst punishment was loss of identity. From the glimpse he'd gotten in a mirror and from the way his companion treated him, Gabe seemed to be his own father, as a teenager.

"Come on, let's find the girls," the boy said. In his haste he almost tripped Gabe, but caught his arm to help steady him. "Sorry about that, Chief."

The boy laughed. Gabe didn't get the joke. His companion appeared to be about 17, with smooth cheeks and an attempt at a sophisticated smirk. A cowlick sticking up at the back of his head robbed him of that. The boy had freckles and sandy hair. Gabe tried to place him, but couldn't.

"There they are. Hey girls!" The boy waved to two teenagers wearing white pleated blouses, one with jeans, the other in a very short blue skirt. Gabe naturally walked toward the latter, because she seemed familiar. She returned his curious stare with lively blue eyes and a sly smile.

The boy said, "Hey, what are we doing here, swapping mates? Holy Bob-and-Carol-and-Ted-and-Alice, Batman!" He gently pushed Gabe away from the girl in the miniskirt and put his arm around her. So Gabe was with the girl in jeans. She stared at him curiously but with a smile. "What's wrong with your friend, Ronnie? Is he on a bad trip?"

"He's overcome by your beauty, Jeannine. Right, Jerry?"

"Right," Gabe answered slowly, drawing out the word. The other kids seemed to take that as a joke, too.

Jeannine had light brown hair, thin lips, and a pert little nose that wrinkled when she smiled. She put her arm around him as they walked. Gabe understood from that contact that this was not a first date, or that this girl was very fast. But who was she? Like the other two, she looked familiar.

They wandered the midway. Again they passed the dart-throwing booth, where the dark-eyed man with the thin moustache gave Gabe another friendly smile. He didn't call to him a come-on like the other barkers, just smiled as if at an old acquaintance. Gabe felt strangely disquieted by his friendly regard.

Outside the Fun House, they stopped to watch people groping through the mirror maze. Two girls emerged from the house and walked shakily across a bridge that moved from side to side. When the girls thought they'd reached safety, a quick blast of air from below lifted their skirts. The other boy, Ronnie, looked down at his miniskirted girl friend's legs and said, "Let's try this place. It's always good for a goof."

"If it's for goofs, you should love it," the girl said. "All you want is a grope in the dark."

Nevertheless, she led the way to the barker's booth. They each paid their admission, fifty cents, and walked through a door into a very dark interior. "Hold hands," the girl with Gabe said. "You can get lost in here."

They heard a scuffle ahead of them, as the other girl said sharply, "That's not my hand!"

Gabe tried to keep track of his position by brushing his hand along the wall to his right, but the wall was shaggy, with creepy things brushing his skin like little reaching hands. He recoiled from the wall, which threw him against his companion. She chuckled slyly, and put her arms around his waist. "Is this why you wanted to come in here?"

Using her hand for guidance, she found his mouth and kissed him, slowly and with confidence. Gabe lost himself in the kiss, until his date drew slightly away and said, "Now pay attention, class. This next part is done very gently."

Her mouth moved along his cheek to his ear. Gabe went stiff as a stucco wall. He hadn't heard anything since her first sentence, because in that phrase he had recognized her voice. It was Mrs. Landry, his fourth grade teacher.

Then Gabe almost shrieked. What was happening to Gabe in the dark was scarier than anything in the Fun House: Mrs. Landry was kissing his ear!

Estela Valenzuela was good at finding things, including people. She had made successful searching her life's work, even a career. So when she began backtracking the route Gabe must have taken, she felt confident of finding him. Or maybe he would answer his phone.

She drove down Olmos Drive, to the intersection with Devine Road, but instead of turning right, the way back to 281, she kept going straight, over Olmos beside the dam. Her instinct served her well, as usual, and if Gabe had still been on the road, she undoubtedly would have found him.

But Gabe's car lay at the bottom of the wildlands of Olmos Basin. Estela drove right past the place where his car had left the road. She missed the skid marks, and drove on down toward the Alamo Heights Pool.

As night fell over Olmos Basin, the unconscious Gabe's only companion was his ghostly father. Jerry had found Gabe's wrecked car, but had no way of calling for aid. He had tried to lift his son out, but his arms had just passed through Gabe's body. That merging seemed to have had some effect on Gabe, though. He turned restless. Jerry heard him mutter the name Jeannine, and wondered what he had done to his son.

In fact, Jerry had landed Gabe in a land much stranger than Playland Park. A place where the young cast off conformity by talking and dressing exactly alike; where even "nice" girls felt an obligation to be fast and loose; where elders learned dress and manners from their young instead of the other way around.

Welcome to the 1960s.

So Gabe remained lost in his own strange journey into his father's past. In the dark of the Fun House at Playland Park, he broke away from the embrace of the teenaged girl with him, having just recognized her as the woman who would become his fourth grade teacher. He'd been enjoying her kisses, but now felt odd. Especially when he understood that it wasn't him she was kissing, it was his father, whose body Gabe somehow had occupied.

The girl's teeth gently nibbling his earlobe cast Gabe's whole past into a new light. This girl Jeannine had grown up to become a teacher – his teacher, on whom Gabe had had his first crush, he suddenly remembered. But his father had been there ahead of him. His father had had parent-teacher conferences with this woman, supposedly talking about Gabe's progress in handwriting and long division. Had they instead been remembering these nights of illicit passion? Had they looked into each other's eyes, forgetting the subject of their conference? And had Gabe's mother been there at the time?

For the first time, Gabe had an adult insight into how unpredictable life is, how its paths tangle and cross each other at the oddest junctions. How wildly unlikely it is that any of us exist at all.

He took Jeannine's hand and pulled her through the dark passageway, emerging into the brightly lighted mirror maze, a series of joined cubicles in which two walls might be mirrors, the third glass, and only the fourth an open passage to the next cubicle. Gabe found himself looking at his father's teenaged face, similar to his own but different enough that he felt he was looking through a window rather than into a mirror.

After the maze, Jeannine trotted quickly across the air blast, even though she wore jeans, so the air lifted only her short hair. Gabe had missed the miniskirted girl's passage through the air, which must have drawn a crowd.

Outside the Fun House they caught up to the other couple, Ronnie and the girl whose name Gabe hadn't heard. Jeannine took Gabe's hand, proprietary now that she'd kissed him in the dark. The other girl noticed, with a sparkle in her eye.

"What next?" Ronnie asked. "Feel like the Rocket?" He pointed toward the rickety-looking wooden roller coaster.

"No. I feel like rockin'," his girl friend said. "Let's blow this popsicle stand."

Ronnie didn't have to be told twice. The quartet made their way out of the amusement park, past the Muzik Express where cups whirled and circled to the beat of recorded music, not even glancing at the miniature golf course, and out past the entrance that demanded 25 cent admission. Gabe stared all around. If it had been up to him, they would have lingered. This lively 15-acre plot, with its diverse crowd of customers, appealed to him. He knew the place only as an abandoned ruin. Looking back, he saw the most improbable locale of all Playland: the Peaceful Valley Chapel. Gabe thought he could have used its solace, but his companions pulled him on.

Outside, Ronnie said to the girl, "Okay, it's your party now, Bet. Where to?"

The girl looked back at the other three, a smile lighting her face. That pose and the sound of her name suddenly struck Gabe like the onset of flu, with fever and chills. He had seen her face look just that way in an old yearbook from Alamo Heights High School. My God, it was Betty Jean McGraw.

His mother.

Veronica Lewis walked into the KSAN-TV newsroom looking less than her fashionable best. Her white capri pants with a beaded floral design were torn at one knee, and her pink T-top so wrinkled one could barely read the word "Babe" stitched across its front. A smoke smudge adorned her cheek like a badly-placed tattoo. Nevertheless, everyone in the newsroom applauded. Veronica dimpled and curtsied, then sat down at her desk to make notes. Thorough professional, that was her. But what Veronica was really doing was waiting for the approach of the news director. She wasn't disappointed.

Roger came up to her already talking. "Good work, Monica." He was getting slightly closer on her name. "Wish everyone in here was that alert," he said loudly. "Okay, you're back on the air. First thing, do an interview with the old broad you rescued. I understand she's somebody important. Does she know you're the one who saved her? If not, make sure somebody tells her before you start the interview. Then we get you a regular beat. I'm thinking Disaster Babe. Every time there's a flood or a fire somewhere, you're there."

"What about City Hall?" Veronica asked.

"Yeah, I guess that's kind of a continuing disaster." Roger shrugged. "If that's what you want." Oh, Veronica wanted, all right. She wanted to get back at the mayor who'd gotten her knocked off the air in the first place.

Watch out, Suzanne Pierce. Disaster Babe is on your trail.

Chester Worthington Delmore V – "Cinco" to his many friends – said to Evelyn Grohman, "Let's get you out of these wet things and into a dry martini." Proving he had read the classics.

Evelyn hadn't, so she thought his line original and very witty. At the same time, she felt bedraggled, standing at the scene of the fire. "Could you give me a ride to my new house? It's –"

"On Grandview. I know, my dear. Everyone's talking about your return to the neighborhood."

Evelyn smiled up at him. For the first time in her life, someone made the idea of people talking about her sound flattering. In the past she'd never been able to think of anything complimentary they could be whispering. But Cinco made her feel like a celebrity.

He took her hand and led her toward his car. Evelyn remembered something at the last moment and said over her shoulder, "Preston? Will you be okay? Shall we - ?"

Young Preston had been staying with his brother Gabe for the last week, and Evelyn hadn't realized that Gabe was missing, nor that Estela had gone in search of him. Evelyn had always been able to count on some family member taking care of her son, and in her distraction had forgotten that his primary caregiver, his grandmother, was in an ambulance on the way to a hospital.

Preston said, "It's okay, Mom, have a good time," sounding adult in his weariness. Most of his blood kin straggled past him, patting him on the head or shoulder but worried about their own troubles.

Then a familiar brown arm went around his neck. "Come on, m'jito, let's go home."

Preston snuggled close against Rosa, recognizing her shape and aroma without even turning his head. A tear swelled in one eye as he felt at home again, and lost his perpetual weary aloofness.

But as they reached Rosa's old green Pontiac, Estela Valenzuela returned. Leaning out of her car window, she casually called, "Hola, abuela. I think I need the little man."

Both Rosa and Preston looked at her suspiciously.

Down in Olmos Basin, cool tendrils of moisture reached through Gabe's car windows after the sun had been down a couple of hours. Fever became apparent in the flush of his cheeks and the labor of his breathing.

In his haunted dream he had fever, all right. Dance fever. The quartet of Alamo Heights teenagers he found himself with had reached the exotic land of downtown San Antonio, a place called the Jam Factory. Frantic bodies jammed the dance floor, to the equally frantic music of "Wild Thing."

Betty Jean McGraw fit the song perfectly, dancing with her arms raised her and her legs flinging out to lift her miniskirt to non-existence. Gabe looked at her with awe and fear, and sometimes had to look away. The couple of times she'd caught his eyes she'd stared at him intimately. Maybe she did that to every boy. If so, Gabe knew how every boy felt as the recipient of that deep, emotional stare.

On the other hand, Betty Jean was, or would be some day, his mother. Which made their exchanges seem sinful.

Sin was the order of the night, though. Midnight approached. Gabe felt sure he'd walk back outside to find that Ronnie's classic 1968 Dodge Charger had become a pumpkin.

But no, the coach awaited. Ronnie, Bet, Gabe, and Jeannine tumbled back into it. Ronnie turned up the radio, and Bruce Hathaway informed them deeply and resonantly that they were listening to San Antonio's number one home of rock and roll. Then disproved it by playing The Archies.

Ronnie switched to Don Couser on KONO and produced a hand-rolled cigarette. "Time to head home?" he asked mischievously.

"Are you kidding?" Bet answered scornfully. "Come on, Ronnie, we're already halfway to the east side."

The driver turned to her with a nervous look that might have been faked or might not. "How do you even know about that place, Betty Jean?"

She just laughed, a trilling, thrilling lilt that convinced Gabe he was in a world that had never existed.

Oh, but it had. And tonight, in the fevered hallucination of what was possibly Gabe's last night on earth, it did again.

Urban dwellers have always known certain universal truths, as instinctively as a farmer knows why the cows are uneasy. City children know that the water from a sprinkler is colder than the water in a swimming pool. A barefoot boy knows which color asphalt is hottest and where the thickest sticker patches grow. And city people know that safety lies in staying in your own neighborhood, especially after dark.

But for some bold explorers, there have always been stronger lures than safety. Gabe Grohman, somehow inhabiting his father's teenage body, found himself in the company of three such dangerous explorers. Or at least one driving the car and one egging him on. "Eastwood," Betty Jean McGraw whispered.

Ronnie said, "Girl, I'm not takin' you there in that skirt."

Looking down at her electric blue miniskirt, Bet answered, "No, I wouldn't advise you wearin' this skirt into the Eastwood."

Both their cadences had changed. Ronnie, driving to Don Couser's selections on the radio, lit a hand-rolled cigarette and passed it.

Great, Gabe thought, *so I'll be good and paranoid when we get wherever we're going.* Nevertheless, he took a hit when it was passed his way. Jeannine, his apparent date, smiled at him slyly. Apparently it wasn't just smoke, it was a bonding ritual.

Gabe had had no idea his father had lived such wild times or run with such a fast crowd, including Gabe's future mother and fourth-grade teacher. He had a sudden inkling of how little we know anyone, especially anyone old enough to have a past.

The quartet drove south and east, toward W. W. White Road and San Antonio's deep east side. The storefronts were small businesses, such as appliance repairs and barber shops. No mall would ever intrude on this urban landscape. The houses were small and lived-in, with people on the porches and an occasional car in a yard. Ronnie drove very carefully, until many cars parked along the streets announced that they were reaching some sort of attraction.

The four got out, looking around nervously. The night seemed darker here than on the north side. Ronnie opened the trunk of the car and produced something in a brown paper bag. "For emergencies," he said, opened the top, and Gabe got a whiff of whiskey as Ronnie poured some down his throat and passed it around.

They approached a low, white wooden building. Gabe barely saw details as they passed inside. A large room crowded with chrome-and-vinyl-topped tables and matching chairs held maybe a hundred people, none of whom paid any attention to the newcomers. The room was low-ceilinged, dark, and smoky. As Gabe's eyes became accustomed to the lack of light, he saw something that would have been a revelation to a north side teenager in San Antonio in the 1960s: there were black people in San Antonio.

In fact, African-Americans comprised a majority in the large room. Weird. Gabe felt tingly and nervous. His companions' bright eyes and chatter said they shared the feeling. That was part of the allure of the Eastwood.

"Look, a booth!" Ronnie pointed and the '09 quartet dove into one of the booths lining the walls. They felt less conspicuous there and had time to look around. On the small stage at the front of the room a remarkable lady danced, her plump flesh shimmying to a different rhythm from her legs and arms. The audience hooted and clapped, and a few called her name: "Miss Wiggles!" She smiled slyly and launched into her own energetic version of "Downtown."

A waitress lounged by, hands on her hips, and said, "'Get you?"

Gabe tried to decide between scotch and soda or a white wine, but Ronnie said, "Four Cokes."

The only beverages served at the Eastwood were "set-ups," glasses of ice and expensive soft drinks, and the management ignored bottles brought in by customers. Ronnie poured bourbon and his cohorts added Coke. Gabe found the whole business so exotic, he might as well have been in a bazaar in outer Mongolia.

On the other side of the booth, Betty Jean McGraw leaned close to Ronnie and whispered in his ear. They laughed. Gabe watched out of the corner of his eye, feeling not simple jealousy, but a conviction that time was out of joint. Sight of his mother growing intimate with another man inspired such odd feelings in him that he wanted to step out of the scene. Or was he feeling the stirrings of jealousy in his father's body? Had this been the beginning of the romance that would one day produce Gabe?

Too confusing. He turned his attention to the room. Other patrons smiled and toasted at him. Twenty feet away, Gabe saw a tall, clumsy blond boy lean back and bump the broad back of the black twenty-something man behind him. The two turned and stared at each other for a moment, but apologies were exchanged instead of challenges. Then one loaned the other some matches, and they smiled. It was as if Gabe were watching a historical moment. This would have been one of the few places in the 1960s where the different races brushed shoulders and dealt with each other. Yet harmony prevailed, on the stage and in the audience.

His date recalled his thought to her by putting her hand on his leg under the table. This was quite an adventure. Only one note marred Gabe's pleasure in reliving his father's teenaged past. A busboy about his own age, a thin lad with large, black eyes slouched past the booth, caught sight of Gabe, looked him up and down, and visibly sneered. Ever after that moment, Gabe felt the young man's scornful eyes on him. What had Jerry done to this boy? Gabe wondered.

There was no one he could ask. In reality Gabe lay alone in his car in Olmos Basin. His ghostly father, apparently unable to take the sight of his injured son any longer, had fled. On the floorboard beneath Gabe, a stain of blood had appeared. Drop by drop as the night deepened, so did this small pool.

If the recently-gathered Grohman clan had worries, it was over the condition of Miz Maddie's health and her virtually destroyed home in Olmos Park. No one worried about young Gabe. They hadn't even noticed his absence from the calamitous family gathering.

Evelyn rode to her home in Terrell Hills on the leather seat of the dashing Cinco's Lexus. He gave the road only casual glances, giving Evelyn long concerned stares. Evelyn began to feel that glow of self-worth that a man's attention always gave her.

Once at her two-story home, she let him in and said, "Didn't you say something about martinis?" She pointed him toward the bar in the dining room while he expressed admiration for her white spaces and rich trim. "Thank you," Evelyn said, going up the stairs.

She threw on some clothes, threw them off again, chose some chartreuse slacks that looked good for lounging, and after much consideration a white blouse with gold filigree. Evelyn undid the top two buttons, decided that looked provocative, and rebuttoned one, but loosely enough that when she bent over the button popped out of its hole again. Oh well, if the blouse had a mind of its own, what could a girl do?

She fluffed up her reddish blonde hair, knowing she didn't have time to wash it, and hoped Cinco liked "smoky" as an aroma.

Evelyn slowly descended the stairs again, feeling her new friend's eyes on her. He didn't have to whistle like a clod; his eyes said it for him. Not that Evelyn objected to a little cloddishness. But Cinco was a smooth change from her recent past. He already had two martini glasses ready, filled to the brim, "To your salvation," he said, toasting. "Come and tell me all about it. If only I'd been there to save you."

"But you did, in a way. I thought of you. I imagined you carrying me out. Isn't that strange?"

"I hope it's not strange that I've been in your thoughts."

Somewhere while telling the story again, Evelyn remembered that she'd left her son Preston at the scene. Well, he would have gone home with Gabe. She trusted they were all right. In Evelyn's world, someone else had always taken care of the important things, like children and money. She barely realized that much of that world had come to an end.

"Here's to us!" she said. Closing her eyes, she felt the martini coursing down her shoulders and chest, and Cinco's gaze following that same path. Evelyn smiled.

"Why do you want to talk to me?" 11-year-old Preston asked. He, Evelyn Valenzuela, and the family maid Rosa were the only people who remained at the scene of the fire. At least the only *living* people.

"Why are you asking me?" Preston said. "Gabe didn't tell me anything. He didn't say where he was going."

"Concentrate, *mijito*, this is important. Does anything tell you now?"

Rosa saw goosebumps pop out on the boy's arms. She put her hands on him. She sensed what Estela had begun to suspect at the coast: of them all, only this boy could hear his late father. But was the ghost even here to whisper to him?

Preston's eyes widened. He turned toward the ruin of the house, but seemed to be looking past it. He nodded. Estela felt a *frisson* of electricity chill her entire upper body. Rosa stood dead still, her fingers tightening on the boy's frail arms.

"Preston?"

He remained silent for another moment, then turned toward Estela with haunted eyes. "Down in the basin," he said. "Hurry!"

Rosa sprang into action. "We'll take both cars. Preston, show me where. Estela, call 911."

"Yes, *abuelita*," Estela said, jumping back into her car and grabbing her cell phone. Preston followed Rosa into her old green Pontiac, thinking about the word Estela had just used. It was the second time she had said it to Rosa.

But his reverie was broken as the two cars raced along Contour Drive, then along Olmos and across the dam.

Gabe may have been on the verge of death, but he remained quite happy, sitting in his imaginary 1960s Eastwood night club. Club regular Curly Maze had just taken a turn on the guitar. It hadn't been a brilliant set, but then again, he'd been playing the guitar with his feet. And better than most could with other digits. Gabe laughed and applauded like everyone else.

He took another slug of bourbon-and-Coke, a nasty drink that grows on the user with repeated applications. His little crowd had grown rather raucous, enough so that "Tiny," the enormous African-American bouncer, sauntered by and raised an eyebrow at them. Gabe also continued to feel the angry stare of the thin, dark busboy, who watched him with fierce concentration from the corner near the kitchen.

But these distractions couldn't deter Gabe's good time. He began to feel lightheaded. Loss of blood often has that effect.

Where the Night Flowers Bloom

A haunted landscape: that was how the Olmos Basin looked at night. Flashlights didn't penetrate it. The beams turned thin and became impaled on the twisted branches of the live oaks that filled the basin, looking like a thorn barrier in the moonlight.

"Gabe is in there?" Estela asked, gazing into the sinister place.

Young Preston nodded. No one asked how he knew, but no one questioned his knowledge, either.

A thousand people could be lost in that thorny maze. Standing on the edge of the road above and trying to peer into the thicket, Estela said, "Why would he go in there?"

Preston appeared to listen for a moment, then said, "I don't think he went in on purpose."

"But how could you – ? Oh." Estela pointed her flashlight at the ground. Some skid marks looked fresh. "Oh, my God, he drove in?"

Estela went over the curb herself, sliding down the steep dirt slope into Olmos Basin. *"M'ija!"* Rosa called helplessly.

Estela fell, got to her feet again, and ran, the light from her flashlight bouncing ahead of her. Branches scratched her. One caught her ankle, but she grabbed a tree trunk and remained upright.

She had been imagining Gabe wandering through this wildscape, which sounded unsettling but not life-threatening. It was a warm night, he wouldn't die of exposure even if he spent the night. But if he had gone flying in here in a car, the situation was much more urgent.

Estela slowed down and started thinking. A car would have left evidence of its path. Sure enough, in a few minutes she found the path. Gabe's BMW had cut a swath of broken limbs and plowed-up dirt. Then she saw it, like a bizarre Halloween ornament half-hanging in a tree. A door hung open.

Estela scrambled up to it, feeling the car shift. But the tree held it. She peered in through the open passenger door and saw Gabe hanging in his seat belt. A gash on his head bled steadily.

Estela climbed into the car beside him. The tree groaned. The car slipped down with a jolt. Ignoring the danger, Estela found a handkerchief in Gabe's pocket and held it firmly against his bleeding head. She knew he shouldn't be moved, in case he had a back injury, but the wound required immediate attention. The flashlight had dropped between them, pointing at Gabe.

Estela gazed at him, remembering the last time she'd seen him, at her place in King William. He'd hesitated before he left, as if he had something to say. Looking at his helpless position, Estela realized she had something to say to him too. He looked so vulnerable, as if he'd been waiting for her. A strong protective urge turned into warmer emotion. Estela huddled close to him and kissed his cheek.

In Gabe's fevered dream, the caresses came from his date, as they danced at the Eastwood. The scene wasn't fantasy, it had happened some time in the late 1960s – but to Jerry Grohman, Gabe's father. At some point Gabe had realized this fact, but by now was just caught up in the experience.

The dance set ended, and he grinned at Jeannine. She smiled back, taking his hand as they returned to their booth. The night had grown late. Tiny, the large security guard, stopped by the table and told them to put their paper-bag-clad bottle out of sight. Even in a BYOB place, people were supposed to stop drinking at 1 o'clock. People were supposed to do lots of things, but laws had never proven much barrier to various desires. Vice finds a way.

An ambulance had arrived. The EMTs managed to get a stretcher down into the basin, and with Estela's help lowered Gabe to it. Estela's breath caught at sight of how limply his body lay. She took a last look around the car, not as if searching for evidence, but nostalgically.

Then she followed the stretcher up that slope and touched Gabe's cheek a last time before the ambulance took him away to the same hospital where his grandmother lay.

"*Abuela*," Estela said, and didn't have to say anything more. Rosa put her arm around Preston's shoulders and led him to her car. It wouldn't be the first time he had spent the night in her south side home. Preston would borrow a t-shirt and share a bed with Rosa's grandson. He had always considered it an adventure. But now he seemed reluctant to go. He looked back at Estela, who knelt on one knee at the curb, examining the skid marks.

"Is Estela coming?"

Rosa shook her head as she started the car. "She has work to do."

As Preston watched, it was easy to imagine Estela wearing deerskins rather than cut-off jeans. Her cheekbones seemed to grow more prominent as the car's headlights swept across her. A smear of blood across one cheek – Gabe's blood – highlighted the effect of a warrior princess. Preston continued to stare backwards until she was out of sight.

Estela completed her examination of the scene. Another set of skid marks, with a different tread, lay sideways across the street. Someone had run Gabe off the road, in the exact way someone had done the same thing to his father months ago, killing him.

Half a mile away, the Grohman family home lay in smoking ruins, its mistress hospitalized. Someone hated this family. But they hadn't understood one thing. Estela Valenzuela was a member of the family, too.

Someone would want to finish the job. Estela's face remained grim. When she stood up, she seemed to have grown taller. Her footsteps fell lightly on the earth.

Estela had a job to do too.

Marty Brewster, chief spokesperson for the least demanding member of the San Antonio City Council, leaned back in her desk chair and said, "I'm thinking Councilman Carter is in the Reserves. What do you think?"

Her fellow staffer Jack Jeffers stopped his habitual pacing to say, "Wouldn't that put our jobs in jeopardy? If he gets called up, doesn't the mayor or council get to appoint a replacement?"

"Well, he could serve around here. Guard duty at the airport or something like that. Strategic planning at Lackland."

The third member of Team Carter, Leonard Bracero, community relations coordinator, said, "How about if we just keep our heads down and try not to draw the wrath of Her Highness again?"

Marty leaned forward. She was thin, with an intensity apparent even when lounging. "But we need to keep the councilman's profile high. That's job security, too."

Jeffers shook his head, and went back to the speech he was writing on a legal pad. "You just keep thinking, Marty. There must be some way to profit from this paranoia about our national security."

She shrugged. "I'm a politician. It's what I do."

The three staff people sat in their councilman's office, Marty behind the big desk, Leonard in an easy chair, Jack dropping down at a table when he wasn't pacing. The three enjoyed unusual freedoms in their schedules and duties because they worked for a councilman who had never been seen in City Hall, at least as far as anyone knew. Mayor Suzanne Pierce had accused Ramon Carter of not existing, and thus far he hadn't stepped forward to refute her claim. On the other hand, Pierce hadn't been able to prove legally that Councilman Carter was a complete non-entity (and not just in the political sense.) So the council staffers clung precariously to their jobs.

The situation instilled an atmosphere of anxiety and cameraderie in the Carter suite of offices. Estela Valenzuela, the newest member of the team, had not managed to fit herself into the group, but didn't seem bothered by the fact.

Jack Jeffers looked up in surprise to find that Estela had joined them. "Estela, hi! You're creepy today. What's up, girl? Supersleuthing?"

Estela remained silent as a ghost, gliding around the room, staring at each of the others in turn. The men returned her gaze uneasily. Marty Brewster just stared back.

"Are you just trying out a new look, Estela, or is something on your mind?"

Her remark referred to Estela's all-black ensemble, with her long black hair flowing. If she let it fall forward, shielding her face, she would have disappeared in shadows.

"I'm looking for some city records. Circa 1888. Any idea where those are kept?"

Marty shrugged. "You asked me before. Answer's the same: I don't know. Check with George Whitfield, he's in charge of records."

"I did," Estela said shortly.

She dropped onto a sofa. No one asked her a follow-up question, and she didn't seem to expect one.

Madeleine Grohman came awake with a startled, strangled cry, imagining someone bending over her holding a cord.

She was right. It was her son Jock. The cord had an electrical plug on the end. "Hi, Mama. You got an extra socket back here?"

He bent beside her hospital bed.

"George, you scared me to death! What are you doing?" Maddie's voice still rasped from smoke inhalation. She was the only person on earth who used her son's real name, the name she had given him.

"Brought you a VCR, Mama. There's nothing but junk to watch on these hospital channels, right? I've been doing some taping."

"George, how thoughtful." Maddie sat up on her pillows, speaking gratefully but feeling slight dread at watching taped greetings from the rest of the family. Or maybe Jock had taped the ruins of her house to show her. That would be just like him.

But the screen showed only darkness, even after he started the tape running. Jock shushed her questions and said, "Listen, hear the birds?"

The view shook then steadied. A thin line of light appeared far off, then quickly widened and brightened. Maddie realized she was seeing sunlight over a wooded horizon.

"It's yesterday's sunrise," Jock said. "Out near Seguin. See, that's the Guadalupe over on the edge of the picture."

Colors deepened and proliferated on the screen. Maddie found herself holding her breath. "It's beautiful, George. But what - ?"

"Wait. Watch this."

The tape went blank, then an image of the sun appeared again, still low on the horizon. No, dropping lower. Jock confirmed. "Then this is yesterday's sunset."

It was beautiful. Again, Jock had found a good location. He and his mother sat contemplating the moving postcards of sunrise and sunset: more interesting than watching paint dry, but the same level of intensity.

When it ended, Maddie's eyes held tears. "That was beautiful, dear. What inspired you?"

Unplugging his equipment, Jock said matter-of-factly, "I just thought you should see everything, you know. In case these are your last few days, you should live them to the fullest."

Maddie felt both exasperated and touched. "George, this is the greatest display of considerate insensitivity I've ever seen."

Jock shrugged modestly.

"But the doctors say I'm going to be fine," Maddie added.

"Doctors don't know everything. Remember that head doctor you sent me to when I was a teenager? He said I was going to be normal."

"Oh, George, you are normal. Just a little off the beaten path."

They remained awkwardly silent. Jock cleared his throat and said, "Listen, Mama, I'll be back. I'm gonna go show the tape to Gabe."

"But why do you have to take the machine? Doesn't he have a VCR?"

"Not here at the hospital. He's right down the hall here. Since they dragged him out of Olmos Basin –" He saw his mother's goggling eyes and said, "Damn! Hadn't anybody told you that yet? Darn."

He went and pressed the call button to tell a nurse that his mother had fainted.

Standing over his mother's unconscious body, Jock made a mental note to himself – like a Post-It note on a refrigerator that no one ever looks at again, and so forgets Emily's birthday or the Boy Scout meeting: Don't spring bad news on Mama when she's already in the hospital.

Once the attendants had Maddie stabilized, Jock said he was going down the hall to see his nephew. One nurse started to say something, but the other stopped her. "That one's still unconscious, he can't do any more damage."

Jock overheard that, and felt insulted. These nurses had to give everybody a reputation. He pushed open the door of his nephew Gabe's room, calling, "Yo, Gabito! Had enough beauty sleep?"

For a moment Jock thought he'd entered the wrong room. What first caught his attention was a woman's rear end. It was clad in a short skirt of faux-lizard skin, revealing shapely white legs in high heels that matched the skirt. Jock wasn't normally one to stare at such a sight, but since she was bent over facing away from him, he didn't have much alternative. Hearing his voice, she rose quickly but not guiltily. Her blond hair swung back away from her face.

"Oh, hi, Jessica."

"I was just trying to wake him up," she said.

Jock looked at her hand resting on his nephew's stomach, and the touch of lipstick on Gabe's ear. "Maybe you could drop by my place some morning and wake me up," Jock said.

Jessica Ambrose looked at him, her expression blank as she made rapid calculations. Jock: older but attractive, also a Grohman, but much too prone to talk about animals and fish and activities involving sweat.

No, thanks: she had a husband for that. She gave Jock a thin, dismissive smile and said, "Tell him I was here, would you?"

Estela had indeed visited George Whitfield, Jr., the gentlemanly, meticulous caretaker of the city's massive store of contracts, correspondence, commemorations, and old paper. He had shown Estela the central storage, an accumulation of paper demonstrating what happens when a bureaucracy grows constipated. Nothing gets thrown away because that would require a decision.

But when Estela asked about contracts from the 1880s, Mr. Whitfield just shook his head. "No such records. We don't have anything pre-1921. They were all lost in the big flood of that year. There were boats floating all through downtown San Antonio. Paper turned to pulp. There may be a few stray bits that were saved because they weren't in the archives at the time, but we don't know what those are."

So it would have been a great coincidence if the Grohmans' contracts with the city had been among the few documents that survived. Estela didn't believe in coincidences. The 1880s contracts Gabe had found in the family condo in Port Aransas must have been the originals or copies that someone had deliberately removed from the city records.

But before 1921? Who would have had that much foresight, or plotted for so long?

An hour later, as dusk descended, Estela lurked behind City Hall, by Panchito's restaurant. Still wearing black, she blended into the dim interior of her black Honda. Everyone seemed to be working late in city government. Estela watched the rearview mirror to see who emerged, and what they did.

Soon she was rewarded. Mayor Suzanne Pierce let herself out a back door and stood on the steps, looking around for her police driver.

And Estela discovered she wasn't the only lurker. As Pierce descended the steps, a man stepped out from a downstairs doorway. A tall, thin man with black hair and a thick moustache. He and Pierce greeted each other. The mayor seemed to hesitate, then glanced around and walked on.

Estela found the encounter suspicious. But the two were separating now, and Estela was only one person. Obeying a hunch, Estela decided to play follow the leader. When the mayor's car pulled out, so did Estela.

And so missed seeing Marty Brewster leave the building a few minutes later. This time the waiting man, who was known as Diablo, not only greeted the city staffer, he casually put his arm around her waist. She leaned closer and kissed him.

"Well, it's been charming as always, my dear." Cinco took Evelyn's hand. For a moment she actually thought he was going to kiss it, but he wasn't that affected. Not quite.

They sat on the terrace of the Piatti restaurant at the Quarry, where they could not only have a drink and an appetizer, but see and be seen. Each had already spotted three people they knew among the passing shoppers.

Cinco's phone rang. He discreetly slipped it out of his pocket and answered quietly. Frowning briefly, he rolled his eyes at Evelyn, but spoke respectfully into the phone. "Yes, of course, but I'm – working."

He made a mimicking face at Evelyn, who felt flattered. He was talking to someone else but actually with her. And given the choice, Evelyn usually preferred eavesdropping to conversation anyway.

"All right," Cinco said smoothly. "You're the boss."

"Damn," he said to Evelyn after hanging up. "Deals, always deals. I hate to cut our evening short, though." He gazed soulfully into her eyes. "Perhaps . . ."

He waited for her to finish his sentence. Evelyn smiled and looked away, at the Quarry smokestacks. "Perhaps so," she said into the quiet evening air.

She smiled. He smiled.

In her city car, Mayor Pierce frowned. What had that weasel been up to? She could tell when he was with someone else while talking to her. She completely discounted his "working" excuse, since Cinco didn't work.

Well, she'd find out soon enough.

Ramos Ramos and Jaime Jones, radical artists, lovers, and recently self-declared *dueñas*, sat over breakfast one morning in their newly-rented home in King William. Ramos, the skinny Anglo, wearing painter's pants and a black t-shirt, said, "Did you see this little item in the *Express*?"

"Is that a joke?" Jaime answered. He sat in his Hawaiian shirt and flipflops reading Talk magazine, imagining being interviewed.

"Seems young Gabe Grohman ran his car into the Olmos Basin. He's in the hospital."

"Wow." Jaime leaned across his coffee and fried eggs. "Is he okay?"

"Says he'll recover, but he's still unconscious. How come Estela hasn't told us about this?"

"She hasn't been around much lately. But you know what this means?"

"She'll be heartbroken and need our support?"

"No, it means we can take a break from guarding her body. Gabe should be out of commission for a while."

"You're right," Ramos said happily. "What do you think, San Miguel?"

The two began making vacation plans, their short happy careers as guardians given a hiatus.

Which shows that even the best-laid plans. . . .

Estela followed Mayor Suzanne Pierce until Her Honor met with Cinco Dilmore at a house in Monte Vista. Estela, afraid her black Jeep would be conspicuous parked on the broad boulevard that no other parked cars perturbed, drove on by. But she went slowly enough to see Cinco throw open the front door and his arms. Pierce brushed by him with a suspicious look and a curt remark, a greeting more intimate than a kiss.

Then Estela packed in her spy duties for the night. She wanted to check on Gabe.

The hospital parking lot wasn't full. In her black outfit Estela felt invisible in the night, but would stand out inside the brightly lit hospital. Nevertheless, she went boldly inside, her stride growing longer as she thought of Gabe. She felt a sudden strong need to see him.

The heavy door to his wing swung toward her face as she approached it. Estela jumped back and went on alert. The way things had been going, she wouldn't have been surprised to be attacked here. But the person coming through the door represented an entirely different kind of threat.

Jessica Ambrose stopped at sight of Estela and smiled. "Is it Halloween already?"

Estela folded her arms. She knew very little about this woman, but had an instinctive dislike for the Alamo Heights blonde who gave her such a lady-about-to-instruct-the-maid stare. Jessica's adding a smile only made it worse.

Looking her up and down, Jessica said, "You must be the new girl."

"That would make you the old girl, then."

Jessica's eyes narrowed. "Anyway, he's – resting. And visiting hours are over."

"Oh, darn," Estela said.

She walked abruptly away, turned a corner, and waited for the sound of Jessica Ambrose's three-inch heels receding. Estela felt a renewed urgency to get to Gabe. Estela felt threats to him from everywhere, not least from the white witch who had just sauntered away.

In a closet she found the perfect disguise: a white smock and a clipboard. Using them, she walked boldly into Gabe's unit, studying the "chart" with a frown. "Where's that nurse?" she said angrily, which had the effect of making nurses flee from her vicinity.

So Estela walked into Gabe's room undetected. He did indeed seem to be asleep. The emotions Estela felt just after she'd found him in the basin flowed over her again. She wanted to protect him, to comfort him, to be with him for days at a time.

She wanted him to wake up.

As if on command, Gabe's eyes popped open. Dazed, he stared at her. Gabe saw a nurse or doctor, with a womanly figure the smock couldn't disguise. She stepped back and slipped off the smock, going into Elektra mode, or Emma Peel, in an all-black clingy outfit. Nurse to lady spy: two fantasies for the price of one. Gabe thought he must still be dreaming. But then he came out of his daze.

"Estela! Thank God. Am I alive? If I'm dead I must have lived a good life. Come here, quick."

She came closer and Gabe took her hands and turned them over wonderingly in his, then looked into her eyes. Brown shot with flecks of green, so that her eyes always seemed alert. Gabe's voice was husky, unused.

"I have to tell you quick, before something else happens. Estela, that last time I saw you, I meant to come back. I thought I should, I almost did."

"Why? Did you forget something?" Her voice mocked him gently.

"No, I realized something. That I didn't want to leave you. That I don't ever want to leave you. I love you."

His voice retained a wondering quality that made him sound more sincere than a firm declaration would have. This wasn't something he said to impress her. Not even something he had sought. Just a simple statement of discovery.

Estela smiled, very slowly then very broadly. "Isn't that convenient," she said.

Gabe looked uneasy, afraid to hope. "You mean - ?"

Estela pulled the covers away from him. She came even closer. "Because I've just realized that you need protection. Your enemies may be anyone. I can't afford to leave you alone, even for a minute."

Her soft hair fell on his cheeks, making a tent for their faces as she bent over him, a tent that enclosed only the two of them. They kissed slowly then more deeply. Neither of them thought of anything or anyone else.

And since this was a hospital room, and not the middle of the night, they had an uninterrupted two hours to themselves.

Life improves at an accelerating pace. One decade one can make a phone call from one's car, the next decade from anywhere. Cars get both faster and safer. Chefs turn spinach from a childhood terror into a crepe-surrounded delicacy.

But some things can't be improved upon. Playing catch with your child. Reading in solitude. Waking up with someone you love.

Gabe Grohman had spent what seemed like days lost in time. He regained consciousness questioning all truths but one. He loved Estela. And when he woke to find her standing in front of him, there was only one thing to do.

Estela had worried about Gabe, struggled to rescue him, schemed to save his family. It was as if he had been with her constantly, for a long time. When he told her he loved her there seemed no course but to stay with him.

And when they woke, and their first sight was each other's face, the moment was flawless.

The next moment, though, when the second thing they saw was an outraged nurse gaping at them, could have been better. The woman stared, openmouthed, then looked down at the chart she held. Obviously finding no box or imagination to record what she was seeing, she dropped the clipboard and said one stern word: "Out!"

At first Gabe had made an instinctive effort to hide Estela, but that, of course, was silly, as two bodies lay clearly outlined under the thin hospital sheet. In reply to the nurse's command, Estela stared back at her calmly and said, "You first."

The lady in the starched white uniform turned on her heel and marched out, her body stiff with outrage and with that spine-stiffened manner of turning one's back on people who are clearly having a better time than you are. She left the door ajar as a further warning. Gabe said, "Who was that? Where am I?"

"Oh, Gabe," Estela said, remembering his condition, and how much she'd neglected to tell him while busy with other revelations. "It's a hospital."

"Oh."

"And your grandmother's in a room three doors down the hall."

"You're kidding. You don't think she'll tell her, do you?"

The quiet serenity of the ward was suddenly interrupted by what sounded like a squawk, followed by a loud conversation from approximately three rooms away.

"I think there's that chance," Estela said.

Gabe grimaced. "Damn, it's hard to keep a secret in this town."

They were in trouble. They'd been sinfully indiscreet. Their lives had just grown infinitely more complicated, both practically and emotionally.

Estela and Gabe broke out giggling.

Madeleine Grohman would never do anything as undignified as burst into her grandson's room to catch him in the act. She didn't even want to envision "the act." But in spite of feeling compelled to portray indignation at the nurse's news, Maddie wasn't all that outraged. A young man's fling was an ancient tradition, particularly for a young man who had just dodged death. Frankly, Maddie was glad to hear that Gabe was recovering.

Nevertheless, she realized she'd languished here long enough. Her family, and the rest of the world, needed supervision. Seven o'clock the next morning found her dressed and already having called her son Jock to come pick her up. (He said he'd be by as soon as he finished taping the sunrise.)

A different nurse came into Maddie's room, and seeing the patient dressed and packing, said in her most cheerfully officious voice, "I'm afraid we can't leave until Doctor has checked us out."

"Doctor can check you out," Miz Maddie said calmly. "And you really ought to learn the poor man's name. As for me, I've been living in this body for 74 years, and I think I can tell when it's doing all right." She snapped her overnight case shut.

"Mrs. Grohman," the nurse said more sternly. "You still need oxygen."

"Of which I'm told there is a great quantity in the outside air." Maddie always grew more formal when angry.

The nurse, who had in fact gone into the profession because she wanted to help people, not boss them around, tried reason. "Mrs. Grohman, you inhaled a lot of smoke. You should..."

"I have an aunt, 90 years old, who's been inhaling smoke since she was 16, two packs a day, and she's doing all right. Trust me..."

"She's beaten the odds."

"So will I," Maddie said firmly. "And before you make any more effort to tell me what to do, I'd suggest you check with your financial office and ask the amount of my annual contribution to this institution."

And Maddie marched out, leaving the nurse speechless. God, it was great being rich.

It wasn't until she got downstairs, and her son Jock pulled up in his hulking SUV and said, "Where to?" that Maddie remembered that she was homeless.

Questions, Answered and Un-

Jerry Grohman found being dead deadly boring. With his power to roam anywhere he solved several mysteries and uncovered more; but he had always been a do-er, not a voyeur. He didn't like being a tourist in his own town, even one with unusual access.

He had spent a couple of nights hanging out with the ghosts of the Alamo, but the ones who remained there tended to be a garrulous, self-satisfied lot, what with hearing their heroism lauded day after day. There were always a contented two or three of them at the IMAX theater, seeing themselves portrayed. And late at night, after the shrine closed, they got even more talkative, and rowdy. Some talked more than others because they were drunk. Die drunk and you spend eternity in that condition, and apparently the liquor supply had held out to the end.

Jerry traveled other byways, but kept being drawn back to his own family. He had amends to make in so many ways. That was probably why he was still here.

After Miz Maddie's house burned the family scattered. Jerry went looking for his younger son, and found him sitting on the porch of Rosa's little house on the south side, a couple of blocks off Goliad. This house, too, had memories for Jerry. He had spent hours here, at first randomly, then on purpose.

Young Preston sat alone on the porch rail, looking lost, listening to the sounds of the night. It wasn't the south side or Rosa's house that made him feel lost. Like many children of wealthy San Antonio families, Preston thought of himself as about half Mexican, since he had been raised as much by the Spanish-speaking maids as by family members. He understood the secret code of gardeners and waitresses, and like them used Spanish to communicate secrets. "*Donde estan todos?*" he whispered.

"*Aquí,*" Jerry said softly. Preston smiled.

Yellow tape still blocked access to the house in Olmos Park, but Gabe and Estela stepped over it. Gabe moved as if in a bad dream. He kept expecting his family and friends to jump out and yell, "Surprise!"

revealing this burned-out wreck as an ugly stage set. "Was anyone hurt?"

Estela shook her head. "No one but your grandmother. But she'll be all right."

Gabe peeked through a front window and saw that part of the second floor had collapsed into the first. The walls stood burned through or smoke-blackened. The ruin looked ten years old.

Estela put her hand on Gabe's shoulder in sympathy. He reached behind himself and pulled her close.

Gabe was a lucky man. Escaped from a hospital, he stood in the ruins of his ancestral home, not knowing where any of his scattered family had taken shelter. A lawsuit hovered that promised bankruptcy and scandal. He didn't know where he was going to sleep that night. But Gabe was lucky because he was a man in love. Such creatures have too narrow a focus for tragedy to touch them deeply. Or what used to be called a one-track mind.

"This is so sad," he whispered.

Estela nodded sympathetically.

"I wanted to be here with you some day."

Startled laughter burst from her. "How long have you had that ambition?"

He pulled her around in front of him and looked into her eyes from a very short distance. "A long time, Estela. You have no idea."

"You don't know anything about me."

Her eyes danced, their green flecks seeming to move against the background of brown. Her lips quirked toward a smile, that knowing smile of hers that drove him nuts.

"I know more than you think."

"So do I, Gabito."

In truth, the two of them put together didn't know as much as they should have. But in a moment they would remember the happy fact that Gabe owned an apartment. So it would be some time before they started again to think about mysteries, genetic or otherwise.

Evelyn Grohman asked a question. This was unlike Evelyn, who seldom knew when she was ignorant of a fact, and usually didn't have enough curiosity to ask about anything. This wasn't much of a question, just small talk, really. But it would set off a momentous chain of events.

And the funny part was, Evelyn didn't really care about the answer. "So, Cinco," she said idly one pleasant afternoon, "what is it you do?"

"Do?" The charming Chester Worthington Delmore V laughed. "What does any of us do, Evelyn? What do you do? Other than this?"

They lay stretched across Evelyn's high, flouncy, canopied bed. Champagne sat on the bedside table, and their glasses were somewhere close by.

They both laughed. Evelyn persisted. "You know, for a living. How is it you have so much free time?"

"I could tell you, but then I'd have to kill you. No, seriously, my dear, I'm a consultant. I'll tell you all about it some time."

Their talk turned to more important matters. Cinco's clothes lay on a chair where he'd dropped them. In the pocket of his suit coat was the cell phone he carried everywhere. It had been a gift from his lover, Suzanne Pierce.

In her car parked less than fifty yards away, Mayor Pierce removed her headphones in disgust. She was a suspicious woman who insisted on confirming her suspicions personally.

So he was cheating on her. And with a woman who asked questions.

A situation that would have to be fixed.

Madeleine Grohman placed a phone call to her lawyer, never a pleasant experience. Javier Gustado was one of the most charming people she knew, and a witty conversationalist too. But talking to one's lawyer almost always yielded bad news. Javier gave her some quickly.

"Maddie we have answers to discovery due very soon. I'm sure I could get an extension because of your house and your hospitalization, but we . . ."

"No, don't, Javier. Just object to all the questions. What will happen then?"

"They'll ask for sanctions, or for a judge to order us to respond."

"Good. That's what I want, a hearing. Or take a deposition or something. I want to see these people. I want to meet them face to face."

"It's a law firm in Houston, Maddie. They don't have faces. There are more lawyers in Houston than cockroaches. If you step on one . . ."

"I want to know who their clients are. You can do that for me, can't you, Javier? Good."

Maddie put down the phone with the satisfaction of feeling she'd taken action. The white phone, a princess model, sat on a wicker end table on the front porch of the house in Alamo Heights. The house the Grohmans used to call "the small house," the one they had kept for years for guests and as a sort of hideout. Maddie had lived here as a newlywed 50 years ago. Now she had returned to the small house because it was her only choice. She had no servants, no one living with her, and nowhere else to go.

Sipping green tea, Maddie gazed at the houses across the street. She felt strangely light, as if the house in Olmos Park had been a burden now lifted from her. In this house she had reached her last retreat, her final fall-back position. From here there was nothing to do but fight back. She felt exhilarated by the idea.

After a moment she put down her tea, and went inside to change into battle clothes.

Estela Valenzuela walked up the lawn of her King William home smiling and wearing a white cap that said "Landman Drywall." She had found it on a hatrack in Gabe's apartment, and pulled it on over her disordered hair.

We live in an age when baseball caps have proliferated and taken on meaning. Sometimes a man's cap makes a statement, of support for a team or a lifestyle. If he wears it backward he's saying that he is so empty-headed as to allow himself to fall prey to teenage fads.

When a woman wears a cap, she's saying, "I haven't washed my hair today."

But Estela could pull it off. Even with the cap shading her face, she glowed. She had a swing to her walk. Gabe trailed in her wake, feeling like an accessory. But he couldn't stop smiling either.

Estela breezed through the front door of the old mansion, calling, "I'm home."

Gabe stayed downstairs looking at the changes in what used to be his father's house while Estela trotted up the stairs to get an overnight bag and some clothes. She passed the open door of the bedroom of her roommates, Ramos and Jaime. The "boys" were packing too, and looked up in surprise.

"What are you doing here?" Ramos asked. "We thought you'd be at the hospital. Has Gabe regained consciousness?"

But Jaime Jones, the burly artist, just stared at Estela. "Oh, my God," he said, gripping his partner's arm.

"What? Ow. What's wrong?"

"Look at her," Jaime said simply.

Now Estela started to blush, laughing at Jaime and putting out a hand as if to shush him. From downstairs, they heard Gabe call her name.

Now Ramos was staring at her too. "He brings her home at 10 o'clock in the morning. He walks her inside, doesn't just sit in the car waiting. And look at *you*; you can't stop smiling. Oh, my God," he echoed his partner. "We failed."

"Failed at what?" Estela finally frowned instead of smiling.

Jaime took her hands with great tenderness. "Girlfriend, we have to talk."

Downstairs, Gabe was studying a work of art that consisted of razor blades imbedded in a large canvas. He was wondering whether anyone would notice if he moved a couple of them, when the air itself was ripped by a woman's scream. It made gooseflesh pop out on his arms.

A moment later he was dashing up the stairs. He skidded to a halt at the sight of Estela staring, appalled, at her two roommates.

"What did you say to her?" Gabe said angrily. "Listen, this is really none of your business. . . ."

"It's not," Ramos said somberly. "But we happen to know something. When we were moving into this house we found something. . . ." He put a comforting arm around Estela.

Gabe didn't understand anything. Jaime stepped forward and said, "Gabe, they were old checks. Cancelled checks. Made out from your father to Estela's mother. And on the memo line, they each said 'child support.'"

Gabe stood frozen, doing the math. He thought of alternative explanations and one by one rejected them. All the while trying to hold at bay the horror of what he was hearing: what he and Estela had felt for each other, so strongly and fast, hadn't been love.

It had been kinship.

Estela and Gabe stood in the bedroom of the old house in King William. They stared at each other, searching for resemblance, and for whether each believed that they shared the same father.

Gabe said, "This can't be true."

As soon as he'd expressed what they were both thinking, Estela, in that delightful way of women, took offense. Hands on her hips, she said, "Are you so appalled at the idea of being related to me?"

"By blood? Yes."

Seeing the anguished look on his face, she relented. Gabe saw her become thoughtful. His heart emptied as he realized she had begun to believe it. Estela's voice sounded hollow as she said, "Haven't you wondered why I just appeared all of a sudden, just when your family needed help the most? Where do I come from?"

"I don't know, Estela. I just thought you were a miracle. Are you saying you believe this? You knew?"

"It explains so much. Why your father spent so much time at my house. What I sensed between him and my mother."

Ramos Ramos and Jaime Jones looked on sympathetically but hopelessly. Jaime nudged Ramos. "Think of something. Say something wise."

"I wish you hadn't found those damned checks."

Jaime looked offended. "It would still be true."

Exasperated, Ramos said, "Who cares what's true? True doesn't matter. It's only what people think that counts. Kids? Kids?" He clapped his hands for their attention. "It isn't true! Sorry. We were joking. Hahahahahahaha."

He trilled utterly false laughter while Gabe and Estela reached for each other, then their hands fell apart, untouched. Gabe turned slowly away and went down the stairs.

Seeing the news director strolling in her direction, television reporter Veronica Lewis picked up her phone and said, "Are you sure about this? You have actual pictures? And nobody else knows about this yet, right? All right, don't call the police yet, I'm on my way."

Overhearing this entirely made-up conversation, Roger gave her a thumbs-up. Veronica grabbed her purse and rushed out, face set with grim purpose. Where was she going to find news in the next two hours? Not regular news, either. They were in another sweeps period, when the battle for viewers became more intense, and the news lost a certain depth, making up for it in boldness. A gang fight at a school would get less coverage than a teacher having an affair with a student.

Having no other ideas, Veronica decided to attend the opening of the Graft Center. That wasn't its official name, of course. But when a place was called the Groft Center for Public Affairs, and had been built partially with city funding, it was bound to acquire a nickname.

The center had been the brainchild of former City Councilman Martin Shill: an institution that would provide a central meeting point for public and private institutions, such as city government, area schools, and arts councils. It had been built as a collaboration between the city of San Antonio and San Antonio School District, along with federal grants and private money. The design and construction had been put out for competitive bids evaluated by city staff.

In other words, the whole boondoggle had been a corruption magnet. Everyone who'd ever applied for public money had come out to try to get in on this one. The bid process had been the Olympics of wheedling and bribes.

Tonight was the grand opening, when the winners would come out to gloat. If nothing else, Veronica could get footage of local movers and shakers moving and shaking. She grabbed a cameraman and headed over.

As with many projects that had started as an excuse for moneygrabbing, the building itself was beautiful. A tall, white, columned structure on the western edge of downtown, it stood serene and untouched by the process that had built it. Veronica fit right in with the well-dressed crowd. She wore tight black pants that flared at her ankles, trimmed with embroidery, and a plain white blouse with sleeves that grew lacy and puffy at her wrists: an outfit that started out stick-figure and ended in flamboyance.

Mayor Suzanne Pierce stood near the bar. Uncharacteristically for a public figure, she held a drink. She stood straight and nodded at everyone, but an occasional flash of her eyes made Veronica think the drink was not her first. Pierce had a reputation for being tightly controlled, but there were also rumors that occasionally she let loose rather spectacularly. And Veronica remembered seeing her once with a martini and a man.

Since then she had inquired about the man: Chester Worthington Delmore V, who was known among the denizens of City Hall.

"He's a paper magnet," one had said. "He attracts contracts." Cinco was ostensibly in public relations, a title that could cover a whole clandestine life, and he was often on the "team" that won city contracts for projects such as the Graft Center. In fact, he'd been doing much better in that regard lately.

At the peak of the festivities, a tuxedo-clad Cinco arrived with Evelyn Grohman. Evelyn on his arm looked elegant and pleased, and oddly wide-eyed for someone with her background.

"And what did you have to do with building this place?" she asked.

Cinco laughed. "Inspiration," he said.

Veronica watched as he went to the bar, approaching Mayor Pierce in the process. "Get a shot of this," Veronica instinctively told her cameraman.

Cinco and Pierce obviously thought themselves alone in the crowd. Without a greeting, Pierce said something to him, her mouth curling into a sneer as she looked across the room at Evelyn. Cinco smiled. Veronica got a directional microphone aimed at him just in time to hear him say, "I have to have someone with me for appearances' sake, don't I?"

He started to turn away, so the mic began to lose his voice. "Of course," he said smoothly, "I'd rather be here wurfle wroof brrr. . . ."

Veronica and her cameraman turned toward each other wide-eyed. "What did he say?" "Did he say what I think he did?"

Veronica spoke slowly. "Did he say, 'with my wife'? Meaning the mayor?"

Scotty the cameraman nodded eagerly. Then his face fell. "But we don't have it on tape."

During the course of a long life, there will be good times and bad. The trick, Madeleine Grohman decided, was to die during one of the peaks, so it would seem as if life had turned out happy.

Well, she had missed that boat, and probably had to live much longer now, because she didn't see any more good times on the horizon.

And when she heard someone walk uninvited through her front door, she felt sure times were only getting worse.

Gabe walked for hours. He might have eaten at some tourist place along the Riveralk, or maybe not. He had no memories of his day, but dusk was approaching when he found himself back at the house in King William. Estela sat on the front porch, staring into space as if she, too, had been lost. Gabe began to smile as he walked up to her.

"It's not true."

Estela looked up at him with enormous hope. What had he learned? "How do you know?"

"Because I so want it not to be."

Estela sighed. She took his hands, noticing that he didn't shy away. "Gabe, is that what life has taught you? That if you want something badly enough you can have it?"

"Yes."

It wasn't that simple. But he had spent the day realizing how life would be from now on, and found it unendurable. He imagined her growing older, apart from him. Getting married, having children. Probably marrying someone he knew. That's how things happened in San Antonio. And he would see her once in a while, at the drug store or a movie. Would they even look into each other's eyes for a moment and imagine the life they should have had, or would they just be two people who used to know each other, who nodded and said hi and walked on past?

"No. I'm going to undo this."

"Gabe, some things are true whether you want them to be or not."

He hated to hear that she believed this. She had introduced him to miracles. Didn't she believe in them any more?

It was almost five o'clock. After Gabe left, Estela went inside and changed into her black outfit, to resume her surveillance of her own private list of suspects. Tonight, she decided, it would be Marty Brewster.

Estela moved with newfound determination. All right, she wasn't going to have love. That part of her life was over. But she would save this family.

After all, it was her own.

In the small house in Alamo Heights, Madeleine Grohman was surprised to hear her front door open. She stood in the kitchen, having just hung up the phone. Who would just walk into her house? Feeling a prickle of danger, she pushed open the swing door and made her way quietly into the small dining room.

The burly intruder almost knocked her over.

"Sorry, Mama."

"Jock! What is it?"

He set down a small suitcase. "I'd like to stay with you for a while, if it's okay, Mama. I'm not going back to the ranch for a while. And I thought –"

Jock looked uncharacteristically shy. Maddie understood. This was how he'd been as a boy, when looking for a chore to do. He wanted to be nice, but didn't want anyone to know. Maddie felt a burst of affection for him.

She put her arms around him. "You want to help?"

Jock nodded uncomfortably.

"All right, dear. How about if you supervise the reconstruction of the house?"

Jock brightened. "And maybe I'll come across some clues to who set the fire."

Maddie doubted her younger son's ability to recognize a clue if one were in striking distance, but she appreciated his enthusiasm.

Their small reunion was interrupted by a knock at the front door. "That'll be the pizza guy," Jock said. "I called Florio's."

But he was wrong. The door opened, pushed by a small hand. Eleven-year-old Preston peeked in. Behind him stood Rosa with a covered dish. "Go on in, *m'ijo*. Miz Maddie, does the oven work? I brought a pot roast."

"Goodness." Suddenly the small house seemed full. So did Maddie's heart. Her family was coming home, even after home had been destroyed. She went to close the door and glanced out on the porch.

"And you brought flowers, Jock!" she exclaimed delightedly.

"Not me."

Everyone denied the gesture. Maddie brought in the large bouquet from her doorstep. One large sunflower anchored the display, but the rest of the flowers featured orange, a bouquet of autumn glory. There was no card.

An hour later the flowers sat in the middle of the dining room table, and the family sat assembled around it, over the remains of a makeshift dinner. Maddie covered her grandson's hand. Preston smiled shyly.

"What are we going to do?" Jock asked.

"I've started making calls," Maddie began, but was interrupted by one last entrance.

Gabe walked in, looking changed. His hair had darkened from going unwashed, and he had it combed straight back. Along with his eyes, sunken from his recent injuries and fatigue, it gave him a hawk-like look. He wore a dark pinstriped suit, as if setting off on a business trip.

Maddie had never seen him with such a solemn air, even angry. But when she asked if he was all right Gabe didn't answer. He sat at the table and clasped his hands loosely in front of him.

"Someone hates us," he said without preamble. "Who? Why? This isn't just a financial scheme, not after they tried to destroy us as well."

"Maybe it wasn't the same person," Jock ventured.

Rosa opened her mouth, then changed her mind.

"Maybe we're not the only victims," Gabe said. "I've decided to meet with the heads of the five families."

Jock looked startled, Rosa apprehensive. Preston just gazed around at the adult faces, obviously with a question but not wanting to speak.

Maddie looked around the table as well, feeling she had somehow called this impromptu war council. She saw determination on every face, but found them rather a pitiful crew.

Strange how good the air smelled, how beautiful the morning. San Antonio was the beneficiary of a strangely extended fall, with cool mornings and leaves beginning to fall. Usually autumn consisted of those ten minutes between the last 90-degree day and the arrival of the first blue norther. But this year for a month or more the air remained crisp and invigorating without being threatening. Individual aromas could be picked out.

What was strange about all this beauty was that Gabe noticed. He had suffered sudden, completely unexpected losses: his father, his home, the love of his life, and soon his family business. He should have been the walking dead, oblivious to his surroundings. But somehow life still stirred in Gabe Grohman. He raised his head, took deep breaths, and gazed into the blue sky.

Ah, the heady smell of despair in the morning.

Veronica Lewis and her cameraman Scotty stood staring at each other. Had they just heard "Cinco" – Chester Worthington Delmore V – hint that he and Mayor Suzanne Pierce were secretly married? Even Veronica, whose knowledge of city government went not much deeper than knowing there were an odd number of people on city council, understood the implications. Cinco had won city contracts. Mayor Pierce had voted on those contracts. At best this would be an ethical violation of the worst kind. At worst, it might be a felony.

"How can we prove this?" Veronica asked. She looked at her tools at hand, a microphone and a videocamera, and sensed their lack of usefulness in this enterprise. Nevertheless, they were all she knew. "Let's circulate," she said with determination.

Evelyn Grohman felt splendid. She knew she looked good in her sky blue evening dress that brought out her eyes and showed just the right amount of cleavage. And she felt at home in this beautiful room, with other well-dressed people, many of whom smiled or waved at her. She remembered her friend Diablo, who had also taken her to a couple of nice places – notably that beautiful penthouse downtown – but there had never been anyone else she knew. Here she had come home to her own crowd.

Evelyn's slumming period had lasted about a week, and she would remember it fondly for the rest of her life, but it was good to be home.

Idly, waiting for her escort to return with drinks, Evelyn began counting. Two boys in college, her late husband Jerry, Diablo... She laughed as her date returned and handed her a glass of champagne. "You know, it's funny you being named Cinco."

He smiled charmingly. "Why?"

"Because you're my fifth –"

"Hello, folks," Veronica Lewis interrupted. "Tell us, what's your connection to this opening of the Groft Center?"

Cinco turned his smile on her. "Just a supporter of public-private enterprise."

He had a practiced way of saying something so bland it would never end up on the air. After a few more tries, Veronica moved on.

But her interruption had left Evelyn thinking. "Dear, why are we here? What is it you do?"

Cinco gave her a closer look. This was the second time Evelyn had asked him this question. It could grow annoying. He'd had a couple of drinks, his control slipped a little. Looking around the well-dressed, affluent throng, he smiled with satisfaction and said, "When people sell their souls to the devil, I'm the collection agency."

"Oh." Evelyn mulled this over. "And do you work for a percentage?"

Across the room, the mayor glared at the two of them.

Estela Valenzuela worked on the theory that a plot involving faked city documents might have begun with someone familiar with city government. Many people knew about the devastating flood of 1921. Many fewer knew that that flood had destroyed most city documents. Even fewer would be reminded of this fact regularly when they needed to check an old source as part of the current workday.

So Estela had talked her way into a job at City Hall, to be close to the source. And now, she devoted all her attention to the task. Quietly, after hours, she searched desks and file cabinets. She eavesdropped on phone calls. She followed people home. Questions of legality didn't deter her. Nor did sympathy or any other emotion. Estela had become all steely resolve.

Some city staffers went to the reception at the Groft Center. Estela followed one who did not, Marty Brewster. Anyone so desperate to keep her city job that she had invented a city councilman boss might be capable of other plots as well, Estela decided. In her black outfit and black Jeep Wrangler, Estela blended into the night as she followed Marty away from the office.

Tonight she was rewarded. Marty drove only a few blocks, into King William, and parked as close as she could get to La Tuna, the thriving neighborhood bar. She joined a dark man who already sat at a small outdoor table. The same dark man with thick moustache Estela had once seen waiting outside City Hall.

The location presented difficulties, but Estela managed to get close without Marty's seeing her. Estela stood with her back to the table, moving glasses at a wait station. The bar was quirky enough that Estela in her spy outfit could be taken for a waitress.

The man leaned across the table, kissed his partner resoundingly, and said, "Great news! Madeleine Grohman wants to meet for a settlement conference." A sneer was evident in his voice as he said the name.

"That is good," Marty answered. "Because we damned sure can't afford to go to trial on this."

"Of course we can." The man scowled. "We have the evidence. We have the witnesses. I want to sit there and see them all at the defense table like convicts. I want–"

"I thought we just wanted money. We have that, Diablo. Let's take a settlement and split. They might offer –"

"No!" He banged his fist down on the table. Noticing the other patrons looking, he said, "Let's get out of here."

Diablo. Estela had heard the name. Fear and elation thrilled along her nerves. She had no choice but to follow. Again, she got lucky, because the surreptitious lovers didn't retreat to a car. They walked along a narrow sidewalk of Baja King William. Estela couldn't follow too closely, but hoped they might stop some place where she could sneak closer, perhaps behind a tree.

They turned a corner and she hurried to catch up, only to find she'd lost them. Ahead was the narrow mouth of an alley. Estela slipped closer, crouching down. She heard Marty's voice.

Then a rough hand grabbed Estela's hair and dragged her around the corner. Diablo lifted her up and pushed her back over a chain link fence. The twisted spikes atop it dug into Estela's back, tearing her blouse and cutting her flesh. She gasped.

Diablo held her arm tightly and leaned down into her face with an awful smile.

"Can we help you?" he snarled.

The Ties That Bind – and Choke

The Grohman family had come to Texas from Germany, bringing Teutonic determination and the physiques of generations of stonecutters and foresters. Over the generations, they tended to marry in such a way as to produce sturdy, heavy-bearded men and lithe blonde women. Sometimes this genetic scheme went awry and produced a wispy blond man or a rugged, broad-shouldered woman. In any event, the generations remained true to their ancestors.

Gabe, though, resembled the thin, pale line of the family, and even before the current crisis he had sometimes wondered if he was made of lesser stuff than his ancestors, who had dug their fortune out of the stony Texas soil.

Looking at Edward Steves reinforced this worry. Edward's family went back even farther into San Antonio history than the Grohmans, and their family business, the manufacture of doors and windows, had begun even earlier, around 1865. Like the Grohmans, the Steveses had been not only hard workers but smart businessmen.

But Edward, with his thick brown beard and workmanlike shoulders, still looked as if he could wrest a living out of a forest or a quarry if need be. He was one of Gabe's best friends, and of course like many scions of old families in San Antonio they were cousins as well. But Gabe had always felt a little inferior around him.

They shook hands warmly as Gabe took a seat at Edward's table in the Plaza Club atop the Frost Bank building. "You look good," Gabe said.

"Thanks. You look like something the cat would leave on the doorstep."

"Camping out overnight in Olmos Basin isn't as much fun as it was when we were kids."

"I thought maybe your love life was exhausting."

"Geez, does everybody know everything? Why do we even need a newspaper in this town?" Gabe shrugged again, more angrily. "No, that was nothing. Just a little – you know. Fling."

Looking at his friend's expression, Edward doubted the explanation. But another member of the table, Bill McMurry, said, "Did we just come here to gossip?"

When Gabe had announced that he was going to meet with the heads of the five families, he meant the people who ran the oldest family-owned businesses in San Antonio – businesses that went back before the 1921 flood. The five at this table weren't exactly the heads of the families, but they were the ones Gabe knew best. His generation: Edward, Pat Frost of the banking family, and Bill McMurry, whose family's business furnishings and supplies company had prospered since 1891. The final lunch guest, Leo Escalante, descended from the original settlers of San Antonio. His family had owned hotels in the area ever since tourists began coming to San Antonio, which went back deep into the nineteenth century.

Leo grinned across the table and said, "What do you have against gossip, Bill? Makes a person wonder."

"I just thought this was a business meeting," Bill McMurry said gruffly. He had thinning curly red hair, a narrow face, and the no-nonsense manner of a 19th century clerk. A green eyeshade and garters on his sleeves would have looked perfectly appropriate on McMurry.

"I'd call it the gossip of business," Gabe said, taking his seat. He looked around the table with his penetrating, red-eyed stare. "I need to know if any of your families have been approached recently by somebody demanding money because your business somehow cheated the city out of money a long time ago."

Pat Frost said, "No one has ever accused this bank of –"

"Take it easy, Pat. I'm not saying it's true. Just a blackmail scheme."

"But those work best when based on the truth," Leo Escalante smiled. "Sorry, Gabe, we've all heard about your family's troubles. But my family's never done business with the city as far as I know. Of course, when you run hotels you tend to learn things that people would rather not have known. But that's as close as we've come to being in bed with city government – so to speak." He smiled. "No one's approached us."

Pat Frost shrugged. "Nor us. We may have had some city accounts over the years, but nothing significant. Sorry, Gabe."

The other two people at the table had remained conspicuously silent. Gabe shot a glance at his friend. "Edward?"

Edward Steves looked embarrassed, but not for himself. "Someone came to me with something like you say. Maybe a year ago. I threw him out, Gabe. Just like you should have done."

Maybe so. But the threat to the Grohman family had involved not only its money but its honor, and it hadn't been Gabe's decision, it had been his father's. Gabe looked at Bill McMurry, who shifted uncomfortably.

"My family furnished the courthouse after it was built in 1896," he said grumpily. "Some bozo came to us and said the chairs were substandard and we'd covered up the defects. Even said some county employee was killed in a freak chair collapse in about 1915. They had a newspaper clipping and everything."

"I'll bet they did," Gabe said grimly. "So did you pay?"

McMurry glared at the table, not meeting any eyes. "*I* didn't."

Gabe knew the meaning of that ambiguous answer: the family had paid off, all right, but in a way they could deny having done so. Someone took a fake order, the actual signer of the check didn't know what he was paying.... They all knew how business could be done in that furtive way.

All eyes remained on the squirming, angry McMurry.

"Tell me about these people," Gabe said.

"So what are you going to do, kill me?"

Estela's voice betrayed only idle curiosity. Even bent backward over a fence, its spikes biting into her flesh, and an angry man's hand on her throat, Elena remained in control of her voice.

"That's the idea," Diablo growled.

Marty Brewster tugged on his arm. "She hasn't heard anything. Let her –"

"Like hell."

"That's right," Estela said. "I know it all."

She grabbed Diablo's arm with both hands. He held it strongly, which she'd counted on. As if on a parallel bar, Estela swung her legs up and over, doing a neat backflip around the angry man's arm. Startled, he released her, just in time for Estela to complete the move, which landed her on the other side of the fence. But she and Diablo still stood face to face. He could grab her again.

Instead, Estela grabbed him. With her words.

"Think about this. Who has as much cause to hate the Grohman family as you do? And I have brand new news that can help us all."

She stared at him with a ferocious intensity. Diablo found himself looking into the eyes of a kindred spirit.

Gabe Grohman stared across the table at Bill McMurry, who had as good as admitted that his family had been the victims of a blackmail scheme similar to the one in which the Grohmans found themselves trapped. Gabe's voice had an uncharacteristic command as he said, "Tell me about these people."

McMurry shrugged uncomfortably. "Slimy character representing the supposed victims. Nobody any of us would know. Some out of town law firm. Dallas, I think."

He said "Dallas" the way all true San Antonians do, like an unpleasant chore that has to be endured periodically, such as a prostate exam.

"So you never went to court?"

"Of course not. That was the point. This character implied he'd drag the family name through the – Anyway, I told you, I never paid."

McMurry looked around for a waiter. His body language and careful phrasing completely contradicted his last statement. Clearly someone in his family had paid. So in two earlier attempts at blackmails of old families, the schemers had batted .500. Their success with McMurry Office Systems must have encouraged them, to the point that they'd made a much more ambitious strike at the Grohman family. This time they seemed willing not only to go to court but to run Gabe off the road if he got too close to discovering their identity.

Edward Steves watched his friend sympathetically. "What can we do to help, Gabe?"

"I think I already have all the help I need. But thanks."

He left the table and walked quickly away. Watching him depart, Edward noticed the stiffness of Gabe's back, and something in his stride that hadn't been there in a long time: an intensity, a purpose.

The last time Edward had seen him this determined had been at the age of 7, just before Gabe had run off his grandmother's roof, a bedsheet "parachute" tied around his neck.

Edward hoped this adventure turned out better than that one.

The paramedics had said there wouldn't be any permanent damage.
Edward wondered.

Madeleine Grohman sat at her dining table studying the lovely bouquet someone unknown had left on her doorstep. It was composed of autumn flowers, blossoms that seemed to defy time by blazing brightly just before the world turned cold and darker.

The bouquet was beautiful. Maddie not only admired it but studied it, like the cryptic handwriting of a coded letter. She felt sure someone had been sending her a message with this floral display. But was it luck or threat? Time to blossom, or time to die?

A soft but insistent knock preceded the opening of the front door. Estela poked her head in. She grew a big smile when she saw Miz Maddie, and entered. "Is it okay?"

"Of course, dear."

Estela gave the older woman a quick hug, then her eye was arrested by the crystal in the hutch against the wall. Dreamlike, she walked to it and lifted down one very thin-stemmed fluted glass. That particular piece had been in the family for three generations, in spite of children and flood and forgetfulness. Maddie watched Estela admire it, but didn't say anything.

"It's a good thing you brought some of the nice pieces here from the big house," Estela said.

Maddie remembered that Estela had said something similar the first time she'd come to this small house – at least the first time Maddie knew of her coming here. The girl had already seemed familiar with Maddie's life before appearing at the funeral of her son wearing a red dress.

The kitchen door opened and Rosa entered, hands covered with a dishcloth. Her face lit up when she saw the visitor. So did Estela's. "*Abuela!*" Estela exclaimed, and put her arms around the long-time family maid.

Madeleine Grohman did not speak Spanish, but she had lived in San Antonio for 70-plus years, and had inevitably acquired some vocabulary. As one aged, so did one's vocabulary: she had learned the names of old things. She knew, for example, that "*abuela*" meant grandmother. It could be simply a term of endearment, but from the way Estela hugged Rosa and spoke to her in rapid-fire, familiar Spanish, Maddie didn't think so.

"You remember Estelita, don't you?" Rosa said to her employer. "She used to follow me around sometimes when I cleaned. But that was years ago."

"Of course," Maddie said. So Estela had an older connection to the family. Maddie began to put pieces together....

But Estela sat down at the table with her. "Miz Maddie, I hear you have a settlement conference scheduled, to meet with these people who are suing the family. That's good –"

Now Maddie understood how Estela had always seemed to have such inside information. The family had no secrets from Rosa, and if she was Estela's grandmother....

The front door of the cottage opened again, this time more slowly. A heavy step fell on the hardwood floor.

Gabe entered. But a Gabe looking changed: darker, more purposeful, and with a deep sorrow, or anger. His face frightened his grandmother.

"Grandma," he began. "I've learned something about these people."

Then he saw Estela, and stopped. Such a strange look he gave her. Delight lit his eyes for just an instant, and yearning figured in his expression as well, but then those emotions shut down, fled whimpering, and Gabe stood just staring watchfully at the young woman, as if he didn't know her.

Her eyes at first on him, then shifting to Miz Maddie, Estela continued. "I think it's a good plan you have, Miz Maddie. You bring these people out of hiding. I'll do the rest."

"I have a plan myself," Gabe said.

Estela continued to speak to his grandmother, sitting and taking the older woman's hands. With enormous earnestness, she said, "I know you didn't trust me when I first appeared. You had no reason to. But please believe me, I have the family's best interest at heart."

Gabe heard this: "the family." Gabe believed at least part of what she said. Estela wanted the Grohman family's prestige and fortune to continue.

Now that she knew she was a member of the family.

Jock, Gabe's uncle, came shambling in from the back porch where he'd been getting a breath of fresh air. He went over to close the front door that Gabe had left standing open, but paused, gazing out. He lifted his face in a questioning greeting and said, "Some weird-looking guy out here staring in."

"Hello? Can we help you?"

Cinco must have been crazy. Chester Worthington Dilmore V's livelihood depended on his weird, secret relationship with the mayor of San Antonio. Why, then, did he want to antagonize Suzanne Pierce by flaunting Evelyn Grohman in her face? Seeing Evelyn secretly was one thing. Bringing her to the reception at the Groft Center, where he knew Pierce would see them together, was quite another. Just being there with both women only a few feet apart left him tingling and feeling drunk before he'd finished his first martini.

Maybe that was the point. He'd never been a cautious man, Cinco. If he had he would have gone into banking or corporate finance and probably been a CEO by now.

And deadly bored.

No: he'd set out for a life of adventure and he had one. Not the swashbuckling kind, heaving a cutlass, nor the behind-enemy-lines-give-the-password-or-die-in-agony sort, either, but one in many ways as exciting. No Afghan mullah or Asian strongman, for example, could devise more insidious tortures than Suzanne Pierce, if he made a misstep. That was part of the fun.

Although this time he may have gone too far.

As he left the reception, escorting the chattering Evelyn, he dared a glance back over his shoulder. Pierce was watching the two of them, of course, with a gaze that suited her surname. Her eyes promised exquisite varieties of pain for him when he got home.

But he knew from experience that if he said just the right things, allayed her suspicion just enough, her intended punishment might take on quite a different tone. Suzanne Pierce was a strange woman, and he was her match.

He laid his hand on the small of Evelyn Grohman's back, exactly as if he were touching fire. "Like to stop off for a brandy somewhere, my dear? I feel the need of some numbing."

"Maybe they weren't married in Bexar County," Scotty said uncertainly.

"Maybe they weren't married in Texas!" Veronica Lewis exclaimed angrily. "Maybe they weren't married on planet Earth. But we've got to start somewhere."

The two sat in a small office at the Bexar County Courthouse poring over record books of marriage licenses issued by the county. Veronica had drafted her cameraman Scotty as her research assistant. He wasn't well-suited to the role, but he was the only other person who had heard Chester Worthington Dilmore V refer to Suzanne Pierce as his wife. Veronica didn't want to let anyone else in on the secret, until she was ready to broadcast it to viewers. Preferably followed by her promotion to news anchor.

But this time she wasn't going to make any mistakes. She remembered vividly doing a flattering piece on Councilman Ramon Carter, only to get demoted and almost fired when news emerged that Carter didn't exist, or at least that no one could prove he did. This had made Veronica look somewhat less than Pulitzer material as a reporter. She still felt sure Suzanne Pierce had set her up for that fall. It wasn't going to happen again. She was going to have her facts in place, including documentary evidence, before she went public with this story.

County Clerk Gerry Rickhoff strolled in, smiling helpfully as elected officials tend to do in the presence of news people. "Finding what you need?"

"No," Veronica snapped. "Someone can't have these records expunged, can they?"

Rickhoff shook his head. "Marriages are public records. You can't hide their traces." The county clerk was justifiably proud of his record-keeping. Bexar County records go back a couple of centuries, and one of Rickhoff's priorities in office had been making those records more accessible.

"Wouldn't there have been witnesses? You can't get married in secret, can you?"

"There would be witnesses, and I would have signed the marriage license. You sure you don't want to tell me the name?" Veronica shook her head, but Rickhoff understood the object of her search must be a newsworthy person. "Personally, if I were a well-known person getting secretly married, I wouldn't do it in this county. I'd go far away, preferably to another state. Or Mexico."

"Great." Veronica realized the paper chase was hopeless. She had to find this out in another way. And quickly, before sweeps month ended.

"Of course, there would be a license somewhere," Gerry Rickhoff suggested. "A lot of people have them framed."

"Her Honor likes to frame people, not evidence against her," Veronica said under her breath. But the County Clerk was right, there would be proof somewhere. Suzanne Pierce would keep it very close. Or perhaps Cinco had it. Veronica saw burglary as her only option.

Time for Danger Girl to go into action again.

"I have a settlement conference in two days," Madeleine Grohman said.

"Good," Gabe and Estela said in unison. Then he frowned at her. "I'll be attending that," he said, as if forbidding her.

"I won't be," Estela said, but smiled. Somehow this meeting fit her plans.

At the open front door of the cottage, Jock frowned out at the dusk. "He's coming up the walk," he said.

"Probably a process server," Miz Maddie said, and went over to close the door. But she was arrested by the sight of the approaching man. A weird-looking character, Jock had called him, but Maddie thought him quite striking, with his thick dark hair, smooth cheeks, and strongly creased, olive forehead. She had thought so the first time she'd seen him, on the beach at dawn.

In his hands he carried a bouquet of flowers, a sister to the one that sat on her dining table.

"Hello," Maddie said pleasantly but uncertainly.

He came into the light but stayed on the porch. "I just wanted to make sure you're all right. I brought the flowers to the hospital, but you were gone already."

Maddie extended her hand. He took it gently. His felt strong, with roughened fingertips. "You remember me?" he asked.

"Of course. We met in Port Aransas."

He shook his head. "We exchanged names in Port Aransas. Our eyes first met long ago. And many times since."

Maddie realized it was true. He seemed familiar to her. And he spoke as if he were her conscience. Or guardian.

She surely needed both, now more than ever. "Come in," Maddie said.

When the stranger entered, Gabe stared at him, certain he'd seen him before. But not here. Perhaps not even in this life.

Madeleine Grohman invited the oddly familiar stranger into her house, remembering his name as she did so. "Mr. Groppe, isn't it?"

He nodded. Maddie waved around at Estela and Gabe and Jock. "Everyone, this is Steven Groppe."

"Stefan," he corrected her pronunciation. He smiled at the assemblage, gesturing with the bouquet he carried.

Maddie took it from him. "Beautiful," she said, not perfunctorily. The bouquet was lovely, of autumn flowers that seemed brighter than their more fragile spring counterparts.

"Yes," Stefan Groppe said, looking into her eyes. And Maddie did something she hadn't done in years, perhaps decades.

She blushed.

Gabe stepped forward and shook hands. He was studying the stranger. "Have we met?" he asked in a puzzled voice.

Groppe shook his head. "Not formally."

Gabe knew him, but couldn't place him. The man's eyes gave him the strangest feeling. He had felt those eyes on him before, but couldn't remember when. It seemed to be an occasion both recent and long ago.

Young Preston was in a bedroom doing his homework, uncharacteristically for him. The eleven-year-old had gone very quiet lately, like a child plotting something, or about to undergo a metamorphosis. If anyone had paid attention to him, they could have heard the sound of a cocoon splitting open.

Feeling a sudden unease, Preston looked up. "What is it?" he asked aloud.

No one else could have heard an answer, but the boy put down his pencil and walked slowly into the dining room. When he first saw Stefan Groppe he had no reaction. A moment later, though, he went pale.

He had heard the sound of his father exclaiming in surprise.

The ghost of Jerry Grohman had been keeping tabs on the family, but only young Preston seemed capable of hearing him. "What's wrong?" Preston said.

"Nothing," Uncle Jock said, and Gabe looked at him and nodded reassuringly. Those were the only answers Preston received.

His father had gone dead silent. Like Gabe, the ghost felt very uneasy in the presence of Stefan Groppe, but couldn't have said why.

Maddie had a completely different reaction to Mr. Groppe. She bloomed in his presence, under his attention. He only stayed a few minutes, and left with condolences on the loss of her home and a hope of seeing her in better health soon. Maddie followed him to the door, out of her family's hearing and said, "Mr. Groppe. Where do I know you from?"

He smiled. "Stefan is fine. And if you don't remember it can't be important. Maybe it will come to you, duchess."

He winked and walked quickly away, to an old pickup truck at the curb. Maddie frowned at his odd choice of nicknames for her. "Duchess"? Had she been acting royal? She vaguely remembered a Robert Browning poem, "My Last Duchess." She'd have to look it up. Maybe . . .

Then as she closed the door she mentally smacked herself in the forehead. Duchess! Coronation. The dark-eyed stranger staring at her, whom she'd never forgotten. But that had been over 50 years ago.

Feeling the past swirling around the room, engulfing her, Maddie looked at the assemblage in her house with fresh eyes. Rosa and Estela stood close together. Maddie remembered what she had just learned about them. How could Estela have been in their lives all these months without Maddie learning that she was Rosa's granddaughter?

But Rosa, semi-retired, only appeared now for ceremonial occasions and family catastrophes. Estela hadn't been at the family gathering when the house caught fire. Was this the first time Maddie had seen them together?

"Did anyone else know that Estela is Rosa's granddaughter?" she said aloud.

Preston was the one standing closest to her, and the only one who answered. "Sure," he said casually.

Maddie shook off her concerns. "Well. You were saying you had a plan?"

Gabe and Estela answered at once. They looked at each other and Estela deferred to him with an ironic nod. After all, he was the family member.

"I'll be at the settlement conference tomorrow," Gabe continued. His face had grown red. "There are some things these people don't know. I think maybe they'll listen to reason once they hear what I have to say. Such as that their clients murdered my father."

There were gasps from Jock and Maddie and Rosa. Preston and Estela seemed to take the news in stride. "If that works, fine," Estela said calmly. "But I think they may have information we don't, as well. I'm sure you'll just be meeting with the lawyers. But when they leave they'll want to meet with their clients right away. That's where I'll come in."

Estela folded her arms. She wore a cream-colored jacket over her black slacks and blouse, and looked capable of anything, from a formal reception to espionage.

"And then," she said solemnly, "I'm going to ask you for a huge sacrifice, and to trust me."

She wouldn't say any more, no matter how they pressed her. When Estela left, claiming important errands, Gabe followed her out. He had the vague idea of trailing her, finding out where she went, but when he saw how she blended into the night, her long black hair falling down over the shoulders of the jacket, he knew he had zero chance of taking her unawares.

He watched her stride down the street. Gabe *didn't* trust her. Estela had brought too many changes, too many revelations, into their lives.

But he couldn't take his eyes off her, either. He dreaded the day when he would know conclusively that he would never see her again.

An Outfit to Make a Man Question His Gender Preference

The **settlement** conference took place in the conference room of Javier Gustado's law offices, located in an old mansion just off Main in Monte Vista. Javier had chosen the location carefully: convenient to most of his clients, but not right in the middle of Alamo Heights or Olmos Park. Respectable people prefer not to be seen going into a lawyer's office. It seems a sign of inability to handle one's own affairs, or of sordid mistakes that need to be corrected.

But Javier did enough probate, real estate, and contract work that entering his suites was not an automatic admission of wrongdoing. And once inside his lavish offices, prison or poverty seemed possibilities too remote to worry about.

The wood panelling and subtle lighting did nothing to reassure Madeleine and Gabe Grohman, though, when they arrived for their settlement conference with the people who were trying to force the sale of Grohman Enterprises. Their representative had shown Maddie a letter from her late son Jerry offering to sell the business to this consortium for forty-eight million dollars, a sum that could never support the extended Grohman family in the style they demanded.

Javier Gustado met with them in his office. Javier had thick, wavy hair going gray at the temples, an easy manner, and a flexible face that could go reassuring or adamant in an instant. The family had relied on his legal expertise for years.

"But this isn't strictly a legal business here today," Javier warned his clients. "This is negotiating. Probing for weakness, and for information. Don't make any offers without running them by me first. Ready? Chin up. Smile. I don't need to teach you manners, Miz Maddie."

So they entered the conference room smiling, to see the "odious little man," as Maddie still thought of him, who had first appeared at her door with the letter. This time two lawyers accompanied him, a man and a woman so perfectly dressed and mannered that they not only resembled each other but sometimes seemed to disappear altogether. Maddie's eyes slipped out of focus when she looked at them, so that the wallpaper seemed to be talking.

After exchange of pleasantries, it was the toad-like man who began talking. He claimed his name to be Otis Feathermyer, which seemed as likely as his hairstyle, consisting of several black strands combed across the top of his shining head. "Of course we accepted your offer of a settlement conference, but really I don't see a compromise position. The President of Grohman Enterprises offered to sell us the company for a certain price, in a witnessed, signed letter. We simply intend to exercise that option."

Gabe tapped a copy of the letter with an angry finger. "My father was under a great deal of stress when he signed that letter."

Feathermyer shrugged. "Everyone has stress in their lives. If you're suggesting this as such an acute psychological condition that it would void the contract – Was your father under a psychiatrist's care?"

Gabe faltered. "Not that I know of."

"Then how can you prove this stress factor, since unfortunately your father is no longer available to testify or be examined?"

Gabe stood up angrily. "And you know something about that, don't you? Was it you who ran him off the road, or one of your partners?!"

Gabe's outburst was so sudden and strong that the opposing lawyers seemed to flicker in and out of existence. If crimes were going to be charged, the civil lawyers didn't want to be in the room.

The odious man stood as well, beginning to put papers into his briefcase. "I didn't come here to be accused."

Madeleine Grohman remained seated calmly, and her voice was calm as well. "Mr. Feathermyer, who <u>are</u> your partners? Whom do you represent in this business?"

"That's not significant," he muttered.

"Perhaps you'll find this significant." Suddenly Miz Maddie was holding in her hand a twisted shape, hard as metal or perhaps very old rock, like a meteorite.

She laid it on the table and Feathermyer took it, staring at it in fascination. "What is it?"

"Your true partners will know," Maddie said. "Take it if you like. We have others. You know its purpose."

Feathermyer kept the object and walked out with his lawyers. Javier looked at his Rolex. "Four minutes. Not a record, but I do usually get to finish my coffee before the meeting ends." He smiled pleasantly at his clients. "I guess it's going to be war. And what do you mean giving away evidence, Maddie? What was that thing?"

"Nothing at all," Maddie said.

Down the street from the office, Estela Valenzuela stood behind her Jeep Wrangler, parked facing the office building. She wore black slacks and a long-sleeved maroon top. Black Adidas completed the outfit.

Ramos Ramos and Jaime Jones were with her, dressed more conventionally. That is, dressed in their usual artists' garbs of painter's pants and Hawaiian shirts. Ramos sat on the curb, Jaime on the back of Estela's car, staring at her. Ramos studied Estela's outfit, the way she lifted her leg to the car and stretched, as if preparing for ballet class.

"Listen, Estela, I have to ask. Were you bitten by a radioactive spider lately? Because you've gone different, and I don't think it's just a fashion look. I mean this whole kitten-with-a-whip thing, while I understand some men find it attractive – Look at Jaime, you're about to turn him hetero. . . ."

"Only bi-, I promise," Jaime answered with an air kiss for reassurance.

"But it seems something else is going on here," Ramos concluded.

"I've found my purpose," Estela said. "What I was born to do."

"And that's always great when it happens, although it does tend to ruin a person as a conversationalist."

"I've already explained," Estela said patiently, keeping her eyes on the law office. "I need your help to follow these people because (a) they might split up, or (b) they may be meeting someone who already knows me. So you – Look, here they are already. Damn, that was a short meeting. Now you two know what to do."

The boys went to their 1978 Suzuki, arguing about which of them had the keys, while Estela started her Jeep and eased out. Sure enough, the lawyers and the odious little man went separate directions. Estela chose the lawyers. In her rearview mirror, Estela saw Jaime and Ramos make the turn after the other man. She hoped they managed to follow him to something important, and, as an afterthought, that the boys didn't get into any trouble.

She also hoped Miz Maddie had remembered to hand over the twisted little object. It had no meaning at all, only a purpose. It was an object that must be passed on, it couldn't be phoned or faxed. It was intended to make necessary a face-to-face meeting between these people and their real clients.

In the car ahead, the lawyers talked on a cell phone. "Damn!" Estela said. They were probably talking to their client now, rather than driving to a personal meeting.

She had picked the wrong car.

"Way leads on to way," as Robert Frost wrote, and the turnings of life's path are so slight yet constant that occasionally we find ourselves doing things that a week earlier would have seemed bizarre. So on the same beautiful, mild day in November, the air pungent with the smell of dead leaves, Veronica Lewis committed video burglary, and Ramos Ramos and Jaime Jones voluntarily faced a man with a gun. Life gets weird, but what else is there?

Veronica had begun as good reporters do, by checking a source. A low-level TV reporter has zero budget for paying informants, so Veronica had to be creative. Sherlock Holmes had his Baker Street Irregulars. Veronica had a similar helper, a neighborhood boy she'd asked to keep an eye on Mayor Suzanne Pierce's house. Since the neighborhood was Monte Vista, and the boy attended San Antonio Academy, his allowance was probably bigger than Veronica's salary. She'd bribed him by letting him into a couple of her live shots and with a backstage tour of the station. The boy had seemed to throw himself into the assignment.

She met 13-year-old Emory in the alley behind Pierce's home. Once in a while they'd peek through knotholes in the pine fence, which was how the boy maintained his surveillance.

"There's this blond guy who's there sometimes," he reported. "Kind of fussy-looking. Little moustache. Sometimes they fight. Sometimes they –"

The boy moved his eyes expressively. So he'd gotten some visual perks out of his surveillance assignment. This, rather than any reward Veronica could give, explained why the 13-year-old stuck to his task so conscientiously.

"Sometimes I've made video," Emory said, face reddening. Together, standing in the alley, he and Veronica reviewed some of the footage on the small screen of his state-of-the-art digital camera. The scenes all appeared framed by the knothole through which they'd been filmed, a constant reminder of the voyeuristic nature of their viewing.

Sometimes the boy fast-forwarded, sometimes he slowed, and a couple of times he even backed up, over Veronica's protests. At the same moment she realized that their heads were bowed close together over the small screen, her hair brushing Emory's neck, and that he was breathing heavily. Veronica stepped away from him, lest she be a party to the boy exploding.

He had an amazing amount of footage, all of it of either the mayor alone or with the man called Cinco. One scene showed the mayor running to the phone obviously from the shower, and mouthing "Hello" over and over again. Veronica speculated that Emory had produced that effect with a cell phone.

Otherwise, the fast-forwarding produced the effect of a love affair evolving through all its changes in a matter of moments, making the whole course of human courtship seem satirical. They watched sly glances, a kiss on the hand, lovemaking, arguments, making up, the angry slamming down of a phone.

Through it all, Suzanne Pierce began to look more and more angry and worried. Veronica remembered what Estela Valenzuela had told her months ago, that Mayor Pierce's love life and financial life were the same. Pierce had been a partner at a large, prestigious law firm and given up that salary for the $20 a week the job of mayor paid. Yet she maintained her home in Monte Vista and elegant lifestyle, all without a husband. Somehow this Cinco was the answer to how that was done. Some of their arguments obviously involved money.

"They're here," Emory suddenly whispered.

Both looked over the fence. There in person appeared the stars of their tape, Suzanne Pierce and Chester Worthington Dilmore V. Pierce was red-faced and screaming. Reflexively, Veronica began taping.

The argument quickly escalated, until Cinco made a caustic remark and laughed. This drove Pierce to a frenzy. She lunged toward a desk in the corner of her den, pulled out a drawer and grabbed a document taped underneath it. She held it up, and Veronica managed to zoom in on it. The next moment, Pierce had torn it into tiny fragments.

Cinco just laughed again. He opened the patio doors and stepped out, making a remark the excellent microphone on Veronica's camera picked up: "Tearing up a marriage license isn't the same as a divorce. There are other copies."

"Ai!" Veronica squealed. She ran back her tape, fiddled with the camera, and managed to freeze the frame where Pierce had held up the document. Emory helped her focus it. They could read the largest letters of print, notably the place where the license had been issued: Cameron County, Texas.

"Got you!" Veronica shouted, then screamed again as gunfire sounded, and a bullet zinged into the fence just above her head.

"Why are we doing this again?" Ramos Ramos asked, as he and his partner Jaime followed the odious little man from the settlement conference with the Grohmans.

"For Estela."

"There's got to be a better reason than that."

"Are you kidding? Did you see her in that black outfit? She's dead serious, man."

"I know. And I'm afraid that's how we're going to end up."

The stranger led them deep into a mysterious region: the south side of San Antonio. After both boys felt thoroughly lost, the bald stranger parked in the parking lot of an abandoned restaurant, next to another car, and went around behind the building.

Ramos shrugged, and he and Jaime followed. Peeking around the corner, they saw their quarry hand over a small, twisted object to a large, angry man with a thick black moustache. "What the hell is this?" he said.

He pushed aside his coat, revealing a revolver the size of Denver in his belt. Ramos Ramos gave an involuntary squeak and stepped backward onto his partner's foot.

In the next moment they found themselves cornered by the odious man and his partner, Diablo, who now had the gun in his hand.

Ramos said, "We're um, um, um –"

"Collectors!" Jaime shouted.

"That's right, collectors. We couldn't help noticing the artifact your friend there was carrying. I think you'll be amazed by its significance."

"Well?" Diablo growled, raising the gun.

Ramos turned to his partner. "Go ahead, tell him."

A world away, Estela Valenzuela appeared at the small house in Alamo Heights. Maddie and Gabe were there, along with Uncle Jock. "Good, you're all here," Estela said.

"What did you find out, dear?" Maddie asked hopefully. "Do you know who's behind this?"

"Yes. I've suspected all along. But more important than that, I know how to get out of this. The only way."

She looked around at their anxious faces, especially Gabe's. He stared at her suspiciously but also with a longing that had no concern at all for the fate of the family business. Estela said, "You must sell Grohman Enterprises. To me."

Madeleine Grohman stared out the front windows of the small house in Alamo Heights. The block appeared to be a frenzy of activity, but it was only the wind, rearranging fallen leaves and making the trees toss their hair in a madcap fashion. "I wonder if he's coming back," she said.

"Who?" asked Jock.

Preston was in school, Rosa back in retirement, and everyone else out having adventures, or so it seemed to Maddie. Jock spent most of his days supervising or interfering with the reconstruction of the house in Olmos Park, but he also seemed to hang around his mother a lot. He gave the appearance of a big dog, anxious to please but unable to comprehend his owner's anxiety.

"No one," Maddie said. "Never mind."

"Mom." He took her hands. Such a handsome boy, and eager to please. Jock had always been the most affectionate of her children, but undirected. This was one of many reasons he had voluntarily exiled himself to the family ranch for most of his adult life. "You need me now. What can I do to help?"

"You can start by not giving your nephew any more concussions."

Jock stepped back and stared. "You knew that was me?"

"Oh, darling, it had your fingerprints all over it. Gabe walking out of the office with Jerry's diary, someone tackling him, you just happening to be standing over him when he came to. It reminded me of your days playing linebacker for Alamo Heights."

Jock looked hangdog. "I didn't mean to. I didn't know it was Gabe, I just saw somebody taking something from the office...."

She touched his cheek affectionately. "I know, son. Don't worry, I think even Gabe's forgotten about it." Indeed, so many events had intervened that no one had given any more thought to the attack on Gabe early in the summer. Except Maddie.

"Just one thing, Jock. What happened to the diary?"

"I put it back in Jerry's desk, where it belonged."

Maddie fought not to roll her eyes. She said gently, "Since he was killed, and he kept a journal, isn't it possible we should read it for clues?"

Jock stared. "You think?"

Jaime Jones thought furiously, an activity to which he was not accustomed. As an artist, he had always been more concerned with getting in touch with his emotions. Puzzles and quick explanations were not his strong suit.

However, nothing so focuses the mind as an angry man with a gun standing at one's shoulder. Jaime looked at the heavy, twisted shape his partner Ramos had just asked him to identify.

"This is obviously, um –"

"Yes, you're absolutely right," Ramos said helpfully. Diablo and the odious little man who wanted to buy Grohman Enterprises scowled at both of them.

Grohman Enterprises! Jaime had an inspiration: ". . . a very old piece of stone," he finished.

"What?" the other two said angrily.

"Where did you get this?" Jaime asked them. "Look at this, I think this is a fault line. Very old. If anything was built with this stone, it's a dangerous structure. Did anyone sell this to anyone?"

Diablo and Feathermyer looked at each other with their own growing inspiration. "Yes, I think so," Diablo growled. "What does it prove?"

"We need to get this back to the lab. Dr. Ramos, do you have an evidence bag?"

"In the car, Dr. Jones."

Jaime held out his hands, the object cupped in it. He and Ramos took two careful steps, began to breathe more easily – and a heavy hand fell on his shoulder.

"We'll help you carry it," Diablo growled.

Madeleine Grohman and Estela Valenzuela sat in a little breakfast nook behind the kitchen of the small house. It was a pleasant room, lit and warmed by western light that bounced off the white walls. A wallpaper border depicted fruits and vegetables that seemed to grow in the light.

Estela said, "You sell Grohman Enterprises to me. I take out a huge loan, collateralized by the company's assets and receivables, to pay you for it. Then if they still want it, they'll find a company burdened by debt and no longer valuable. Maybe they'll drop their claim. Maybe they'll take the company but you'll have been well paid for it. It's the only way out. Have you talked to your lawyer?"

Maddie didn't answer. She studied the young woman's face. "Why didn't I recognize you, Estela? I do now. Rosa's granddaughter. I remember you toddling after her years ago. I would have remembered you if I'd given it enough thought. I've seen so many faces in my life. Where did you disappear to for so long?"

Estela seemed all business lately, desperate plans and dangerous assignments. For a moment she looked impatient at being thrown off her course. Then her face softened. "Do you remember my mother?"

"Of course. She became an artist."

Estela nodded. "Luz," she said, with an obvious mix of emotions. Her mother had explained Milagro Lane to Estela, an imaginary street of inspiration. Lately Estela had felt inspired, but not artistically. She felt as if she walked down a dark alley off Milagro Lane.

Estela shrugged off reminiscence. "She took me away for a while. Mom has conflicted feelings about the old hometown. Don't ask me why." Although Estela had a better idea now. If Jerry Grohman had been Estela's father, the relationship between him and her mother was obvious. And Luz had always fled emotional ties. She wouldn't be tied down by anything, not even a daughter's needs.

Miz Maddie laid a tender hand on Estela's. "It sounds like a good plan, dear. I'll ask Gabe . . ."

"Ask me what?"

Both women looked up, startled. Gabe stood in the doorway from the dining room. He looked taller than in the past. His eyes sought Estela's, who looked back at him without flinching. They didn't nod or speak to each other. Only their eyes held for a moment.

"Look who I found outside," Gabe added, ushering a guest forward from the front room. Stefan Groppe appeared, looking apologetic. But Maddie smiled at him, obviously pleased.

"Good morning," Mr. Groppe said, the few syllables carrying heavy freight of emotion. "I am sorry to disturb you. I wouldn't intrude except I think – no, I'm certain – you could use my help."

After a bullet whizzed over Veronica Lewis's head as she crouched in the alley behind Mayor Suzanne Pierce's house, Veronica sent her fellow spy Emory home. Veronica could get killed in the pursuit of news – in fact the idea held a certain glamour – but putting a 13-year-old boy at risk was another matter.

She practically had to push the boy toward his home. So far Emory's surveillance of the mayor's house had rewarded him with both sex and violence: better than any movie he had ever seen. Veronica escorted him most of the way home before returning to her post, only to find the debonair Cinco gone. Through the knothole in the alley fence she saw Suzanne Pierce storming around her den, obviously cursing a blue streak, then finding her car keys.

Too late, Veronica realized the drama was about to go on the road. She rushed back to her car, but by the time she drove around the block Pierce's car had disappeared, leaving only a smell of burnt rubber.

But Veronica had some good footage already, including a closeup of the mayor's marriage certificate. Veronica understood enough about city politics to know that if Pierce had voted on contracts awarded to her secret husband's companies, she had committed serious ethical violations, if not actual felonies.

Feeling both elated and oddly uneasy, Veronica hurried back to the station to study her footage and make phone calls.

And to wonder idly if the mayor had taken her gun with her in her pursuit of Cinco.

"Darling, there's been a sort of – development."

Evelyn Grohman looked at Cinco – Chester Worthington Dilmore V – with slight puzzlement: the way she responded to so many of life's events.

Cinco gazed at Evelyn fondly. God, he felt comfortable here, in this lovely Terrell Hills house, with this lovely, unquestioning woman.

Her guileless face offered the comfort of not having to worry whether she was plotting against him. He felt he'd come home.

He wanted to preserve this at all costs. "Listen, there's this crazy woman. . . ."

Cinco didn't have to say more, because there was a pounding on the front door, then it crashed open, and the crazy woman stood glaring at them. Suzanne Pierce looked disheveled and distraught, tendrils of blonde hair falling down across her red face. "There you are!" she cried, glaring at Evelyn.

It was a situation awkward to the point of danger. Nonetheless, Cinco's well-bred manners did not fail him. "Evelyn, this is Mayor Pierce. I'm afraid the cares of her office –"

"Mayor!" Evelyn cried delightedly. "This is an honor. I didn't get to meet you the other night at the reception. I wanted to tell you how much I admired your campaign, standing up to the male establishment the way you did. I only wish I could have voted for you, but I was a resident of King William at the time –"

"King William is part of San Antonio," Pierce said, staring at this creature.

"Really. Now you see, that's the kind of voter education you should have done *before* the election."

Pierce shifted her hate-filled gaze to her lover. "The depths of your taste never cease to amaze me."

Cinco shrugged modestly. Evelyn continued, "Much as I'd like to go on talking politics, Cinco and I have plans, and I just have to wonder what you're doing here."

Evelyn's use of the nickname seemed to enrage Pierce all over again. "Because he's my husband!" she screamed into Evelyn's face.

Then she shook her head at herself in self-admonishment. Turning to Cinco, she said, "Damn. Now we have to kill her."

After his initial declaration that he had come to help the Grohman family, Stefan Groppe grew reluctant to talk, as if he had overstepped his place. He chatted pleasantly, offered advice, and seemed to know all about their predicament. When he talked Maddie nodded along, as if he offered wisdom she had never heard.

Maddie watched him, lost in the past, or in a present unlike the one in which she lived.

Gabe watched him too, then suddenly began staring. Then he went hastily outside, muttering that he needed air.

When Mr. Groppe finally departed, with a touch of Maddie's hand, he found Gabe in a dark corner of the porch. "I remember you," Gabe said, in a voice so pointedly neutral it was obviously the product of strict control over emotions.

"I don't see how you could, son. Except from the beach this –"

"No." It was complicated. Now Gabe understood why he'd been given glimpses of his father's teenage past when Gabe had been lying comatose in Olmos Basin. There had been clues to the present crisis in that past. One had been this man, who Gabe had noticed staring at him – that is, at his father. "Did you ever work at Playland Park?"

"How could you possibly know that?"

Because Gabe had seen him there, in his fevered dream, his hallucination that contained glimpses of truth. But he didn't understand nearly enough. "So you caught a glimpse of my grandmother years ago, and you've watched us ever since – ?"

"It was more than a glimpse, son. It was an exchange, a promise. Maybe I made too much of it in my mind, but –" He shrugged. "It didn't matter. You can't understand how it was. In your life anything is possible. Fifty years ago, a woman from her background, and a man like me – it was unthinkable."

Gabe thought of Estela, and wondered how much things had changed. "I'm not the only one who lives in this brave new world. You're still here. Why not – ?"

Stefan Groppe shook his head sadly. "Now it's become impossible again. I want to help because I feel responsible. This monster who's pursuing your family's ruin: I created him."

Suddenly Gabe remembered another pair of eyes glaring at him from out of the past.

Stefan Groppe explained his life to Gabe. The small front porch, darkness acting as curtains, felt like a confessional. The old man twisted his large hands together as he spoke.

"It wasn't as if I obsessed over Maddie. I never forgot her, but I went on with my life. But then I'd see her picture in the paper, I'd see her somewhere – this is a small town, you know – and I'd remember

214

again. Sometimes our eyes would meet and I'd think she remembered me, too."

He laughed hoarsely. "This didn't break up my marriage. It'd be ridiculous to say that. But it wasn't a good marriage, and let's say I didn't work at it as I should have. It ended. And I had a son. Somehow over the years he learned about my . . . interest in your family."

Gabe remembered a young man with dark, dark eyes glaring at him when he'd inhabited his father's young body, 30 years ago. "Did he work as a busboy at the Eastwood Country Club?"

Groppe stared. "How do you know these things?"

Gabe held his secret. "And so he began to hate us. My father in particular?"

Groppe nodded. "Somehow he developed the idea that Maddie had stolen his father, and that her son had the life he should have had. Even that Jerry had stolen his place. You can't imagine the resentment."

Gabe had made the inevitable leap of imagination. "And so he killed him."

Stefan Groppe hung his head. "I hope to God not."

Gabe stood lost in thought, and finally asked, "What's your son's name?"

With a hoarse laugh, Groppe said, "That's another silly thing. We're not even Hispanic. We're Czech. But he calls himself Diablo."

When Estela left the house, she found Gabe still in the front yard, pacing then stopping to stare into the night. He seemed lost, and she understood the feeling. They had lost each other.

Gabe turned and looked at her. He suffered his usual moment of joyful recognition followed by sharply hurtful memory. Since he had been told that Estela was his sister, he didn't know how to feel about her. He couldn't still love her, but no feeling of kinship had replaced that lost emotion.

So he had come to mistrust her, everything about her, why she had appeared in their lives. His memories were mangled.

But his body remembered. His eyes, his hands. They reached for her and she responded. "Goodbye," he said, and inclined his head to give her a sophisticated, "Tonight Show"-style goodnight brush of the lips. But their lips refused to brush. They caught. They held.

Time passed. Or maybe it didn't, they couldn't tell. They were both breathless when they drew apart.

Estela tried to make light of the moment. "We've got to stop that now, I guess."

"Then one of us needs to go far, far away," Gabe answered. "I think it will be me."

Estela just smiled and walked away. She had people to meet and plans to lay. But before stepping into her car she turned and saw Gabe still watching her. Estela thought he was right.

One of them had to go.

Evelyn Grohman turned to the love of her life, her soulmate, Chester Worthington Dilmore V, and slapped his face as hard as she could. "You're married!? No, don't touch me. Ick! Get your nasty eyes off me, too."

Mayor Suzanne Pierce watched, bemused. Having just blurted out her deepest secret, she'd then realized she could never allow Evelyn to reveal it. But Evelyn seemed concerned only about the romantic implications of the news, not its political consequences.

"Go away! Get out, both of you!" Evelyn pushed his chest, and Cinco stumbled backward into his other lover, who shoved him roughly away. Putting out a warning finger to Evelyn, she said, "If you tell anyone about this . . ."

"You think I'd want anyone to know I was involved with a married man? I feel dirty, I need a bubble bath."

Pierce found it hard to believe this woman didn't understand the blackmail potential of a marriage between the mayor of San Antonio and one of the city's best contract-grabbers. But when it came to displays of ignorance, no one was more convincing than Evelyn.

So Pierce let herself be ejected from the house. Evelyn slammed the door and walked away wiping off her hands, angry and unhappy and completely unaware that she had just saved her own life.

Everything was going according to Estela's plans, except the way she felt. For years she had ruled her emotions instead of the other way around, but now her control had slipped. One of several emotions that kept overcoming her was a deep curiosity.

So on a sunny Saturday afternoon, driving around and switching stations on the radio, she became caught by Michael Black's legal advice show on KTSA.

"Welcome back to Legal Line, where the city's best attorneys try to answer your legal questions. My guest today is Sue Hall, board-certified family law attorney, which means issues of divorce and adoption and child custody. If you have questions…"

Impulsively, Estela pushed buttons on her cell phone.

In the studio, Michael Black and Sue Hall sat on opposite sides of a counter, headphones on and watching a screen where the producer typed the names of callers and short versions of their questions. Slowly the letters formed "ESTELA: Can an illegitimate child inherit?"

Sue seemed oddly struck by the question. Covering her microphone, she said, "I'd like to take that one off the air, Michael."

So at the commercial break she picked up the phone. "Hello, this is Sue Hall. Is this by any chance Estela Valenzuela?"

Estela pulled her car to the side of the road. She must have become more famous than she realized. "Yes. I think I need to hire you for some legal work. I even think I can pay you a retainer."

In the studio, Sue smiled. "Well, it's always nice to be paid. But you don't have to hire me, Estela. I've been your lawyer for a long time."

A Falling Out Among Thieves?

A **bright day** makes a ghost feel especially wispy. In the darkness he can pretend to have substance, night filling and extending his make-believe body. Sunlight pierces that illusion.

So Jerry Grohman stood under a pecan tree on a bright Saturday afternoon, watching his 11-year-old son play catch with Jerry's brother Jock, and felt himself fading away.

Preston had changed in the last few months, from a sullen, withdrawn child into a thoughtful, observant one. And he had family support. Earlier his brother Gabe had come by to help him with his homework (until the 6th-grade math assignment passed Gabe's abilities). Preston and his grandmother had baked two pecan pies, from a crop in their front yard. Even Evelyn, Preston's mother, had called to say she'd be picking him up later and bringing him home.

Preston's network went further, too. A child's conscience is a shifting, formless apparition. It works best when assisted. In a small community such as Alamo Heights, there was always an army of observers willing, even eager, to report a child's behavior. Even deeds teenagers thought had been performed in private soon had wide circulation. This sense of observation assisted a child's decisions on how to behave. It takes a village to intimidate a child, and Alamo Heights was very much a village in that sense.

When Jock took a break and went inside, Preston turned to his father. He tossed the football toward him, and saw it pass through ghostly hands. "Why haven't you just told them what happened to you?" Preston whispered.

Jerry answered deliberately. "You're the only one who can hear me, son. Besides, to tell you the truth, I don't remember very well any more."

Preston looked around at the bright day, which he could see through his father's form. His father – a frequent presence, a reminder of what Preston had lost. "Why do people have to die?" he asked bitterly.

It was a very big question. A month ago it would have been too big for Jerry Grohman. He had spent months after his death railing against his fate and mourning his own death. Now he could understand, though. He, too, looked around at the day, fall but springlike, both cloudy and sunny, a breeze blowing smells of death and renewal. If people lived forever, would they appreciate anything as Jerry appreciated this day? He had become so much closer to his younger son, too. He understood Preston, appreciated him, and loved him as he never had in life. Why should anything have to die?

"Because that makes everything precious," the ghost said.

Jerry put his arms around his son. Preston couldn't feel the embrace, but he could feel the love. When his uncle returned he found Preston with a tear in his eye, but whistling a happy Christmas carol.

In Javier Gustado's office, Madeleine Grohman picked up a pen. Her attorney put his hand on hers, stopping her. "Maddie, let me repeat. This is very dangerous. There aren't enough safeguards in place. Once you sign the business over to Estela, there'll be no going back."

"I understand."

Curiously, Javier asked, "Why do you trust her?"

Maddie considered the question, thinking back over the mysterious arrival of the young woman who had appeared at her son's funeral wearing a red dress. It was odd how strongly a part of the Grohman family Estela had become in only a few months. As if by design, a cynic might have said.

But Maddie didn't think that. "I don't know," she answered. "I only know I do."

And she signed her name to the contract of sale.

Estela walked up the sidewalk to her house, unlocked the door, and went in. A baseball bat came at her head and a heavy walking stick toward her knees. She had nowhere to duck or run.

At the last moment the objects stopped short of her face and torso. Her roommates Jaime Jones and Ramos Ramos called her name and embraced her. "You boys have gotten more affectionate," she said wryly. "And I haven't seen you for days. What happened?"

Quickly they described their frightening experience after following a stranger on her instructions. "How'd you get away?" she asked.

The artists smirked at each other. "We told him our laboratory was upstairs from the Bonham Exchange. Of course we had to pass through the bar and the dance floor to get to the stairs. It was a fun crowd. Somehow we squeaked through and the big guy with the moustache didn't."

"Rough trade but good-looking," Ramos added. "Some people like that kind."

"And we're taking no more assignments from you," Jaime added.

"That's okay, you've told me what I needed. I thought Diablo was behind the lawsuit as well as the blackmail. Thanks, boys."

There was a knock on the door. Fearlessly, Estela opened it. Her roommates gasped and scrambled for their weapons.

Diablo stood on the doorstep.

He glared at the two artists. "So you're with her. I might have known it."

"Meet my bodyguards," Estela said casually. She led the mean-eyed newcomer into the under-furnished old mansion, to the nearly empty dining room. Turning, her eyes glittered. "I've got it," she said. "The papers are being signed today. Grohman Enterprises will be mine."

Diablo's eyes glowed with satisfaction as well. "Now we just need to figure out how to cheat the family of the sale price."

"It won't matter," Estela said. "In a few days I'll have so wrecked the company that when they get it back it'll be ruined. Bad stock trades, horrible contractual obligations. They'll never climb out again."

Diablo said, "Excellent work, *la Estrella*. But we must also –"

Estela's tone suddenly grew hard. "What do you mean 'we'? If you want in on this, tell me how it worked. I may have to defend all that old city contract business. How did you fake that?"

She lowered her voice. "And tell me how you killed Jerry Grohman."

A few minutes later Diablo returned to his car and drove away. From the passenger seat, Marty Brewster said, "How'd it go?"

"Going okay," Diablo replied slowly. "Grohman Enterprises is in play. The family's poised on the brink of destruction."

"And Ms. Valenzuela? Somehow I suspect her intentions."

Diablo grinned. "Have I ever trusted anyone? No, she has to go. Luckily, that's exactly the kind of problem I've handled so successfully before."

Who Is Estela Valenzuela?

The Bexar County Courthouse is more than 100 years old, and has heard many, many strange, twisted, sometimes deadly stories. It takes a genuinely curious case to rouse interest inside the old building. But on a sunny, cool afternoon in December a few court observers had gathered in Judge Michael Peden's third floor courtroom.

When one of the city's best-known family lawyers obtains a special setting for something as ordinarily simple as a motion to unseal a record, court personnel figured something must be up.

Estela Valenzuela stood by one of the counsel tables, looking uncharacteristically nervous. Her attorney Sue Hall put a hand on her shoulder and said, "Are you sure you want this?"

Estela could only nod.

Sue had come poorly equipped by lawyer standards, with only a small briefcase holding one thin file. No boxes of evidence, no video equipment. On the other hand, her efficient office staff, Karen Ruff, Rose Broll, and Brenda Ybarra, sat watchfully on the front row of the courtroom, a very unusual event.

Judge Peden entered from a door behind the bench and took his seat. An informal man who nevertheless took his work seriously, Judge Peden had even put on his robe for this occasion. "What's up?" he said, by way of announcing the case.

Pushing her client down into a seat, Sue Hall said, "Your Honor, we're here today asking the court to unseal a record that was ordered sealed some time ago. I was the attorney who represented the infant when the case was decided, about twenty years ago."

"When you were a teenaged attorney fresh from your remarkably early graduation from law school," Peden cracked.

"Exactly," Sue answered. She pushed back a strand of wild hair, smiled, and continued. "That child is now here today asking the court to unseal the record and view its contents."

Judge Peden picked up the file from his desk. It was in a large pink folder, bound securely. Estela thought the pink a cute touch. Did they have blue folders for cases involving boy children?

"What about the other parties?" the judge asked.

"Your Honor, the only living party is Ms. Valenzuela's mother, Luz. We informed her of this hearing by certified letter and have received no response."

Characteristic, Estela thought, for her mother to learn of a major event in her life and be conspicuous only by her absence.

"What about the father?"

Ms. Hall went forward and spoke quietly to the judge at the bench. Whatever she said seemed to satisfy Judge Peden. He motioned Estela forward.

She came shakily. Estela had faced threats and weapons without fear. She had little respect for institutions. But something about the courthouse setting made her nervous. The place inspired solemnity.

There was also the lurking knowledge that she was about to learn, finally, about her past. That had suddenly become a frightening prospect, possibly worse than the unknown with which she had lived all her life.

She stood before the bench. Judge Peden looked her in the eye and said solemnly, "Ms. Valenzuela, this record was ordered sealed long ago, by a very wise judge and good attorneys, including Ms. Hall. People don't make that decision lightly. This file contains information that they thought should be kept from public scrutiny, that might hold facts that would embarrass people, including you, and that therefore should be kept secret. Are you sure you want to undo that decision?"

Estela took the question seriously. She looked much younger than usual, like a teenage girl. But curiosity ruled her. She nodded.

"Okay," Judge Peden said casually. "Here y'go."

He handed her the file and a pair of scissors. While the judge signed the order unsealing the record, and Sue Hall smiled encouragingly, Estela opened the folder. A small pile of 20-year-old documents tumbled out.

On top was one titled, "Order Granting Termination and Adoption."

The whole file was labelled "In the Interest of Estela Valenzuela." And no one had a more intense interest in its contents than the subject. She read quickly through the order.

"It says 'Father unknown,'" she said. "What does that mean?"

"It means exactly what you'd think 'unknown' means," Sue explained. "Your mother signed a sworn statement that she didn't know who your father was, and after a diligent search the attorney appointed to represent that unknown man couldn't find him. Believe me, we questioned your mother pretty closely on that point."

"But – I thought . . ."

"And whoever that man was, he never supported you or appeared in your life, so we had his parental rights terminated. Luckily, there was someone else who wanted to step into that role."

Estela read down. ". . . the Court finds that it is in the best interest of the child to grant the petition for adoption of Gerald Grohman. . . ."

Estela suddenly had tears in her eyes. "He adopted me? So that's why Jerry paid child support to Mom. But why didn't he ever tell me?"

"He wanted to be there for you but not give you the burden of having to treat him like a father. He wanted to be a friend instead. At least, that's what he told me."

Estela whispered, "But couldn't this have been a ruse? He really was my father, so . . ."

Sue shook her head again. "Then we would have done a decree establishing paternity. Believe me, I asked him that very closely. Jerry Grohman insisted he was not your biological father, and I believed him."

A new participant had slipped into the courtroom in time to hear these revelations. Gabe Grohman walked slowly forward, staring at Estela in yet another whole new light. Estela looked up and saw him. Her face lit up with a joy that wasn't tarnished or diminished as it had been lately when he'd appeared in her view.

"Gabe!" she cried delightedly. "I'm not your sister!"

Gabe ran the last few steps to her and caught her in his arms. The darkness he'd carried under his eyes for weeks fell away. "Well, you are, sort of," he stammered. "But not . . ."

"But we're not related by blood," Estela declared happily.

They were done talking. There in the middle of the courtroom, they kissed, completely unaware of the small crowd of observers. Sue Hall looked on unabashedly, smiling. Judge Peden commented, "I think this is the happiest I've ever made anybody by unsealing a record," and left the bench.

Back at the courtroom doors, there was a new entrance, by someone with no sense of decorum and in fact a flair for the dramatic when it came to entering a room. The stir through the spectators even managed to separate Gabe and Estela, who looked toward the doors and stared in shock.

"Oh my God," they said simultaneously, "it's my mother."

Feeling a tingle of horror down his spine, Gabe turned to Estela. "Please God tell me we're not talking about the same woman."

The Return of *Las Dos Madres*

Luz Valenzuela had given herself her first name. Luz, meaning light: the perfect name for an artist, and one reflecting neither modesty nor shyness. Luz had never shown those qualities in person, either. She was of average height but gave an impression of tallness in her high-heeled boots and with her mass of wayward black hair. She appeared both angular and voluptuous, a neat trick that may have been achieved surgically. Her outflung arms took up even more than her share of space.

Luz stood just inside the doors of the courtroom and stood smiling as if this gathering were a reception to unveil her latest work. Then she saw her daughter and cried, "Estela, darling!"

Betty Jean (McGraw) Grohman had never been a shrinking violet, either. But traveling in the company of Luz made Betty Jean lean back and roll her eyes indulgently. Seeing her son Gabe, she wiggled her fingers in greeting. B.J. wore jeans and a simple white shirt and looked almost as young as her son, with a few strands of gray only emphasizing the authenticity of her otherwise auburn hair.

Gabe hadn't seen her in more than a year. She hadn't even returned to San Antonio for her ex-husband's funeral.

It had been almost that long since Estela had seen her mother, too. As Luz came toward her, arms open, Estela stared at her as if she'd never seen her before. Before her mother could embrace her, Estela said simply, "Jerry Grohman adopted me?"

Luz stopped. Her generous lips quirked into a wry smile. "So you know about that?"

"I know more than that, mother. Like, my father was 'unknown.' UN-KNOWN? As in, you don't know who he was? How can that be?"

Luz did something Estela had never known her to do. She blushed. Then she shrugged. "As you might imagine, the explanation is a tad embarrassing. Could we have this revelation somewhere less public? Like maybe the courtyard in front of the Alamo?"

Taking her daughter's arm, she led her out of the courtroom. Estela, who at times could appear dazzlingly exotic, looked positively ordinary walking beside her flamboyant mother.

Gabe lingered with his own mother. "What brings you back?" he asked casually, though Betty Jean heard the resentment in his voice.

She told him seriously, "Someday you may understand that San Antonio gets a little stifling. Everybody knows everything. Sometimes I've had these strange desires to be among people who haven't known me and everything that's happened in my life since I was born.

"But lately everything seemed to remind me of home. I'd run into reminders in San Francisco, New York. Finally when I was in Paris and ran into Luz, I realized it was time to give up. Either push on to Mongolia or come home. And when Luz got the notice of this court hearing, I thought maybe I should be here. And Luz thought it might be a hoot."

Gabe said, "So now the two of you are like – friends?"

Luz had heard her name and stopped. She put her arm around Betty Jean's shoulders. Now here was an odd coupling: Jerry Grohman's ex-wife and the woman everyone assumed had stolen him away.

"Of course," Luz said. "We have so much in common."

The west side Bohemian artist laughed, and a moment later the Alamo Heights social leader turned gypsy thrill-seeker joined in.

Outside the courthouse, Gabe and Estela and their respective mothers found the party joined by others: Madeleine Grohman and Stefan Groppe. In the general melee of greetings, Gabe managed to pull Estela aside.

"Whatever they tell us, I don't care," he said. "No more revelations. Nothing's going to change the way I feel. Let's run away now. I don't want to know anything else except this: I love you."

He kissed her. As usual when this happened, the world went away. He felt her breath, her body, the flutter of her eyelashes. Just as they seemed about to meld into one person, Gabe felt a tap on his shoulder. He looked around irritably to find Stefan Groppe giving him a significant look.

"Do it now," the older man said solemnly.

"I beg your pardon?"

"That's what you're thinking, isn't it?"

Gabe lowered his voice. "As a matter of fact, yes. But a gentleman doesn't discuss –"

Stefan shook his head impatiently. "I mean marry her. Now, before anything else can go wrong. Believe me, waiting is bad. Here you are where they hand out marriage licenses."

The older man gestured toward the courthouse. Gabe looked him in the eye and said, "I have more time to think about it than some people." And he glanced past Stefan Groppe at Madeleine Grohman. Maddie heard her grandson, glanced at Stefan, and looked away, with an embarrassed smile and reddened cheeks.

This blushing thing seemed contagious today.

The group found a vacant bench, but no one sat, merely congregated around it. Estela folded her arms and stared at her mother. "So why didn't the two of you explain all this?"

Luz looked innocent, an expression to which she hadn't been entitled for many years. "Darling, we didn't know we'd left any mysteries behind. We were simply pursuing our lives. How were we to know you were delving into all these sordid stories behind our backs? If you'd asked me, I would have told you."

"I did ask you, mother, about 15,000 times while I was growing up."

"Yes, but I never thought you sincerely wanted to know."

Estela sighed. Betty Jean took her son aside and said, "Gabe, I'm sorry. I never wanted you to know all this. You were one of those babies who are supposed to save a marriage. But frankly you weren't up to the job. Let me start earlier. From the time your father and I first met, he was – how else can I put this? – fascinated with me."

Gabe, having weirdly experienced one of his father's first meetings with his teenaged mother-to-be, knew this to be the simple truth.

"Unfortunately," Betty Jean continued wryly, "the fascination wore off pretty quickly. We were married by then, but… Well, you don't want to hear all that. I knew Jerry had found someone else, but I frankly didn't care all that much."

She saw Luz listening in, and acknowledged her. With a hand to her chest, Luz took a slight bow, as if being introduced as the other woman.

Betty Jean continued, "But there was still a lingering, you know… God, this is so embarrassing. We were headed for divorce, but we had one of those, you know, after-a-party, the-old-magic-remembered, 30-minute kind of, you know, reconciliations –"

Luz interrupted, reaching toward her, "It's all right, darling, I forgive you."

"Thanks ever so," Betty Jean said, returning her attention to her son. "And the next thing we know, you were born. And Gabe –" She turned serious for the first time, putting her hands on her son's shoulders. " – your father loved you more than he ever did me. He wouldn't leave me then, because he wouldn't leave you. I swear, son, this is the truest thing I've ever said, or seen."

Tears glistened in her eyes, and in her son's matching ones. After a long, long moment, everyone turned and looked at Luz Valenzuela.

"Oh," she said brightly. "My turn for hideously embarrassing revelations? Well, if you must know, I don't want to go there. I didn't come back to town for that, I came for Mexican food.

"Is there a cab stand around here?"

Veronica vs. the Mayor: The Finale

In the newsroom of KSAN-TV, Veronica Lewis made a decision. The latest rating period had passed, TV news had become a bit more sober. But the news director still wanted something to interrupt the constant flow of anthrax and Afghanistan, and Veronica knew the story she had could make her the queen of the local news set.

Confirming this idea, Roger the news director strolled by. "It's getting on toward 5, Veronica. There's a rumor that you've got something juicy. True?"

Veronica fingered her videocamera, which among other things held footage showing the mayor's marriage license. And Veronica made that decision. She stood up decisively. "I think so. I just need a last quick interview to wrap it up."

Not bothering to grab a cameraman, she headed for City Hall and Mayor Suzanne Pierce's office.

"What the hell do you want?"

Mayor Suzanne Pierce greeted the visitor to her office with the warmth usually reserved for a process server.

"To give you some information," Veronica Lewis said. She closed the door and confronted her long-time adversary.

"That will be refreshing," Pierce seethed. "Of course, if it comes from you, I'll have to check its accuracy."

"That's why I've been so careful with this story," Veronica said. "Because I screwed up before. With help from you. This time I checked out the story of your marriage very, very carefully. Even more carefully than you did, I'll bet."

"Marriage?" the mayor said feebly, knowing the game was up.

"From Cameron County? Forget it, mayor, I've got the license on tape. I know the consequences, too. You've voted on contracts that went to your husband. Not only should you have abstained from those votes, you should have resigned once the city had a contractual relationship with your husband. I don't know how many votes and contracts you've invalidated. What do you make it, about a dozen?"

Suzanne Pierce nodded slowly. She slumped back to sit on her desk, took a deep breath, and looked relieved.

"I've been planning to resign. I've just been looking for a good excuse. Also . . ." She looked nostalgically around her office, the flags, the certificates, the commemorative pen set: the slight trappings of power that represented so much more.

Veronica understood. "You hate to give up this job. And I don't think you should. You're good at it. Don't let some bloodsucking con artist drive you out of office."

Pierce looked at her in surprise. "How can I stop you?"

Keeping her poise, Veronica said, "Tell me about your wedding. Was it lavish?"

The mayor laughed. "I'm not even sure I was there. It was a border conference in Brownsville. I was on city council, there were several of us attending, and local people. At night the hosts would show us a good time, you know. Cinco was there, I knew him slightly, and one night we went bar-crawling together – an expression that became more accurate as the night progressed."

Veronica had heard rumors that the mayor could be quite a party girl when she let her rigid control slip.

Pierce shrugged. "He's a charming guy, you know. Some time during that long night we came across a friend of his, who lightheartedly pronounced us man and wife. It seemed very romantic. We had a . . ." She clicked her tongue. "'wedding night.' The next morning we made light of it, had a few laughs, came back to town. The next time I voted on one of his contracts, I felt a little funny about it, but his group had the best proposal, I didn't feel any qualms. Until a couple of weeks later, when he came to my house and showed me the marriage license. Seems that friend of his was a judge, and he'd actually made the ceremony legal. I didn't remember any of it very well, but Cinco told me that's what had happened."

"My lord," Veronica breathed. She hadn't turned on her recording equipment.

"Then what could I do after that?" Pierce said. "I'd already violated my oath, a city ordinance, maybe the Texas Constitution. If anybody found out I'd be ruined. You know how marketable a lawyer who's done jail time is? But Cinco said it would be all right. He said he'd make sure no one *did* find out – as long as we kept going as usual."

"So he's been blackmailing you?" Veronica asked angrily.

Pierce shrugged. "My plans to run for mayor had already been made, I couldn't back out. And I didn't want to, damn it. I was born to do this job."

Veronica paced around the office. She had a good walk, with a long stride and swinging arms. If she ever got the TV pilot she wanted, she hoped it involved a lot of striding across town.

She had the key to Suzanne Pierce's problem, but couldn't decide what to do with it. The woman had been hateful to her. But now Veronica understood better than anyone the pressures Pierce had operated under for months.

Slowly, she said, "You didn't look into the marriage very closely, did you?"

"No. I didn't want to draw anyone's attention to it. I hoped it could just lie there. I do know there's a Judge Ramon Briseno in Brownsville, the one who signed the license."

"Yes, there is," Veronica said. "But he checked out of your border conference early. By 4 o'clock in the afternoon of the day you were supposedly married, he was on a plane to California for an Alaska Cruise. I checked. Like you should have done."

Pierce's jaw dropped open. "I never wanted to open up the story, I never . . . Are you sure about this?"

Veronica nodded. "Absolutely. You and Chester Dilmore V were never married. There's no marriage license on file in Cameron County. He just came back to San Antonio and forged that document and has been holding it over your head ever since."

"And now you will." Pierce's mind was reeling, but she reverted to cynicism.

Veronica shook her head. She popped open her old-fashioned videocamera and handed the tape to Pierce. Pierce's stare asked a question.

Embarrassed, not looking her in the eye, Veronica said, "The whole thing is so sleazy it makes my skin crawl. I don't like the way I think it would play out. He used your vulnerability as a woman against you. That's how too many people would look at it." She shrugged, and looked her antagonist in the eye. "I don't like the way it plays."

Holding the tape, Pierce stared at her, waiting for the punch line.

"You do what you want," Veronica said more briskly. "If it were me, I'd make a date with the bastard and have the cops waiting. You haven't violated any laws, but he has: forgery and blackmail for a minimum."

"I've misjudged you, Lewis. I thought you were only in anything for your three minutes of fame every night."

"Yeah, well..." Veronica smiled brightly. "Of course, if you want an extra guest at the arrest scene, you could give me an exclusive."

Suzanne Pierce smiled. She put her arm around the other woman's shoulders and led her out of the office. "Lewis," she said, "I think this is the beginning of a beautiful friendship."

The Magic of Disappeared Places

Gabe began to feel over-revelated. His discovery that Estela was not his sister, of how his own father had felt about him, left him feeling lightheaded. When the party outside the courthouse seemed about to move on to a restaurant, he whispered to Estela, "I've got to get my own car. Can you and I meet, soon, without them?"

She knew exactly what he meant. With a quick kiss, she whispered back, "Your place."

Gabe walked slowly away as Estela said, "Now, mother. El Mirador is only a few blocks away, but you don't get even a *tostada* until you tell me about my father."

She folded her arms resolutely. Luz looked at her, then away, measuring the idea of walking several blocks in her beautiful but impractical high-heeled boots, sighed, and began talking.

Gabe paid the parking attendant, found his BMW, and drove it slowly out of the lot. He rolled down the window, wanting the rush of air against his face. He would have liked to see his father at that moment.

A voice from behind his seat said, "Roll it up again."

A dark-moustached face came into view in the rearview mirror. He held a pistol. Gabe could feel its barrel near his shoulder.

"Let's keep this meeting private," Diablo ordered.

"After Gabe was born and Jerry decided to stay in his marriage," Luz Valenzuela said, "he came and told me. I didn't take the news well."

"You, mother? Really? You weren't gracious in loss?" Estella laughed, having seen her mother's reactions over the years to not getting various awards or fellowships. The walls still bore scars.

"I let him walk out, but I was seething. I decided to hurt him worse then he'd ever been hurt. I wasn't sure how to do that, but I thought a drink or five might help me decide. After a couple of bars,

I realized what would really crush Jerry would be if I took up with his best friend. Or one of his friends, or at least someone close to him. So he'd have to see me with this man all the time.

"Having come up with the plan, of course I put it into operation at once. There was some kind of party, German Club or something. Lot of single young 09er types. At the Country Club, I think. I wormed my way into it and started making conquests left and right."

"Who was it?" Estela asked, growing horrified.

"This is the unknown part, darling. I kept drinking. I think I had one tryst right there at the club, a room upstairs. All right, I'm positive I did. Stop staring at me, this was the 70s, we had different standards."

"Or none."

"And I was mad as hell. So anyway, I left with someone else, and we went somewhere else, and to tell you the truth things were kind of confused. I'm not even sure someone didn't drug one of my drinks. And I ended up at home and nine months later, whoops, here you were." She shuddered. Then smiled. "Which was how I knew God forgave me, Estela. Because He gave me you."

"And Jerry?"

"Jerry somehow felt responsible, because he'd broken my damned heart and all, and he came back around and felt protective of you and sort of hung around and, well, you know the rest." Luz looked at her daughter ironically. "So if Gabe Grohman hadn't been born, you wouldn't have either. Life is funny, isn't it?"

"A laugh riot," Estela agreed.

A car pulled to the curb. Jock Grohman emerged carrying a book. "Look, Mom!" he called. "I found it."

He hurried over with the late Jerry Grohman's desk diary. Opening it to a page from March, he pointed dramatically. "Look at this."

In Jerry's hasty scrawl was written, "Going to meet Groppe."

Everyone turned to Stefan Groppe.

"Oh, no," he said, color draining from his face. "I was afraid of this. It doesn't mean me. It means my son."

Voices rose, clamoring with questions. Only one made an exclamation.

"Gabe!" Estela said, with sudden insight. She ran.

"I don't believe you can do this," Gabe said with a confidence he didn't feel. Driving slowly through downtown traffic, he added, "I don't think you murdered my father. It was an accident, wasn't it? He was chasing you, he thought you had the original of that supposed city contract, he lost control of the car – Isn't that the way it happened, Ms. Brewster?"

Slowly Marty Brewster rose up off the back floorboard, to sit beside her lover Diablo. But she didn't say a word.

Gabe continued as if she'd asked a question. "Estela figured out you were in on this. There had to be somebody from the city involved. Somebody who knew about the destruction of all the city records. But it's gone a lot farther than you planned, hasn't it?"

"Shut up," Diablo said flatly. "Go straight. You know the way to where we're going."

Half an hour later, having taken a twisty, roundabout route while Diablo glared around suspiciously, they arrived at the burned-out shell of Madeleine Grohman's house in Olmos Park. Diablo gestured Gabe out of the car, and they walked across the front yard. The house still looked imposing and solid. Construction equipment sat in the yard, but no workmen. Diablo must have had them called away.

When they opened the unlocked front door, the illusion of solidity fell away. Part of the front hall remained, some of the rest of the flooring, but the interior walls had collapsed and so had a huge part of the ground floor. A hole yawned into blackness.

"They may not find you right away," Diablo said speculatively. "I hope when they do it's a member of your family, not just some workman. It will be too perfect, won't it? The mansion destroyed, the family fortune lost, and the young golden boy dead all at once. If this doesn't give someone a heart attack, I don't know what will."

"That's what this is all for?" Gabe asked. "Because your father cared about my grandmother?"

"Shut up! It's because you know the scheme."

"Did you sign up for this part of the plan, Ms. Brewster?" Gabe still sounded confident, but that hole made him shaky. He knew the basement floor that lay many feet below was solid concrete. And there might be scaffolding to bounce off on the way down. If he planned carefully and fell just right, he might only break ribs and puncture a lung. But a broken neck seemed far more likely.

Marty Brewster stepped up and whispered to Diablo. She did seem the most frightened person in the place. But Diablo shook her off. He put his gun in his jacket pocket and looked around the littered floor. "A board or a crowbar," he muttered, obviously intending to initiate Gabe's plunge with a blow to the head.

Gabe had no place to run except back toward his captor, and Diablo would surely be able to draw the pistol again before Gabe could reach him. The only other option was the hole.

Far across that expanse of nothingness, coming through the opening where the french doors into the back yard had stood, a figure appeared. Black against the sunlight, the figure appeared only as a slender silhouette, but Gabe recognized her immediately.

So did Diablo. "Estela!" he said angrily, drawing his gun.

But Estela only had eyes and instructions for Gabe.

"Jump, Gabe," she said quietly. "It'll be all right."

She came up and stood right on the opposite edge of the huge hole in the flooring. Light was lost falling into that space. Gabe couldn't see more than a few feet down.

"There's a safety net down there," Estela continued calmly. "I checked it out earlier. "It's right in the middle there. Just jump out."

Diablo whispered to his partner, "She's doing our job for us. So she'll be sole owner."

Gabe stared across the space at his "sister," his lover. With a slow smile growing across his face, he leaped toward her.

And fell.

Estela smiled across the opening at Diablo. "Are we done now?"

Diablo nodded approvingly. Marty Brewster, looking sick, turned and ran. She threw open the front door, incidentally letting in the sound of cars arriving.

"The family?" Diablo said. "Perfect." He put his gun away and looked for another way out of the house.

"It's better than that," Estela said. "Not just the family. It's the police, too, Mr. Groppe."

She took two steps and jumped high, cutting a graceful figure as she disappeared into the hungry darkness.

Everyone came to the wedding, including at least one who didn't technically exist. Though hastily arranged, it was the event of the Christmas season. The simple ceremony and large reception took place at the former Jerry Grohman home in King William, now leased by Estela Valenzuela and the artists Jaime Jones and Ramos Ramos.

The hosts had arranged the food. From art to food seemed a natural extension. Looking at the spread, Ramos said, "It almost looks like performance art, doesn't it?"

Jaime answered, "Natural medium, food. I'm surprised no one's ever used it."

A moment later two pairs of eyes lit up. "I thought of it first!" they both cried, running for the studio.

Even the former owner attended, though he had been dead these many months. Jerry Grohman, paler than ever, wandered among the guests looking for a certain one. He found young Preston standing with his mother Evelyn. Evelyn looked lovely and Preston both manly and boyish in his blue suit.

"Thank you for being my date," Evelyn smiled at her son, her arm around his shoulder.

"Did you see on the news that that Cinco guy got arrested?" Preston asked.

Evelyn was looking over the crowd. "Who?" she said.

Gabe, strolling through the crowd, suddenly recognized the golden back of a head, and stiffened. But of course Jessica Ambrose, his former secret lover, would be here. Everyone was here. Jessica wouldn't miss a social occasion – or a chance to embarrass Gabe. They had not parted very cordially. Jessica was not one to leave a slight unavenged.

But Gabe boldly walked up and said, "Hello, Jessica," then as she turned and he got a look at her stomach, added a long, "Uhhhh –"

"In your dreams," said the happily pregnant Jessica, tossing her hair. "As a matter of fact, Jim and I have had a renaissance in our marriage."

"That's great, Jessica. I'm happy for you. I guess he'll be James Ambrose III. Or is it the Fourth?"

"Maybe," Jessica said with the twinkle of trouble brewing. "Or maybe I'll name him something else entirely. Happy day, Gabito."

Upstairs, Luz Valenzuela had found her daughter's studio, a small white room with good light from large windows and a skylight.

Luz strolled around glancing at the simple portraits and still lifes Estela had attempted lately. They looked like preparations, practice. A large covered canvas in the corner drew Luz's attention. As soon as she drew off the cover she gasped.

As if Estela had heard that sound, she came quickly from another room, to find her mother studying her work in progress.

"It's not finished," Estela said stiffly.

Luz turned, her eyes blazing. "Estela, I've been trying to paint this painting since before you were born."

"You know what it is?"

"Let me guess. It wouldn't be called 'Milagro Lane,' would it?"

Estela came forward with an unusual shyness. She and her mother studied the work together. The canvas was as crowded as Hieronymous Bosch. An old-fashioned gas streetlight held a central position, and the further from that light the less distinct the figures: two hand-holding lovers, a "chili queen" from the 1800s, a rambling drunk, a teacher, several children. One corner of the canvas was blank.

"What goes here?" Luz asked.

Estela studied that blank spot. "Unsolved mysteries," she said. She looked at her mother. "Like the identity of my father."

Luz sighed. She patted her daughter's cheek. "Darling, some mysteries are best left unsolved. Trust me on that."

Estela's bright eyes held on her. Looking into those green-flecked eyes, Luz could understand why people had thought her Jerry Grohman's child. But that had been true only in law.

Downstairs, Gabe stood with his little brother, and noticed Preston turning a coin in his fingers. It turned out to be a wooden nickel. "Found it upstairs in my old bedroom," Preston said.

"It looks like the ones they used to give out at the old magic store. The Elbee Company. I wish I'd taken you there, Pres. It was a great old shop. Dark, mysterious, crowded with weird stuff."

"Uncle Jock took me," Preston said casually.

"Really?"

"Sure." Jock came up beside them, made a sudden gesture with his right hand, and produced a carnation, which he casually fastened to his suit coat. He winked at Preston, who laughed.

The ghost of Jerry Grohman smiled along with his son. Jerry realized why he'd been left on this mortal plane. Not to undo his business mistakes, not to save the family honor. He'd clung to the living out of guilt over leaving his son so young and alone.

But in the last few weeks he'd seen Preston increasingly surrounded by family, and happier than he'd been when his father had been alive. In a few minutes there would even be a new addition to the family.

Jerry's smile grew wistful, and his form even less distinct. Preston suddenly looked up. He could barely see his father. He was gone except for his eyes and his smile. Preston smiled back.

And Jerry Grohman faded away, at peace at last.

A clapping of hands announced the beginning of the ceremony. The crowd began to move toward the unfurnished dining room. Jock Grohman found himself bumping into an old acquaintance.

"Hello, Luz. I heard you were back."

Luz smiled. "Why, Jock, you're back from the ranch."

"Yeah. I think I may be in town for a while. They seem to need me."

He gave an embarrassed little laugh, his green eyes sparkling. Luz put an affectionate hand on his arm.

"I feel silly," the bride said.

"I have never seen you more beautiful," Rosa said sternly. "And that covers a lot of ground."

Rosa, former maid and continuing confidante, was serving as matron of honor. She stood with the bride, and both turned to see the blushing groom enter from a side door.

Stefan Groppe looked very handsome in his tuxedo. He approached Madeleine Grohman, splendid in pale blue. The minister spoke. The ceremony, as it does for the participants, passed very quickly, until they had both said, "I do," and the minister gave permission to kiss the bride.

A heart shouldn't be put to such a moment. Stefan Groppe had imagined this moment for a lifetime. Its reality was too much for him. His hands trembled as he took Maddie's.

Then she smiled, and she looked 19 again, as when he'd first seen her. He smiled joyfully back, kissed her quickly, and the crowd cheered.

Then it became a party, one that threatened to go on for a long time. As night descended Estela found Gabe in her studio, studying her painting. "I've been thinking," he said in an odd hollow voice that she had heard before. "About the old magic shop. And this house, all changed. Did you ever eat at the Red Carpet?"

Estela shook her head, watching him closely.

"It was a beautiful old place," Gabe said. "I'd like to take you there. There's magic in disappeared places. I think I could plan a whole evening for you and me in some of those places that aren't there any more. I can see them so clearly...."

Estela knew very well the magic of disappeared places. She knew reality, too. She and Gabe studied each other's faces. She looked at him lovingly, and with wonder.

"Gabe, I only know a couple of people who have walked on Milagro Lane. I don't think anyone's ever spent the night there."

They walked out, holding hands, ignoring the crowd. "But if anyone could manage it," Estela added, "I think it would be you and me."

They walked out of the old house, across the front yard, strolling down toward the Lane.

The End

About the Author

Jay Brandon is a successful attorney and an award-winning mystery novelist. He holds a Master's Degree in writing from Johns Hopkins University and a law degree from the University of Texas. All of Brandon's novels are set in San Antonio and South Texas. His extensive experience as an attorney with the District Attorney's office in Bexar County and with the Fourth Court of Appeals has provided him with plenty of insights into the workings of the legal system, local politics, and the multicultural realities of the region. A native Texan, Brandon lives in San Antonio with his wife and three children – but not on Milagro Lane.

Wings Press was founded in 1975 by Joanie Whitebird and Joseph F. Lomax, both deceased, as "an informal association of artists and cultural mythologists dedicated to the preservation of the literature of the nation of Texas." Publisher, editor and designer since 1995, Bryce Milligan is honored to carry on and expand that mission to include the finest in American writing – meaning all of the Americas, without commercial considerations clouding the choice to publish or not to publish. Technically a "for profit" press, Wings receives only occasional underwriting from individuals and institutions who wish to support our vision. For this we are very grateful.

Wings Press attempts to produce multicultural books, chapbooks, CDs, DVDs and broadsides that, we hope, enlighten the human spirit and enliven the mind. Everyone ever associated with Wings has been or is a writer, and we know well that writing is a transformational art form capable of changing the world, primarily by allowing us to glimpse something of each other's souls. Good writing is innovative, insightful, and interesting. But most of all it is honest.

Likewise, Wings Press is committed to treating the planet itself as a partner. Thus the press uses as much recycled material as possible, from the paper on which the books are printed to the boxes in which they are shipped.

As Robert Dana wrote in *Against the Grain,* "Small press publishing is personal publishing. In essence, it's a matter of personal vision, personal taste and courage, and personal friendships." Welcome to our world.

Colophon

This first edition of *Milagro Lane*, by Jay Brandon, has been printed on 70 pound paper containing fifty percent recycled fiber. Chapter titles and text have been set in Adobe Caslon type. All Wings Press books are designed and produced by Bryce Milligan.

On-line catalogue and ordering
available at
www.wingspress.com

Wings Press titles are distributed
to the trade by the
Independent Publishers Group
www.ipgbook.com